EDITOR'S COLUMN

In my 'letter' later in this issue, I talk about a photograph taken when I was fifteen. I was leaving school, and the photograph is of my particular group of friends. At the time, one of us was out as gay, but now, in 2015, all but one of us has come out as gay. There was something about the six of us, something other, that had pulled us together, as if we were somehow all able to sense that secrets we were keeping.

But it's taken until this year—ten years later—to finally reveal the story of that photograph. Raised in an extremely conservative Christian household, one might have expected it to be me who left coming out until past the quarter-century mark, but instead the two lagging behind those with no obvious reason to lurk in the closet. But the thing is, the process of learning ourselves, figuring out who and what we are isn't a predictable or smooth road. We are shaped by things huge and tiny, in ways it can be hard to fathom until looked at from a distance of years, if at all.

Being queer is a passport into the 'other', and whilst at points in our life it might seem like something that seperates us, I have always felt that it is something that unites those that fall under its banner. And we all have stories to tell—'the stories of our tribe' as other, more articulate people than me have described it—and more importantly, the stories that built us.

Read, and enjoy.

Matt Cresswell
April 2015

NIGHT SWEATS
MARK WARD

Everyone knows what a homo is

He's not a fey boy fancying

himself subsumed by a city

being swallowed by it

relearning the system

and coming out triumphant

monarch of his patch, barstool, apartment

He is a single man

that society shuns

controlled by a wilfully perverse intent

that causes him to cajole boys

into his truck

using the gravitas he's seen

real men with

that paternal patter plied

that could sate his slickness

his only interest, destroying innocence

to still his sickness

eyes locked to similar skin

boys who'd hate him but someone like

searching for some sort of signal, and then

a mind's eye consummation he's

nervous at visible tells

at the end of the fairytale

and nothing else

almost at that age where the prefix presupposes

boys unwilling, unable to conform

that blossoms behind eyes in sleep

that don't feel like men yet

these are just teenagers fumbling

and the confidence he's coveted from

out this fear of failing the tongues

those magic, unthinkable words

must be known before one can speak of

he swaddles himself, trying

but his fitful sleep continues to bear witness

AERIAL
JOHN HUBBARD

"He wanted a son, of course,"
Ma poisoned in my ear,
and as their lips and marriage thinned,
Pop took himself to the shed like a damaged bird.

I loved its smells: cedar wood;
the balsa, dope, of wide-spanned
kits for flying; polystyrene glue and paint
of static Airfix scaled one to seventy-two,

no longer than his hand, in fish-line hung
formation; the slipstream of his days in the RAF
framed in taped photographs.
"Canvas, comrades, camouflage," he winked.

But I was not to be a tomboy,
was always fetched for some domestic chore,
kitchen lesson or flounced party frock.
"Those fumes aren't good for you."

I toyed with the strangeness of words
'Flammable' and 'Inflammable'
meaning the same on almost every
tin and bottle that he used.

He never built with motors;
an airborne accident had made him fearful
of fuel and fire, brought him nightmares
of cockpit flames in which he shouted.

So we took gliders to the Chilterns
when Ma was away enjoying her sister's
ill health. On the lift of clean air
we launched bright colour on great wings.

I chased, ran and soared with them,
tumbling under his round laughter,
looping loops and figures of eight,
arms outstretched, eyes on the horizon.

One day, flickering orange and blue woke me
amid small explosions. The ashen dawning
that he could not be found.

Damped, seared rafters in collapsed
awkwardness, a powder of matt granite
(Humbrol No. 16). Ma's narrow voice,
"Where's Elsie, where's my little girl?"

I stood silent by the singed holly hedge,
the only sound, a gentle unsettling
as supple charrings lifted, fused as strut
upon strut, forming leg, torso and lifting edge.

Ash skirled upwards, a light breeze
wrapping all in a taut covering of mica
and there stood a man, young, strong
with wide glider's wings grafted on broad shoulders,
who launched tiptoe onto air.

I followed his tiny lights, white, red, green
into the thickening dark, winking,
higher and higher until they stilled
beside the distant stars.

WAYNE'S WORLD
STEVE STEED

Third grade can be challenging, even when you're in public school. Not quite sure exactly what to make of it, I'd recently discovered while working on a book report that I was a Thesbian. Of course being a boy only complicated matters, seeing as how most of them were predominantly angry, muscular actresses living in sin and deprivation on a Greek island called Lesbos, but somehow I knew they were closer to my kind than my own family or any of my classmates at Motley Elementary.

We were Southern Baptists living in suburban Dallas, and by the advanced age of ten I'd been an actor long enough to know I was destined for the stage as well as hell. I also knew instinctively not share my hidden talents or proclivities with anyone for any reason at any time. "Peculiar" was how my family described me when they were being kind. That didn't happen very often, mostly when we had company. There were no such terms as "gay" or "queer" in those days and I wouldn't have known what they meant anyway. Like I said, we were a good Christian family and didn't know any people of ill-repute. My parents never, ever used such coarse fucking language while disparaging the deranged, depraved denizens skulking about, reputedly ready to snatch us on our way home from school and do unspeakable things to young boys such as myself. I wanted to know more, but considering I was in 3rd grade, it seemed inappropriate to ask.

Miss Skidmore, my long-legged, brunette teacher hadn't even been married once by the ripe old age of 27. My own mom was on her 5th husband by then, and I could only assume that was the reason she held the woman in such poor regard. It was the scandal all the fathers silently adored and the mothers overtly abhorred. Hearing the snide remarks and rumors circulated about a secret love-child born out of wedlock, I never told anyone how desperately I wanted my genes to be from that pool rather than the ones I was forced to wear from Sears and Roebuck.

Our church and its fiery brand of pathological congregants had taught me a great deal about fear, hatred, condemnation and loathing, but life as a love-child sounded infinitely more appealing than dying nailed to a wooden cross or spending eternity in the smoldering flames of hell. Two years before, I'd suffered the unfortunate revelation of what sticking a fork in an electrical outlet could do. *Go and smolder no more* had had been at the top of my commandments list ever since. Besides, picking and arranging wildflowers without being mocked, shocked or barbecued seemed a much nicer way to live out one's days, at least from my limited perspective.

Mother saw things differently, as I imagine most of her five husbands would have wholeheartedly agreed. That particular November, like most others, I sat cringing at the school's open house in horror while she grudgingly listened to my whorishly attractive teacher prattling on about how adorable and artistic I was.

"I know. He's the same way at home. Maybe he'll grow out of it someday." Shoulders slumped, she sighed disappointedly. "He reads too much and his grandmother thinks he can see the future. Please try not to encourage him."

More nuanced than Miss Skidmore at gauging the mood of the moment, I stood behind Mother's back shaking my head indicating she might want to change the subject. Mercifully for both our sakes she at least tried. "Here Mrs. Kendall, let me show you Carson's Christmas project."

Clearly annoyed and distressed like an angry bleached-blond blue jay, she swooped in. "Christmas project? What exactly are you teaching these children? It's not even Thanksgiving. So this is why he's been bothering me for weeks about a second tree and more lights? This is your fault!"

Straightening her skirt, the hapless harlot (I'd learned the term "harlot" in Vacation Bible School that summer) stood up and ushered Mother to the back of the classroom. "I'm sorry ma'am, but Carson's considerably ahead of his classmates and we have to find things for him to do. He's worked very hard on his piñata."

I damn sure did. It's the fucking Marlboro Man with a white beard, just so you know. See that cigarette hanging outta' his mouth? My Santa's smokin' hot!

"Such detail. I don't think I've ever seen such a handsome Santa." I had to admire her tenacity, if not outright bravery. Crossing a bridge too far, I watched helplessly as she proceeded to screw herself by grabbing hold of my dangling wrist. "See these little fingers? They cut and curled each strand of that beard all by themselves. I'm sorry, but I find it extraordinary. I still can't figure out how he got the plumes of smoke to stand up like that. You may have quite the little sculptor or hair stylist on your hands."

Sensing she'd dug herself a grave far deeper than necessary, she attempted to exhume the body by laughing nervously and flipping a finger around a lock of my hair. "Maybe he could do something with mine? Carson's very talented, don't you think Mrs. Kendall?"

Too much... too soon... too everything. You are so fucked lady. It's been real nice knowing you.

Snatching my adorably artistic tiny fingers from Miss Skidmore's sin-stained hand, Mother snapped. "Carson, please go wait in the car. It's time for supper and we don't want to keep your father waiting." Hoping she wasn't referring to the *Last Supper,* I assumed she meant father number five, who'd recently fallen from grace and was himself, like Miss Skidmore, about to become another sad statistic, even if I was the only one tallying the body count.

Either way, I felt terrible for my 3rd grade strumpet teacher. Pulling blond curls as far down into the turtleneck of the highly-fashionable maroon cable-knit sweater as possible, I ducked my head in silent dread of the Wagnerian opera about to be performed on yet another unanaesthetized audience. I'd have suggested Handel's Messiah, but knew better than to try and temper the score mother had in mind. Having heard it all before, I quietly exited stage left while she schooled Miss Skidmore in the fine art of coming-to-Jesus.

The next day was no laughing matter at school. Miss Skidmore had obviously been persuaded to see the light. My instructor had been instructed to be nothing more and nothing less. Once or twice I caught her looking at me as if she wanted to cry, but when I'd meet her gaze, she'd look away or yell at Roosevelt to remove the colored chalk from his nose. I didn't know what a fetish was back then, but he was always sticking things where they didn't belong. Not very creative in my opinion, his piñata turned out to be a deep-sea diving helmet he wore screaming around the room asking people to hit him. I still wonder if I'd smacked him hard enough, whether or not he might have shit Tootsie Rolls.

Fish sticks? Not again lady, I'm a Thesbian not a fucking amphibian! Muttering under my breath had become a favorite way to pass lunch while sitting alone. I was still protesting the day's menu silently when *He* walked up with his tray and asked if he could sit beside me. *Shit, and they call me adorable.* No puppies were harmed as I fell in 3rd grade love at first sight. Sort of goofy and blond, he was just my type, or so I imagined. He even smelled new, like a car fresh from the dealer or underwear just out of the package. I was elated when I found out he was going to be in Miss Skidmore's class, *my class.*

Feelings are not the same as stirrings. I definitely had stirrings. So engrossed was I by his mouth on the straw, I offered him my second carton of chocolate milk which he slurped down with such gusto I wanted to stand and shout, "Bravo! Bravo!" He even thought my Santa was "bad ass." Surmising he couldn't possibly be Christian and say such words out loud, he was everything I'd ever secretly hoped for in a first boyfriend. It was a Wednesday, I was in love and for the very first time a boy walked me home from school. By Friday, my stirrings had moved on to bigger and better things, but we'd become best friends, which was fine with me.

Over the weekend, attempting to put the past behind us, we went sailing in the drainage pond at the end of the street. Of course the boat I'd worked so tirelessly fashioning from wooden pallets and heavy-duty plastic, much like the Titanic, sank on its maiden voyage. Screaming with delight and soaking wet, we did manage to salvage the expedition by bringing back a live baby water moccasin. The look of relief writ plainly across mother's face wasn't the one I expected upon our return from distant shores. Startling as it was, I could still read behind the smile and half-closed, watchful eyes. For possibly the first time, she was thinking I might be a real boy after all. Had I known nearly drowning and handling a venomous snake was all it would...

Taking measure of me as a swarthy seafarer, what she failed to notice and I carefully neglected to point out was the fact that my infatuation was not a fleeting interest in boating, but rather a rapidly-forming, as time would undoubtedly demonstrate, life-long preoccupation with seamen of a different sort. Strong swimmers, especially the ones who also played baseball, were the latest rage on my dream team. Among the rarest of breeds, my best bud David happened to have one laying around, much to my astonishment, cradling a half-eaten bag of Cheetos in the finest arms I'd ever seen. Wearing nothing but gym shorts and washboard abs, Wayne had me eating out of his hand in a matter of minutes. When he laughed at the bright yellow-orange drool running down my chin, I melted faster than a crayon on the sidewalk under a scorching Texas sun.

Inexplicably, I suddenly felt weak, warm and nauseous. Unaccustomed to such *advanced* stirrings, at first I thought I was coming down with something. When I got home mother checked and I wasn't running a temperature, so I quickly adapted to living in a constantly fevered state. Watching him work out in the garage, lifting those impossibly heavy weights, sweating, flexing and smiling... it was the hardest week my young life and libido had ever endured. Each night I went to bed praying that a tall building might fall on me, crushing me flatter than a pancake. Hell be damned, I wanted to lick his biceps as he rescued me from the imagined rubble, sweeping me up, up and away into arms stronger than steel, which I knew for a fact they were, because I'd nearly fainted when he let me feel his muscles.

Believing Wayne's warm lap and strong arms to be my ultimate destiny, I spent the next week plotting and scheming, devising new and improved ways to be near him. Once I discovered he and David shared a room with twin beds, my obsession grew to such an extent, it would've easily merited a centerfold spread in Psychology Today, if not Popular Mechanics due to my inventive machinations. Life had ceased to have any meaning other than the constant, maniacal desire to awaken next to the man of my dreams. Lust and longing filled my every waking, aching moment until the following Friday, which is a very long time when you're ten, and David finally popped the question. "Hey, do you wanna' spend the night at my house?"

Birds fell from the sky in mid-flight, Lassie no longer cared whether little Timmy drowned and Gilligan, as far as I was concerned, could rot on that damned island. God himself could do with me as he pleased on Sunday. *But fuck it! I'm spending Friday night at Wayne's house.*

Mother couldn't have been more delighted I'd taken up snake handling and lost interest in fixing Miss Skidmore's hair. Surprisingly agreeable about the sleepover, she said she'd have to talk to David's mom first and make sure it was okay. I was trying to thrust the Princess phone into her face when she spoke the words I'll never forget. "David, I don't even know your mother's name."

"Barron, Linda Barron," he said without either of us understanding what he'd done. I watched all the color draining from her face as she shakily asked, "What's your dad's name, David?"

He was writing down the number on a scratch pad without noting how white she'd become. "David, same as mine," he replied, scooting the paper across the table.

Wayne had a football game that night and naturally I was planning on waiting up. Since we weren't in any particular hurry, we took the long way to David's on our bikes. When I spotted mother's car in the driveway, my own complexion must've turned a ghostly shade of Casper white. Confirming my fear of the unknown, she and Linda met us at the door. "You boys come in and sit down. We need to talk to you," Mrs. Barron said cryptically. I wasn't nearly old enough to drink, but the glasses of Merlot they were nervously needling in their fingers looked infinitely more inviting than the expression on either their faces.

She can't know. She's a psycho, but she's not psychic. Turning to Linda I tried playing dumb by asking, "Where's Wayney Boy?" That's what they called him at home. It had recently become my favorite phrase. Having said it so often by then, I'd begun to wonder whether I could've been a parrot in a former lifetime, although I strongly suspected a rousing debate about reincarnation wasn't on the agenda. Possibly the end of life as I'd known it, but not reincarnation...

"Wayney Boy's got a game tonight Carson. You know that," the nicer, more attractive of the two replied calmly before Miss Congeniality rudely interrupted by shoving open the screen door and raising her voice.

"Carson Wayne! Wipe your feet and come inside. I'm not going to tell you again." Wayne was my middle name and she never used it under any circumstances other than when she was extremely annoyed with me. Terrified, it was rapidly dawning on me that this was exactly such an occasion.

Oh fuck me Jesus! I don't know how, but somehow they know. I'm a dead man.

I was barely listening when Linda ended my young life just as I'd entered the Big League of puberty. Shifting wildly between my teary-eyed, wine-sodden mother and the rust-colored roosters pecking away on Linda's kitchen curtains, my own cock had ceased crowing back in the driveway.

Somewhere in the midst of "A long time ago..." and the words, "I was married to your father, Carson," I heard Linda saying, "We had a son. His name is Wayne. Wayney Boy is your brother. I know you're not old enough..."

The screen door slamming behind me was the last sound I heard. The voices in my head were shouting and screaming too loudly to hear my mother yelling out all my names as furious, frightened feet pumped away at the bike's pedals. Relentlessly, the bone-crushing words kept ringing in my ears. "He's your brother. Wayney Boy is your brother."

When my forehead finally exploded as it slammed into the telephone pole, those were not the last words I heard. Flying through the air after flipping the bike against the curb, I wasn't thinking of Superman or his incestuous arms of steel. My last thought was about my own secret identity. *They don't know. They don't know I'm a Thesbian.*

SO MUCH TO SAY TO A YOUNGER GENERATION
DENNIS MILAM BENSIE

Another newspaper story:
A nice, well-behaved gay boy
Attacked
At the hands of the cruelest brutes.

All of us are sick of the disparaging remarks:
Fairy,
Queer,
Fag,
Queen,
"Those people."

Government measures against you
Idiotic political situations.
Church sermons judging character.

People can't accept that God wishes to see people happy.

Get over it, bad, hypocritical Christians.

America lives in crazy times.
There have always been prejudices.
Not being able to speak
Of love.

But you still came out.

Be proud of your own ideas and principles.

Gay people are pretty tough .

The only cure for "queer"
Is courage and strength.

—a mashup using only words found in
The Diary of Anne Frank *(1947)*

LOOK AT ME

HANNAH TARA FAYE

THE HARVEY MILK DOLL
DENNIS MILAM BENSIE

Now that Harvey Milk
Has his own stamp
(Which I use to mail all my letters)
I wish someone would make
A Harvey Milk doll
For gay little boys
Who like to play with dolls.

I would love to see my
Ten year old son
Play with a doll of
America's first openly gay elected official.

He could wear a dark suit and tie
And maybe come with his own
Play platform where
He could give cool speeches.

Pull Harvey's string
And he has three important things to say:

"Gay brothers and sisters,
You must come out.
Come out …to your parents.
I know that it is hard
And you will hurt them
But think about how they will hurt you
In the voting booth."

"If a bullet should enter my brain,
Let that bullet destroy
Every closet door in the country."

"Hope will never be silent."

Hell, I say we give
The Harvey Milk doll a cape
Or even a gown and a crown.

God knows that despite his assassination
His work shaped every generation of gay people
Until the end of time.

I think it is very important that
We let kids know that
The Harvey Milk doll isn't just a doll
—He's an American action figure.

—a mashup using only words found in Stephen King's Carrie *(1974)*

OFF THE RACK
C. CLEO CREECH

Young formless, I saw only one way to be,
like a single suit in an empty closet
a hand-me-down threadbare but safe
"This one, put this on, this uniform."

My skin burned and crept, knowing
this costume foreign, alien but expected,
but it was this or go naked, exposed
and I was not ready to reveal myself.

Then independent, but ill-defined, still vague
other options opened up from leather to chiffon,
endless accessories, options, communities, trying
each one for size, fit, function—but failing.

Conning myself I could create something
the best of this or that, scraps, rags
some hybrid piecemeal Chimera,
but even that was self-deception.

Only in deconstruction was there hope,
stereotypes broken down to snails and buttons,
to be carefully rewoven by warp and weft.
Into something entirely new—and off the rack.

CRAYON. INK. BLOOD.
FLINT

Telegram to the Reader

encrypted message **stop** sense of self at stake **stop** yours **stop** mine **stop** ours **stop** theirs **stop** code to follow **stop** code enclosed **stop** blood will roll heads will spill **stop** stop shuddering **stop**

———————————

All my life I have tried words on like clothes, slipping my limbs through the semantical holes in life's long argument. Girl. Woman. Womyn. Daughter. (Adopted). Sister. Lover. Wife. Pretty. Poor. Victim. Survivor. Shipwreck, trainwreck, wrecking ball. But what if I wanna call myself queer? Or dyke? A swaggering bulldagger? A tube of fuck-me red lipstick in search of a pouting mouth?

———————————

FACT: Walking any Christopher-less Street, I am held hostage to some scumbled vision of hatred—the knife-wielding punk ready to cut the queer right out of me, the frat boys with the proper fuck that I never knew I needed zippering their pants, the His&Hers married couple dropping their eyes and raising their guard against the sight of my lover's fingers twined through my own.

———————————

Witness the dim pollution of discrimination.

———————————

FACT: Discrimination is an awfully useful tool. As a writer, discrimination is part of the job description.

> WANTED: Someone able to pour language
> from a pitcher and fill it at the same time.
> Willing to puuulllll the wings off p.u.p.p.i.e.s.
> Prerequisite: Advanced Knifework Studies.

———————————

What if I want to bend my neck for the collar, buck the system like a bronc, bare my breasts and open my wallet and be paid the price of the ravening Male Gaze? What if I want to raise the hand that raises the whip that raises the welt in raw, s/t/inging bliss? What if I want to cry *Uncle!* and call it a day, just call myself writer and scribble it down on a palimpsest of parchment and quarried stone?

Telegram to the Reader

don't tell me i asked for it **stop** this waxy crayon tongue **stop** these ink-stained hands **stop** the blood running down my leg **stop** don't you dare **stop** i know exactly where my skirt hits my thigh **stop**

I WAS NEVER FUCKING KATE BUSH
DENNY SAZE

Even when I was young and semi-pretty and
unencumbered by incipient osteoarthritis
and an irritable bowel
I was never fucking Kate Bush.

I never had:
waist-length Alice-in-Wonderland hair
Biba-droop eyes
sex-doll lips
sinuous hips
balletic poise
or a baby-hushed fuck-me voice.

I was prone to cold sores
and spilt ends
and hindered by an unattractive
congenital slouch.
My only claim to Isadora Duncan-type antics
was an embarrassing tendency to get ensnared by
sartorial accessories;
scarves in escalators, pockets in doorknobs,
skirts in knickers.
You get the picture.

So imagine my dismay in 1983
when I discovered that my undergraduate lust-object
- a badly-scanning poet from Warrington
with a penchant for hard-porn and knitting in purl -
was in love with a ringer for KB.

I persevered for a while
though I knew when she looked at me
in post-coital contemplation
that I wasn't a potential bride in her eyes
and each weekend she'd bounce like a rubber ball
back to her doe-eyed,
petite, long-haired, Bush look-alike.

They moved in together a long time ago
but from time to time she reappears
and despite her comments on my still-short locks
and other such withering slights
she still gives my senses a rush.

But I'll never again let her in at my window
oh no no no
because I am not
and now never will be
fucking Kate Bush.

DERWENTWATER
KOREY WILLIAMS

 Midnight walk from the hostel. Seven of us,
strangers really,
               made intimate by the buddy system,
so as not to get lost,
                       so as not to be lost alone. This way,
we're all somehow already found, assured
by someone else's light—torches,
                       they call them,
like stepping through history or a fairytale, stepping through
the kaleidoscopic blackness of wood and field,
                               almost hoping
to come across an ogre, almost
                       giving in to that hope, now
almost plunging down a muddy fell, clutching someone's
sleeve—the name floats off as when
                               everyone is nameless
in a state of panic, but when nameless doesn't mean
unidentifiable—saved
               by this bough of a forearm, longing
to shine my torch on the face it belongs to,
                               but I won't
for fear of losing track of my feet, for a second time, for
this sleeve may then be just out of reach,
                       so we hold
hands instead, without speaking, without plodding
in unison, without feeling the warmth of skin beneath
the other's glove,
               just watching each other's graceless steps,
hoping the batteries don't give out.
                       But then, "Lights off.
We're here," and suddenly, the lake, invisible,
                               save for ripples
of starlight as water pulses against the stony shore. Nestled
together for body heat, we sip mulled wine on the dock,
and I strain to tell apart their voices,
                               scattered in separate
conversations, since I can't make out their figures, forgetting
what they looked like in any other light, now
                               just a kind of motet,
a chorus of shadows.
               I think to relight my torch,
even fumbling for the slide switch,
                       but don't.

A MAN REFLECTS ON HIS ADOLESCENCE
DAVID M. LYDON

Under warm bath water
And the happy click of
The lock or under sheets
In the nighttime hours -
I held their sinewed arms.

They were teachers and friends
And strangers passed on streets.
My evening hours spent
In rehearsal for when
They leaned across their desks

Or held a hug too tight,
And fixed a gaze too long.
Until finally in
The night we succumbed to
The inevitable.

But in the day their looks -
Bewildered when my eyes
Would linger. Our nightly
Rituals forgotten
In the flashbulb glare of

The day.

NOT ACCEPTING THE DRAGON
ALICIA COLE

"The feminine manner of defeating the dragon is to accept it." – Amor and Psyche

I am tired of accepting the dragon.
I am tired of being stolen and charred and eaten.
I am tired of a society that polishes women
into bright
jewels

that only dragons will desire.

I prefer a sword and armor and a horse–
indeed have spent much time
cobbling them
together–

so that I am capable of defeating the dragon.

I am my own knight in shining armor.
I am my own myth brought to light.
I am my own fight against oppression.
I am outside of the norm.

I am battering dragon scales into blue jeans.
I am eating lamb chops over a roaring fire,
lamb chops the dragon shared with me.
After I proved I could win.

ON THE TRAIN TO ROME
MARK ELLIS

An old lady tries to teach me to count,
uno, due, tre, quattro, cinque...
and another
holds out something wrapped in paper.
"She's offering you some food,"
I see him then,
look over at him, startled, another American.
Exiled from my friends in the next cabin,
other passengers speak Italian to me,
wanting to teach me.

Then I glance at his eyes and
see, know. On the Rome train
and I told him I didn't know where to stay
what I should do, but I didn't care,
a cheap hotel, he said he would take me if I wanted,
but not my friends, too many of them,
When the train stopped he left,
I hesitated—
uno, due, tre, quattro,
and then slipped away
to follow him.

FALLACIES TO SWEAR BY
JON BREDESON

I would have sworn—
Just for a moment—
I saw a crescent icon in the sun
For the rest it offered me.

A childhood bully
Became other than he'd been,
How he touched me changed,
And I promised him
No jealousy because
He had a girlfriend,
For I'd abandoned bitterness.

But people crave disease
In unending succession,
And as I think this then I know
That whisky soon will follow.

UNTITLED - SHAUN WOODSON

A BIT OF COLOUR
CRAIG BARRON

By the time I was fourteen I was quite aware of my mother's keen powers of observation. Women were sluts or saints, children were dirty things or darlings, old people were cripples or characters, and the men they were either bad or good providers. The observing wasn't too complicated in our town in the late '60s, with its population still under ten thousand. And my mother had excellent posts of command: her days at work in a too tight blue uniform behind the counter of the George Street Cafe, and her evenings at play in her fake leopard skin jacket at a table in the American House lounge.

The exceptions, a rare enough thing in those days, were what my mother called the imports, the out-of-town arrivals. And her suspicions would last for years, as was the case with Leigh and Pastel; three years after they arrived in town they still muddled her point of view. Leigh originally arrived to look after Mr. Todd's harness-racing horses. Then a couple of years later Mr. Todd sold the horses when he went whole hog into real estate, subdividing his land on the edge of town into small lots. Leigh stayed on to caretake the remaining bits of the farm; mostly he kept the barn clean, cut the lawn, cleared the snow. Otherwise he did odd jobs around town.

Leigh and Pastel were unpropertied tenants in a town where even the poorest Catholics owned some sort of shack. Sad was how my mother described the house where they lived: cast to the side in the bare rocky field behind the barn, with chalky green stucco walls and a stove pipe stuck up at the centre point of the roof. "Like a summer cottage dropped onto Mars," she said. "Peculiar," the word my mother liked to use when she spoke about them. Their names for example: "Leigh, no name for a man. Pastel? What the hell is that to call anyone?"

"It's a nickname," I'd tell her.

"Well I know that, but what does it mean?" Though Pastel was rarely seen in town, and usually in the cab of Leigh's Ford pickup, my mother knew full well that the name fit. Probably some of the older local teenaged girls had started it; they distrusted her pallor, absorbed as they were with shades of red hair, powdery gold tans and bright makeup. No one could remember Pastel's real name. "She could be a Ruth or a Robin and be better off for it," my mother said.

"Maybe she's a Rebecca?" I said.

"And you read too damn many books."

My mother and I were mostly fine so long as we stayed out of each others' way, and so long as I didn't interrupt or contradict her talk too much. And I learned I didn't have to let her know everything that I knew, the particulars about our town that I collected on my early morning paper route. The silent hours before dawn: the muddy grooves in the lanes; the sweet summer mist on the grass; the wet clumpy fall leaves; or the fresh winter cold after storms—except for the odd cat or dog, the occasional rabbit, I was the one who made the first tracks in the snow.

The only lights would be in the house windows behind the barn. Leigh and Pastel's place was my first stop; Leigh had asked if I could deliver the paper early, in case he went out to work before seven. That was the only time he ever spoke to me, asking my name before I left. "Terry," he repeated, not seeming to know what to make of me; he stared at me for a moment, touched the curl on my forehead. "Almost white," he said.

Each morning, as I dropped the paper in front of the door, I looked through the sheer curtains, sought out and memorized different details: the lighted lamp with a shapely fringed shade, like something from an old detective movie; the fancy decanter of dark liquid on the shelf; the glass-doored cabinet crowded with books of the paperback kind; and a beaming Moffat stove with space-age dials. Pastel would always be sitting at the kitchen table, a book open in front of her, a yellow teacup resting against her lips. Sometimes I glimpsed Leigh naked, his muscled body moving from room to room. Once he stood behind his wife, his skin like sandalwood against the strange birch colour of her arms and neck.

"A woman who looks like that couldn't be a healthy mother," my mother said. "Skin like rice-paper, you can see her veins; dried up like an old beach bucket tossed aside." I laughed at her strange meanderings and she swatted at me. I knew there was something ruined about Pastel but not in the usual local sense of what people called a tramp.

"Unnatural." My mother had settled on a word to describe Leigh. "Just a bit too beautiful, you know what I mean?" I didn't know what she meant. It made sense to me that Leigh looked good, the effect of a bit of tone from physical work, the tan from the trips he took to the Carolinas. He often went to the States, New York, New Jersey too. I knew these things because I could see scattered maps and racetrack schedules through the windows of his truck parked under the barn light. Pastel never went on his trips, safer in her kitchen reading then in a roadside hotel while Leigh did whatever his dealings were. At dinnertime my mother, still following Perry Mason on the TV, would sometimes get down to brass tacks: Pastel and Leigh were childless and that was unnatural in a family-centred community. She questioned me, "Do you hear things up behind the barn?"

"Sometimes Leigh yells." I answered. I did hear him, just once, and it might've been at someone on the phone.

"Does he hit her?"

"I don't think so."

"And no one ever visits? She never goes out? Is there ever laundry hanging on the line?"

"At six thirty in the morning?"

My mother was disappointed. She wanted to hear stories, have some connection to another world, maybe trigger some memory, a movie she might have seen years ago, some dream. But likely she just wanted to hear dirt, make sure someone's life was worse than her own.

I did tell her about my paper deliveries to the one better street up on the hill, new $40,000 houses with fieldstone chimneys and dark glass walls, luxuriating on big foresty lots. I embellished with other sordid details: liquor bottles sunk in rancid birth baths; tire tracks in petunia beds from Cadillacs that always managed to disappear at dawn.

Sometimes I thought about telling my mother that people watched her too. The immunity of her tragedy was wearing thin, too long a widow—that spidery word that had frightened me when I was nine years old; my father had suffered from an aberrant leukemia.

I was maybe the first to know. The papers were piling up at the door, their house was always dark, and the burning bulb over the big barn door had burnt out. There was no sign of the truck. After a week I stopped their paper but continued my visits, circling the house in the still black mornings. I took a flashlight, shone it through the windows, tossed the beam of light from the bookcase glass to the chrome on the stove, up the pipe from the heater to the ceiling, shone a spot on the naked hanging light bulb. But mostly what I saw was that the rooms were empty because Leigh and Pastel were very much gone. I could've tried the barn doors, but the darkness there was too big and quiet.

"I heard Mr. Todd there is looking for that Leigh." My mother said.

"Yeah, they're gone."

"And why didn't you tell me?"

I was no help to her, and she was busy enough already with the around-town stories, the rings of rumours rippling into others, tossed into the pond from all sides: Leigh had stolen some money; Pastel had given birth to a monster child, half horse; Leigh had killed his wife in a sexual passion and buried her in the dump; Pastel had axed her man and burnt his parts in the stove. My mother was frantic with interest, welcomed any new theories, unwilling to restrict herself to any one fiction when reality might be wild beyond belief. She sometimes looked at me strangely, maybe considering a possibility that I was keeping something from her.

Mr. Todd was a solid little man with a red face and hairy ears—when you look like that your life is over. But from the lilt to my mother's good morning, good afternoon greetings, I knew she thought he was something special. Since Leigh and Pastel had disappeared Mr. Todd was more evident in town, making visits to the city hall and the land surveyors. Most days he ate at the George Street Cafe. "Always a hot beef sandwich and fries, coffee white with good heaps of cream and sugar," my mother coolly revealed. "A man who knows his own mind." She kept her reflections about him simple, no garnishing at all. Mr. Todd now lived in a house with pillars in the next county, was rich from his land speculation, but yes still an ordinary guy.

Mr. Todd had been inside Leigh's house and was emptying the mail box. Finally one day he added his own twist to the plot: Leigh was getting correspondence from a southern religious community. What the problem had been with Pastel, Mr. Todd didn't know. Everyone in the restaurant was listening. "Good riddance, goddamn hippies!"

This set off my mother, "Too different they were." And then breathless she asked, "Is the hippie revolution coming to town?"

I was in the corner trying to eat my own grilled cheese and of course I heard Mr. Todd come to her rescue. He bought a piece of peach pie, extra big I saw. Lingering, he admired her new hairdo, an auburn shade scalloped high and that I hated. "Over my dead body, would I sit at a table with a long-hair man!" We had all seen on the street some shaggy university students come home; Mr. Todd I guess not knowing that at my school one of the teachers and a couple of the boys were already just a little bit over the collar. And surely we always had the current music in town, You Can't Always Get What You Want.

I missed the destruction, the pushing down of the little house, the breaking timbers and dust. I was on a school trip to Ottawa that day, the only excitement a dropped strawberry shortcake on the new Sparks Street Mall. When I got home that night my mother didn't ask me about my excursion. I was ready to tell her a lie about sighting our dashing new Prime Minister. But not wanting to hear again the only French my mother knew, her usual words for the technicolor Trudeau: "Á la mode, s'il-vous plaït."

She didn't keep me waiting for her details of the day. "Nothing more than a tinder box." She said. "Mr. Todd's orders. Building lots, ranch-style bungalows, he wants." The barn would be gone soon too, but a big job, the foundation three feet thick. My mother said nothing about the big white Moffat stove now waiting in our front porch—this for a woman who had long envied those who possessed Coppertone.

I couldn't wait until the morning. I walked to the edge of town with my flashlight. The maple and ironwood buds were bursting in the warm night. I moved slowly past the barn and stood by the rubble. The remains were mainly pieces of wood, plaster and asbestos, an oil tank lying on its side. The house hadn't even had a basement, just a couple of feet of cinder blocks, broken-off water pipes still bolted to the sides. The site had been picked clean of anything useful, probably by the locals who'd hacked the house into the ground. But under a board I saw a bit of red: a new book, a romance novel with a picture of a man and woman locked in a painful embrace. Small enough to hide in my windbreaker pocket.

I took the book to bed, fully knowing its outcome, though I was still just a kid. It didn't penetrate my dreams. But the Moffat stove did, lying on its back out in the clay, ready to sink or fly, or burn orange. And I dreamt about the barn: the roof was gone and it was full of sun; two ends of a thick rope hung from a crossbeam. I was in the hay, touching wavy, dark hair. Leigh was sitting in front of me naked and shivering. Above us there was a whoosh of pigeons; Pastel in an old housecoat was moving across the beam, a slow dance looking up at the sky.

In the morning there were beer bottles and dirty coffee cups crowded to one end of our kitchen table. I looked out the window and saw that someone was up earlier than me. Mr. Todd's light yellow New Yorker was edging out of a spot just across the street.

"Why didn't that Pastel ever go out? Where are they now?" My mother kept up her questions a long time after. Now and then she would break my silence by raising her lemonade glass of foamy beer to her chapped lips. She expected no answers, as if the sound of her words deflected something, a real threat, a damaging dream. The only thing that made sense, I could've said, that some do get out of this trap of a town.

When I brought home my class picture, grade eight, 1969, my mother was fascinated: the girls in white blouses and dark skirts, one row seated, one standing behind, and the line of boys in dark sports jackets at the rear. One very tall girl stood dead centre of the photo. She was African black, the only not-white person in town, adopted by a childless engineer and his wife. "That's not right, making her the centrepiece, like a rare flower."

"Nobody else thought about it that way."

"I would've been offended." Once again my mother was mixed up, disapproving, but approving. Adopting a child was certainly a fine thing. Then she pointed to another girl in the first row with clips in her long blonde hair. "Thinks she's the prettiest one, doesn't she? Surely a troublemaker. And in for a big surprise; she'll be 250 pounds when she's thirty."

My mother took the perilous, puzzling photo, measured it two or three times, bought a Kresge's frame, and stood it on the TV. She never did say a thing about me: back row left, the almost white curl on my forehead quite visible.

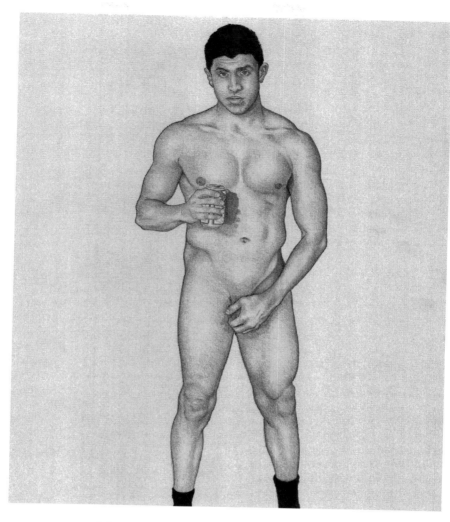

ADRIAN - MATTHEW CONWAY

"My work is an investigation into contemporary masculinity, male performance, and queer desire. I asked several of my straight male friends to pose for me in various states of undress, to explore the art historical "male gaze" through a queer lens. Female bodies have been the subject of western art for thousands of years, generally as eroticized objects of the fantasies of male artists. My work shifts the focus to the male form, to make it subject to the same erotic depiction. Queer desire for straight or "butch" maleness can be problematic but is indicative of a yearning for the taboo, the ultimate forbidden fruit that dominates many secret fantasies. In making this work, I had to confront my own attractions and question my own conception of gender performance. I wanted to show the men in my work as they are; irreverent and humorous, sometimes sexy or pathetic. My attempt to showcase men as they are, some bearded, tattooed, in sneakers and underwear, abandons the classical nude, that men can be beautiful in their imperfections. As the images are of my friends, many of whom I have close personal yet platonic relationships with, this work traverses boundaries of social conventions as well." The choice to use color pencil was a conscious rejection of the lofty associations with oil paint for a medium that seems more juvenile. The name of my current series being shown at The Road Gallery (http://theroadgallery.com/artists/guest-artist-matthew-conway/) is called Paper Dolls, as the reference to the gendered ephemera that teaches children the correct social conventions they should follow."

VISITATION
LEWIS DeSIMONE

He appears at the most inopportune moments. I'll be in the kitchen, coating the chicken in breadcrumbs for my parmigiana, and he'll sneak up behind me and nibble at my neck. Or I'll be taking out the trash and find him waiting by the recycle bins on the side of the house, his face lit only by the flare of a joint as he inhales, then offers it to me, holding his breath, eyes smiling.

But mostly he creeps into the bedroom at night, as I'm just about to drift off to sleep. His body carves a black silhouette out of the patch of moonlit sky framed by the window, and he slithers toward the bed, dropping first his shirt and then his jeans before lifting the covers and sliding in beside me. His fingers glide gently along my side, and he ducks his head against mine, rubs his cheek along the stubble on my neck. He opens his mouth to kiss my shoulder and pulls gently at the skin with his teeth. I can't make out his face in the dark, but my senses are overwhelmed by the smell of him, that odd mix of orange and vanilla, a trace of cumin—his smell, unlike any other man's, unmistakable as an olfactory fingerprint.

The first time, he didn't slip in so stealthily. The first time, there was an insistent rap at the door, loud enough to wake the neighbors if not the dead. Roused from a just-beginning dream, I jumped out of bed, the hardwood floor like ice upon my feet, and raced to the door. I opened it without peeking through the peephole—not that that would have done any good at midnight. I pulled open the door and saw the familiar swirl of hair spilling over his forehead, and I fell against him. He half-dragged, half-carried me down the hallway and back to the bedroom, and covered me in kisses, held his arms so tightly around my chest through the night I thought I'd lose my breath.

Since then, I've taken to leaving the door unlocked. Not the smartest thing to do, perhaps, but it's a rare practice in the city, rare enough to be safe. I can't imagine burglars prowling the streets, testing every doorknob on the block, choosing their victims on the basis of who's foolhardy enough not to fasten a deadbolt.

He doesn't speak, doesn't say a word. He was never a loquacious man, not the type to keep you up all night with musings about the universe or stories about his daily adventures. He always chose his words carefully, saving them for when they were absolutely needed. Silence, to him, was a precious commodity: if it was to be broken, it had to be for a good reason. Better to sit and just be, hold hands on the sofa and gaze without comment as the stars stole the sky from the sun. When you're one with the night, there's nothing to say.

I've become superstitious in my middle age. When I was young, when every relationship felt so special I assumed I had invented love, it never even occurred to me to keep it to myself. I couldn't resist telling the world, dropping my new boyfriend's name into every conversation, cornering friends to offer details of his past, his job, his dance moves, his sexual prowess. In the beginning of an affair, I couldn't keep my mouth shut because it was all so new, so exciting. And when it was over—inevitably—even that couldn't put the brakes on my lips: I would talk endlessly about my heartache and twist everything I had once praised about my lover into a fault, performing a personality autopsy over cocktails as whatever friend I had chosen to unload on grew less and less attentive, the look of sympathy in his eyes turning gradually to judgment, impatience, boredom.

At some level, I recognized the pattern of failure, the lure of the familiar forms of dysfunction, the cliché of insanity—expecting different results from the same old behavior. So after a while, the logorrhea was less about my own excitement than overcoming everyone else's resistance: I exaggerated my enthusiasm to convince my friends that this time would be different, this time I really meant it, this time I wasn't deluding myself.

Wrong again. And again.

Eventually, I decided that the talking was the problem. I was jinxing every relationship by discussing it too soon. That was as surefire a romance killer as renting the proverbial U-Haul. I resolved to keep my love life to myself. It was safer that way. At the very least, my failure wouldn't be exacerbated by humiliation.

So now, all this waiting for him in the dark and thinking about him in the light, I keep it all—the only part of my life that makes me feel alive—a secret.

"What did you do last night?" Theresa asks, standing in my office doorway embracing a mug of coffee in both hands, Pepto Bismol–pink fingernails tapping gently against the ceramic.

"Nothing," I say. "Dinner, TV, you know."

"You really should get out more often," she says, and that look reappears on her face—head tilted, eyes hooded. I've come to think of it as her shamed puppy face. It's supposed to connote sympathy, I suppose, but her expression is so strained it looks like it's her own pain she's displaying.

"After a day in this place," I say, "who has the energy to go out and do anything? I'm lucky I can lift the remote control."

She laughs. I've become an expert at deflecting pity with jokes.

"Well, maybe we could go out for a drink after work sometime," she says. "We can commiserate."

"I'd like that," I tell her. And I would. It would be nice to hear about someone else's problems for a change.

In the meantime, there's another day to get through, piles of paper that need to be moved from one side of my desk to the other, emails that need to be opened and deleted, meetings that need to be sat through—meetings that amount to little more than an opportunity to postpone decisions in favor of listening to various people boast about how busy they are and how many decisions they have to make.

I live instead for the evenings, for the anticipation, wondering how he'll surprise me next. Because it's always a surprise. He always hated predictability. If I expected him to call, he never would. But then, when I had given up on hearing from him ever again, the phone would ring, or flowers would be delivered to my door, or a romantic card would show up in the mailbox—and whatever it was would be made more special for having come out of the blue.

If there was one thing he taught me, it was to appreciate the moment rather than demand it as a right. Demands are a recipe for disappointment, even when they're obeyed. It's always better to have no idea what's around the corner, or when it will appear.

Theresa has a friend.

"He's a really great guy," she says, a telltale glint in her eye. "You don't mind if he comes along, do you?" She's affecting a casual indifference, as if she were suggesting something as inconsequential as the color of a suit, but she knows I can see through her. She knows I know what she's doing. She's doing what she thinks is right. And this is the best she can come up with.

"Sure," I say. "The more the merrier."

Her tentative expression breaks abruptly into a wide grin, even wider eyes. It's as if I'm the one who's doing her a favor. Who knows? Maybe this guy is even more pathetic than me. Maybe it's really all for him. Maybe I'm the catch.

It's supposed to be a casual evening—impromptu drinks after work at a seedy bar around the corner from the office—but I've learned that nothing is quite impromptu with Theresa. Theresa's a planner. She's hardly a role model for living in the moment, unless that moment is situated firmly in the future.

He's already there when we arrive. Even before Theresa spots him, I have him pegged. He's the blond nebbish in the last booth, white shirt and brown suede vest, like some ersatz Midnight Cowboy. A moment later, when he opens his mouth to greet Theresa, I expect him to call her ma'am.

Theresa catches his eye and waves frantically, as if she's just discovered a spider on her hand and is desperate to swat it away. She practically races to the booth. Aaron steps out and gives her a hug. His arms fall to his sides a couple of seconds before hers. She introduces us, and he scoots back into the booth, Theresa sliding in beside him. I'm grateful to have the other side to myself. I sit in the center of the vinyl cushion, legs spread to claim territory.

"Martinis all around," Theresa proclaims. She orders her own extra dirty.

Aaron's never been to this bar before. "Old San Francisco," he says, scoping out the dark wood, the dingy furnishings.

"Barbary Coast charm," Theresa adds.

But none of it feels old to me. Nothing anymore feels any older than I do. I remain silent during the initial chitchat.

"So," Aaron says finally, "you guys work together."

I nod politely. Theresa, sipping her drink, stares at me over the rim of the glass. "He's the only sane person in the office," she says at last. "It was kismet."

I laugh. It's true in a way: Theresa is the only person at the office I can stand to talk to, but until tonight our friendship hasn't strayed beyond those industrial gray walls. I hardly know a thing about her. And most of what she knows about me is pure speculation.

"It's so important," Aaron says, "to have someone to talk to at work. Especially someone you can laugh with."

"I couldn't agree more," says Theresa. "We laugh all the time, don't we?" She reaches a hand across the table. It falls flat onto the aged wood, beside a set of jaggedly carved initials.

"Sure," I say. I'm on my second drink now. At this point, I would agree to anything.

"It's so nice to be out for a change," she says. "I'm usually rushing home to relieve the babysitter and make dinner." She hardly ever mentions her son; I'd forgotten that she had one.

"So, the sitter's staying late tonight?"

"No," she replies, "Cody's with his father for the weekend. That's our visitation agreement, every other weekend." She plucks an olive off the spear and lodges it in her cheek, her words swerving their way around it. "And holidays. Well, some holidays."

"So," Aaron asks with a mischievous glint, "what else are you going to do during this weekend of freedom?"

"Oh, I have all sorts of things planned. I might take myself to the movies. Hell, I might go totally crazy and make chicken Kiev for dinner. You have no idea how boring it is to cook for a child. Macaroni and cheese is Cody's idea of a delicacy."

I've never seen her this animated. But after a few more sips she quiets down a bit, and Aaron hesitantly takes up the slack. There's a delicacy to his features and a softness in his voice that go a long way toward explaining their relationship. He's her counterweight.

On the sidewalk, as we say our good nights, Theresa is leaning precariously against Aaron. One too many Martinis. "We live near each other," he says, flagging down a cab. "I'll make sure she gets home all right."

"Great," I tell him, "then I'll just head for the subway. It was nice—"

"Here," he says, digging into his pocket. He has to reposition himself to keep Theresa from falling as he pulls out a business card. "Call me sometime."

I accept the card with a perfunctory nod. "Good night," I say, uncomfortably aware of the quaver in my voice. Theresa tosses me a lopsided grin.

"Good night," Aaron says. A cab stops abruptly beside us and he pulls open the door. He smiles, the streetlight catching the crinkle beside his eyes. He has his own ghosts, I see. He hasn't gotten through unscathed, either.

He guides Theresa into the cab and follows, slams the door behind them.

The night is warm. I walk to the subway with my coat open to the breeze.

He used to be there all the time, even when all I longed for was a few minutes to myself. I would come home from work and he'd be there, waiting, making dinner. I'd wake up in the morning, and he'd be there, at my side, gently snoring or watching me greet the world.

He was there all the time.

Until he wasn't.

A watched kettle, my mother told me, never boils. But when you're desperate for a cup of tea, you can't help watching. I run from the subway now, hoping to find him on my doorstep. And once inside, I look everywhere—in each room, each closet, behind the shower curtain—as if we're playing an extended game of hide and seek. But tonight he doesn't want to be found. I wait—in the living room for over an hour; finally in bed, gazing up at the ceiling until my eyes adjust to the dark and I can make out the cracks, the brown stain where the neighbor's tub once overflowed and dripped down onto our bed.

He doesn't come when I'm waiting for him. He doesn't come when I call out his name, whisper rambling prayers to the indifferent night. He doesn't come on my schedule—only, as ever, his own.

"Did you have fun the other night?" Theresa asks. She's standing in the doorway again, this time with two Starbucks cups in her hands. I take one with a smile. She's forgotten the protective sleeves; the cup is so warm I have to put it down after a few seconds.

"Yes," I say. "But I'm surprised you remember it."

She grins. "Oh, I remember everything," she says. "I'm like an elephant."

I'm not sure what she wants me to say, so I just sit on the edge of the desk and smile.

"I think Aaron had a really good time. He isn't often that comfortable in front of strangers."

"Who is?" I pick up the file beside my computer and tap it against my knee. "Did you enjoy your weekend alone?"

She sighs, reddish curls bouncing around her head as her smile widens. "Oh yes. Mani-pedi, bubble bath, romance novel. The whole shebang. Well, minus the bang."

She's a very attractive woman. I can see that better now, when she smiles, when she's more relaxed. "How long have you been divorced?" I ask, immediately sensing the inappropriateness of the question.

Theresa answers without hesitation. "Four years." Her eyebrows are raised, as if even she can't believe it.

"Anybody else since then?"

She rolls her eyes. "One or two. But mostly they hear about Cody and run for the hills. Even the ones who claim to want children seem to be talking only about their own children. It's better this way," she adds. "I've become pretty picky over the years. Once burned, you know."

"I know."

Her eyes fall to the credenza behind my desk, and I can tell she's looking at the photograph. I keep it behind me so I don't have to look, but I still know it's there.

"Well," she says, "I'm sure you have tons to do. I'd better let you get to it. Maybe we'll do lunch this week."

"That would be nice," I say. "Thanks for the coffee."

She holds her cup out in a caffeine toast. "Any time."

My phone seldom rings anymore. I canceled the landline long ago, and am very careful about who gets my cell number. Thankfully, most communication these days is more impersonal—email, texts, media that can be easily ignored, easily forgotten in the welter of oversharing.

Surprised to hear the phone ring at all, let alone with an unfamiliar number flashing on the screen, I answer more out of curiosity than any genuine interest. It's probably a robocall, a wrong number, something relatively safe.

"Hi," the faint voice says with a stammer, "it's Aaron." There's a long pause as I wonder how to respond. "I hope you don't mind; Theresa gave me your number."

Something's flickering outside the window. I get up to check it out. It's just a headlight illuminating a street sign. There's nothing more out there.

"How are you?" Aaron asks.

Still grasping the curtain, I gaze out into the night. "I'm fine," I say. "How are you?"

"Good, very good." He's uncomfortable. I'm not being friendly enough. No one likes feeling that they're disturbing you. "I was just wondering if you'd like to join me for dinner."

There's nothing out there. Barely 8:00 and the street is empty. Even the dog walkers have left the park.

"I know a nice place on Valencia—good food, quiet."

Nothing. No one.

"Sounds lovely," I say at last.

"Great!" With one syllable, the nervousness in his voice begins to disperse. "Would tomorrow work for you?"

Tomorrow.

I let the curtain fall back against the glass and turn away from the window, the street, the world. "Yes," I tell him. "Tomorrow would be fine."

I don't even want to think about the last time I went on a date. Instead, I choose to assume that this isn't one. Aaron is a new friend, someone to talk to, someone who doesn't know anything about my past, someone who can see me and not the baggage. I don't have to talk about it, any of it.

He's already seated when I arrive at the restaurant. Two data points: his punctuality is now officially a pattern. He rises when I approach the table, and I'm relieved when he doesn't reach out to touch me.

We talk about the restaurant, the neighborhood, and, once it arrives, the food. He's wearing a pair of gray-framed eyeglasses that give him an academic look that seems incongruous in a hipster-dominated Mexican restaurant.

It turns out he's a grade school teacher. "That must be challenging," I say, imagining a roomful of squirming 10-year-olds.

He asks how I ended up in banking, the number crunching that passes for a career. "I try not to think about it," I tell him. "It pays the rent."

He chuckles politely. "What would you rather be doing?"

What I'd rather be doing is lying in bed, waiting. "I used to work at a nonprofit," I tell him, "an AIDS service organization. But I burned out on that. I decided I wanted a job where I didn't have to … where the only thing that mattered was the paycheck. I learned to love compartmentalizing, if you know what I mean."

"I get it," he says.

"But your work must feel different," I say. "You must have a sense of accomplishment at the end of the day. I mean, what you do is important."

"And lending people money isn't?"

Now it's my turn to laugh. "Where were you in 2008? Most of the time I'm ashamed to tell people what I do for a living."

Baby steps, my therapist told me. Like Theresa, like everyone, he encouraged me to get out of the house, to get to know people. He might have scripted this conversation—the small talk getting gradually larger, like medicine in increasing doses to get your liver primed.

After dinner, we're walking through the Mission when a bicycle whizzes past, not even hesitating before blasting through a red light. The neighborhood is as busy and disjointed as a beehive, people moving in seemingly random patterns, voices and languages overlapping, laughter competing with sharp words. I start to walk faster, toward the quiet.

"Can I walk you home?" Aaron asks, and I realize we're probably already blocks away from his own place.

"It's a bit of a hike," I tell him.

"No worries. It's a beautiful night, and I could use the exercise."

By the time we reach Dolores, the streets have calmed down, only the occasional pedestrian passing us, the cars taking turns at the intersection. We take a circuitous route to skirt around the heart of the Castro, away from the bars abuzz at this time of night. As we reach 14th Street, I'm suddenly aware of a pounding in my chest. "Would you like to get a drink?" I ask.

I lead him to the bar on the corner. It used to be one of my favorite haunts—a somewhat seedy place where the drinks were the perfect combination of cheap and strong. I haven't been here since they spruced it up. It's brighter now, with a refurbished floor and pendant lighting, tables so new they don't even have water stains. Unlike the old days, the clientele is predominantly straight and loud, voices lifted in friendly conversation as opposed to the hushed tones of cruising that used to mark the place.

We find a table in the back and Aaron offers to fetch the drinks. Alone for a moment, I find myself inspecting the crowd. They're all young, of course. San Francisco has always belonged to 30-year-olds. Now that the AARP invitations have started filling my mailbox, I'm officially ancient. I have only vague memories of being in this particular space before, this now unrecognizable room. But it's not the place that matters at the moment. It's the feeling. The room is heavy, a fog hovering in the air, dense with lost energy.

Aaron returns and places a glass before me. There's still a quarter inch between the rim and the surface of the booze. Things have definitely changed.

He takes the seat across from me. "Are you all right?" he asks.

I wonder what he sees. I wonder if he can feel what I feel in this room. The fog swirls through the air, wrapping around the woman in the corner, muffling her laugh, encircling the bottles behind the bar, graying everything. Only Aaron seems unaffected, still bright and glowing and alive.

He leans toward me across the table, fingers entwined around the stem of his glass. And I start talking. I'm not sure exactly what it is I'm saying or where it comes from, or why it comes, but I tell him everything, a year's worth of pain. I tell him things I've never before expressed in words.

I spend half the time gazing into my glass, measuring as the olive floats lower and lower with each sip; the other half looking up at him, gauging his reaction. I don't see Theresa's pity. Instead his lips are flat, slightly open, his eyes focused and soft. It's not pity, it's something else, and I keep talking, talking about the past, about all the ghosts.

Aaron's face grows misty, as if under water. Finally, the words spent, I turn my head away and look out the window, at the stragglers on Market Street, walking to or from somewhere. When I turn back, Aaron's face is clear again. He still wears that look, a look that says he knows everything, and that in the end there's nothing to know. I want to believe that. I want to believe that this is all there is—this room, this moment, this feeling in my chest that can change at any moment and be replaced by peace.

At the end, he just looks at me. It's his eyes that reach across the table, not words, not his hand. He daren't touch me. My skin is on fire. His touch would incinerate us both.

He walks me around the corner, and we stop in front of my house. "This is it," I say, nodding toward the building. It looks so dark, so empty.

"Are you okay?" he asks again.

"Yes," I tell him, "I'm fine."

"You should get some rest," he says.

"Yes. Thank you." I move past him and, in the doorway, turn around to say good night.

He's still standing there as I close the door behind me—double-checking that I've gotten in okay, as if the simple act of opening the door isn't enough to reassure him.

Inside, something has shifted. It's as if a storm has passed, sucking the air pressure out with it, leaving behind that clean feeling, when everything's washed away and you suddenly find yourself waiting for something to replace it.

I don't bother turning on the lights. I just walk through the apartment, guided by shadows.

The bedroom curtains are closed against the stars. I crawl into bed and curl into a ball, the covers up to my neck, the pillow soft and cold on my cheek. For months I've lain like this, praying to nothing, waiting for something, summoning the past out of the indifferent present.

The telling has exhausted me, each word pulling energy out of my body as if with pliers. Everything feels empty—arms, legs, shoulders, all free of the weight they've been carrying.

I hear a faint click. In a moment, the bed shifts behind me. A sudden draught washes delicately over me as the blanket is lifted. And then the warmth as he sidles in, chest against my back, legs curled to echo my own. An arm drapes slowly over my side, fingers splay against my chest. He taps a steady rhythm upon my skin—a heartbeat, a lullaby singing me to sleep.

GIRL CRAZY
ROSE YNDIGOYEN

There's a minute it hits her, watching a classmate on a swing, school shoes pointing into the blue, head tilted back and laughing. It's an ordinary day, only unusual because she's never noticed that girls are beautiful before.

Once she's seen one beautiful girl, there are lots. Giggles and fingernails and hair and the way they chew their bread and butter sandwiches. Our sweet girl can't eat much herself, sits quiet at meals and listens to a constant churn and gag in her stomach. It's a thrilling sick when theres a girl on the other end of her gaze.

She's trying to learn by watching the boys, watching the ways they call and catalog, following their swagger down the halls. But all she gets for her trouble is the brush off.

"Leave us alone."

"Ugly."

"Weird."

"Dyke."

She's not sure what it means but it's hard and sharp and the pain it brings when it lands, seems to fit about right. From her ears to a piercing pinch at her temples. Dyke.

She's strange but not stupid; she can't very well go calling after the boys to insult her again. There would be marks she'd have to explain to her parents.

So she goes it alone, finds a broken bottle in the empty lot, smashes it to the ground once more for good measure and finds a fat shard in the glittering wreckage to press into service. Press there, and there, right at the soft skin just at the bend of her elbow. No one will notice it there.

"Dyke," she hisses to herself as she finally breaks the skin. "Dyke." she whispers as she watches a dot of blood appear.

There's a war coming and the dot dot dash on everyone's mind is on her skin. She always wipes up carefully, rolls her ratty sweater sleeves down and heads home in time for dinner.

And in those empty silent spaces between the dot and gash, something starts happening. There are glints of glass in other girls hands. Ruthie, Dotty, Lois, Rose, at turns they all glitter.

Annie has tangled brown hair and a broken front tooth that scrapes her bottom lip when they kiss. She's fifteen in an air raid shelter, and they never ever look at each other again once the lights go back on.

War is a convenient cover. Everyone is sick to their stomach now. No one is healthy enough.

Those boys who taught her to hate herself best are gone. She's even sad sometimes to see their mothers and sisters and wives weeping in the street. She offers comfort. She's 17 now, thin wrists, cold hands, dirt under her fingernails from her work in the community gardens. One widow says, come in, sit close, touch here, like this. Sweet girl, just like this.

After, she feels a certain lightness in her belly, now that her diagnosis is confirmed. Her empty womb dances; she is thrilled.

But young widows move back home to take care of their parents and eventually remarry, settling for boys they remember fondly enough from high school dances. And our sweet girl is left alone in the grit gray city, digging at her skin again.

Her mother tries to coax a smile out of her with dress patterns, her father frowns and wonders if she needs fresh air. Her cousin brings her out on a double date once or twice, but she takes the cover too far - a boy tries a kiss, she ends up with her hands plunged down the front of his pants, laughing at the shock on his face.

Her cousin doesn't tell, just looks at her strangely and says, "Maybe no dates for a while, huh? You know how these boys in uniform get."

She wishes for a uniform of her own. She's seen the way some boys in uniform get, when their flushed gazes seek each other out in a dark alley. They feel the same wave of fear she does but they're riding it, making a game.

The war ends. Instead of a uniform, she gets a job, wiping plates amid the clattering of a long tabled cafeteria. She doesn't mind it. It's loud enough for everyone to leave her alone.

One old woman notices the scars, when her sleeves are rolled up and her hands sudsy.

"You shouldn't, you know."

Sweet girl shrugs.

"I have to."

And our girl always does what she has to do. Life falls into patterns. Work, and widows, a drink to celebrate and a shard of glass from her beer bottle to make sure she's punished good.

Some of the women tell her about girls who are happy. They tell her about bars that are underground, duck when you go in.

She tries. She steals a few kisses in dim smoky rooms, goes home alone. In the mirror she kisses her reflection, just where those girls kissed her.

On the brow, on the cheek, on the mouth - dyke. Dyke. Dyke.

She smiles at children in the park. Mothers hiss "stay close" until she's passed. Her sister has a baby. She'd like to see it, offers to drive the hours with her mother for a visit.

"You've got your work." She says. You've got that haircut, she means. "Maybe next time. I'll just take the train."

Once upon a time she thought things might change, but the older she gets the more convinced the more sure she is it will go on forever like this, pain and pleasure confused and conflated - a stomach full of sky blue butterflies vomited out as hissing leathery bats.

PIROUETTE
JOHN HUBBARD

Uniformed, a bag slung across your back
on the suburban trek to grammar school,
there you were
dancing.

Dancing in that world of your own.
Two sidesteps, a shuffle, a slide
arms bent, hands poised in air
for a Sinatra finger-click but
innocent.

Innocent yet of weariness,
of the ranked 'must's and 'now's
of others, brim full with your
Plans, Collections, Ideas, Lists,
Songs, songbirds, trains, boats, fish,
astronomy -

Astronomy which twinkled down
on your awkwardness with bat and ball,
the words that glimmered as jewels,
loving the sound of 'isthmus' and 'azimuth',
jostling with dinosaurs and magnesium flares,
equations shrinking line by line,
the cornered tritons of engraved maps, plains
seen first by discoverers or adventurers in books.
Delight– a terrestrial globe in slow
pirouette.

BLISSFUL TOUCH

HANNAH TARA FAYE

OUT FOR ICE CREAM
DENNIS MILAM BENSIE

Did he come out too fast?

My eight year old son
Looked at me with confident, loving eyes
And came out.

My little man made it quite clear.

He would only
"Fall in love someday with another male
—Sleeping with a female
Would never be my thing."

He knows for sure
Because he's in love
With a boy in that band,
One Direction.

"It's permanent", my son says.

Some men, much older,
Still fear coming out
—Yet my eight year old boy
Has changed the course
Of his life
Forever.

There is so much going through my mind now.

Is there a scar
From something or someone
His mother and I don't know about
That hurt him?

Is there something wrong in his brain?

Is he going to have a harder life?

Will he lose his faith?

He's always been masculine around me.
Is he going to become feminine now?
Wear dressed and do drag?

Would that even matter to me?

He said,
"I didn't want to lie to you, Papa."
"Now I'm free."

I'm confused and a little hurt,
But I accept my son.

I'm proud of him
And love him
No matter what.

It's October—
Still warm and sunny.
Coming Out Day is next Saturday, I hear.
I'm going to take my son
Out for ice cream.

—a mashup using only words found in Ernest Hemingway's
The Old Man and the Sea *(1952)*

INKPOT
DENNIS MILAM BENSIE

Being openly gay is like getting a tattoo.

Once it's done there's no turning back.
You're out there for the world to see.
Your body is your own personal gay pride flag;
An influence in our society;
A peg on which to hang your favorite gay topic.

Every tattoo has a need to be seen;
A permanent theatrical gesture
Of political style and identity.

A bear paw on your pierced tit;
    Some super-masculine tribe arm band;
        Six colors of flames on your groin;
            A tramp-stamp of a queer devil;
                One sleeve of gay Chinese;
                    Madonna, Cher or Divine's face on your butt;
                    A pink triangle that won't get you executed.

                    Even gay words of equality, English or Hebrew,
                    That say something (clearly worded, please).

                    The pain was not ill-spent.
                    A brotherhood of queer men
                    United in a melting inkpot.
                    Carefully studied carelessness;
                    Gay expressions, pricked up

                —And an excuse to take your shirt off in public.

                —a mashup using words only found in Leo Tolstoy's
                    <u>War and Peace</u> *(1869)*

HUMAN FORM
MARK WILLIAM LINDBERG

It stumbles down the black street, getting used to knees that bend in this way. It misjudged the acuity of human eyes in the dark, so it finds the night much more difficult to navigate than expected. It drifts from one side of the street to the other, no specific destination in mind, just out for a test drive. Not many cars park on the street in this part of the city, and not many people hang out around here this late at night, so there are thankfully few things for it to walk into. It still manages to shoulder-check a telephone pole, scrape a wall, get its feet tangled in a plastic bag. Two tall and shiny humans with physics-defying hairstyles approach, laughing.

"Girl, you ok?"

"Mira loco, I hope you're heading home."

"Hey. Drunkie. Do you know where you're going?"

"Seriously, person. Speak to us."

It studied speech. It practiced. It's too nervous. It can't remember.

"Shit, girl."

"Ok, how many fingers?"

One of the humans opens their hand, extending three of what it knows are fingers. Numbers it knows. It's always been good at numbers.

"Three."

"It speaks!"

"Ok, yes, three, very good, now what's your name and where you going?"

Nope, it's all gone again. The humans seem to give up on it and start addressing each other instead.

"What do we do, we can't just leave them here."

"It is not our responsibility."

"No, no, no, we're not pulling that walking away shit."

"Fine, what do you want me to do, call the cops?"

The bluer one regards it.

"Let's take him back to Bart's. He must have to deal with this a lot."

"Oui, oui, bonne idée."

So it finds itself arms-in-arms with two tall shiny human figures, one silver and bluish, one silver and greenish, being led forward through the night. Conversation it feels helpless to track flies over its head.

"Santana was so wasted, she didn't even know she was on fire."

"He had this ass was like butter made out of a rock."

"I tasted pine cones for the rest of the week."

The humans turn and push open a door. They guide it ahead of them and follow it into an almost empty bar. Behind the bar a human with a dark beard wipes his glasses and puts them back on.

"Ladies. I told you. Closing."

"Bartholomew…"

"Mija, we found this one wandering on the street, can you call someone?"

"Just what I need."

"Bartholomew…"

"Mija, we can't just leave them."

"Ladies, you're killing me."

"Bartholomew…"

"Mija, you gotta help them."

The human behind the bar breathes a heavy breath.

"Ok. Ok. Drop your friend on a stool here, and I'll figure things out."

"Bartholomew!"

The greener human jumps over the bar to put its lips to the beard human's cheek. The bluer one drops what it recognizes as money on the bar.

"Here for whatever they wants. But really only give them coffee. No more booze for this one."

"Understood."

The silvery humans are gone. The beard human continues doing things behind the bar. He says things to another human who leaves the bar. The beard human comes back to stand in front of it.

"I can call you a cab, where are you going?"

It gets nervous again. It knows speech is important. It must make an attempt.

"Oh boy, you're pretty far gone, aren't you. Ok."

"I'm from out of town."

The beard human regards it.

"Oh. Ok. Where are you staying?"

"I'm staying here."

"I hope you mean here like the neighborhood because you're not staying here like the bar."

"Like the neighborhood."

"Ok. Good. So, walking distance?"

"Walking distance."

"Ok. Me too, so, I guess, give me a couple more minutes, and I'll walk you out."

"Ok."

It remembers an important lesson.

"Thank you."

The beard human regards it.

"No worries, man."

The beard human walks away, but it has understood that he will be back and they will walk together. It feels a strange sense of something in the center of itself. An excited uneasiness. This test drive has already gone far deeper into human territory than expected. It had expected that this late in the night, in this particular location, it would not be likely to run into any humans at all. But it had been in conversation with three already, in physical contact with two of them, and would be walking more alone with one of them. It identifies the anticipation of that next walk as the source of its excited uneasiness. The beard human returns. Its uneasiness intensifies. The beard human causes it. Looking at the beard human causes it. It has a feeling about the beard human.

"I forgot I've gotta clean something up. Drink this, by the time you're done I'll be ready."

He puts a white cup on the bar with a dark liquid in it. It must be coffee. It knows all about coffee, and now it is about to actually ingest some. The beard human is still there.

"It will help more if you drink it, not just look at it."

It feels like it has done something wrong, but when it looks back at the human he is smiling. It has a feeling about seeing that.

"Ok."

"Yell to me if you need me, I'll be in the back. I'm Bart."

The human extends a hand. It has practiced this. It takes the hand with its diagonally opposite hand and clasps it, holds it with a slight firmness for a moment, then retracts its hand. Bart seems to wait for something else, then smiles again and walks away. It feels that feeling. It looks down at the cup of coffee and doesn't even realize that it licks its lips. It knows to sip but isn't sure exactly how large a sip should be. It lifts the cup and takes what it figures is an average-sized sip of coffee. No amount of study could have prepared it for the sensation in its mouth. It grimaces. It opens its mouth and lets the coffee spill out onto itself and the bar. It spits and spits. The taste will not leave. Bart has returned.

"Oh, for-. Man, I don't need this right now."

Bart throws a cloth at it which lands on its lap. It understands what the cloth is for and begins attempting to soak up the coffee on its clothing. Bart has another towel with which he wipes the bar, taking the cup of coffee away and dropping it somewhere behind him. It remembers an important lesson.

"I'm sorry."

"It's ok. Coulda been puke, I guess."

"I didn't like it."

"That's fine, just spit it back into the cup next time."

It files that lesson away in case it has a similar experience in the future.

"I definitely think we're done here. Let me get my jacket."

Bart walks away again. Its clothing has already soaked up the liquid, so the cloth gets none. It now smells strongly of coffee. It puts the cloth on the bar and gets off of the stool. It feels the feeling, the uneasy excitement, excited uneasiness. Bart comes toward it in a dark, smooth jacket. It automatically reaches out a hand to feel the texture of Bart's jacket. It does not consider how its action will be interpreted.

"Uh, you like it?"

It realizes what it has just done was perhaps inappropriate.

"I'm sorry."

"It's ok."

Bart laughs softly. The sound causes an intensification of the feeling inside it.

"It's a new jacket, actually, so it doesn't mind the attention."

Bart smiles.

"It's not real leather, of course. I got it at the place right on the corner here. You know it?"

"I don't know it."

"Well, if you're in the neighborhood for a while longer, check it out. New shit for old prices. That's what their, whatever, tagline is."

For the first time it attempts a smile and laugh. It can not tell how it goes. Bart leads it outside. It stands looking up at the sky while Bart does things at the door. Bart comes up beside it.

"You're not cold?"

"No."

"Ok. So which way are you going?"

It stifles panic. Thinks for a moment. The silvery humans encountered it walking from that direction, so it should say the opposite.

"That way."

"Great, me too."

Bart begins to walk. Back out here on the open road, moving forward feels different than it felt shuffling around inside the small space of the bar. Here, it has to take actual steps forward again, and it still hasn't mastered these knees. It takes steps slowly. Bart is already several steps ahead. He turns and looks back. He laughs.

"I didn't think you were that drunk until I looked at you now trying to walk."

"I'm sorry. I'm not drunk. I just walk like this."

Bart's expression changes completely. It's fascinated by how fast the change happens.

"I am so sorry."

"Why?"

"I… I am so sorry. I was not trying to make fun of you. I feel really bad."

"No worries."

"I have a cousin with a fused hip. I'm sorry, that means nothing to you. I really do apologize."

"No worries."

Bart slows his pace to walk beside it. It feels feelings.

"So the ladies who brought you in just assumed you were drunk?"

"Yes."

Bart breathes a heavy breath.

"Well, I apologize for them, too."

"No worries."

They reach a corner.

"This is the place I was telling you about, where I got the jacket."

Bart motions to metal grating covering glass. Because Bart didn't seem to mind, it touches his jacket again.

"I like it."

"Thanks."

It runs its hand up and down Bart's arm, unsure if the feeling happening inside it has to do with Bart or just the smooth texture of the jacket. Bart is watching its face.

"So, which way from here?"

"It doesn't matter."

"I meant which way to the place you're staying."

"Oh. Yes."

Bart takes a small step back, and it lets its hand fall from his jacket arm.

"I live two blocks that way, by the bus stop?"

"Yes, that way. For me, too."

"Ok."

They cross the street and continue on. The sidewalk begins to incline. They're walking uphill. This is different. This is difficult.

"I'm sorry."

"Really, it's ok."

"Thank you."

"You don't have to thank me."

"Thank you. For letting me figure this out. On my own."

"Of course."

They cross another street.

"You're staying with a friend?"

"No."

"Is it a sublet?"

It realizes it will have to lie. It does not want to lie to this human.

"Yes, a sublet."

"So you're here for a while."

"Yes."

"Well, come by the bar anytime. If it's open, I'm there."

Bart has stopped walking. It stops with him.

"This is my place. How far from here are you? I don't mind walking you the rest of the way."

"Not far."

"Which street?"

It studied the maps, but right now it can't remember any location names.

"Two blocks that way."

"Ok. So, really close."

"Yes."

"Do you want me to walk you there?"

It will try to be as honest as it can be.

"I would want you to walk me there, but I'd also like to stop walking."

It is impressed with itself for putting that sentence together on its own. Although Bart looks like he can't quite grasp its meaning, so maybe it was not successful at all.

"Ok, I guess, do you want to sit on the stoop here for a few minutes?"

"With you?"

Bart smiles. It feels.

"Yeah, with me."

"Yeah."

Bart sits on the stoop. It sits beside him. There is silence between them for a minute.

"So, where are you visiting from?"

It studies Bart's face. The eyes behind the round pieces of glass, the lips surrounded by the dark beard. It begins to reach out a hand, then remembers.

"Would it be ok if I touched your beard?"

Bart's expression is hard to read. It panics for a moment. It has made a mistake.

"I'm gonna say yeah? Yeah, it's ok."

The human heart inside it is beating harder than it would have thought possible. This is a distant concern in its mind. It reaches a hand slowly to come into contact with Bart's dark beard. It runs its fingers through the hairs along the line of Bart's human jaw. Its feelings are loud voices shouting in incomprehensible languages.

"It's not soft."

Bart's laugh is so loud and sudden it pulls its hand back.

"No, it's not."

Bart laughs.

"Can I ask? You said you weren't drunk, but are you on something else?"

"I'm not on anything, I'm just like this."

Bart smiles.

"Ok. Well, you've touched me, now, so... Can I touch your face?"

Feelings shout. It attempts another smile.

"Yes."

"Good, that's only fair."

"Yeah."

Bart brings both of his hands up. It is unprepared for the sensation as Bart cups its face in his two hands, his fingers along the upper jawline, by its ears. His thumbs stroke its cheeks.

"You have a nice face."

It can not tell him it designed it itself.

"Thank you."

"There's definitely something about you."

"Thank you?"

Bart is looking into its eyes. It is afraid he will see things in its head. He doesn't seem to. It looks into his eyes. It also can't see anything in his head. This trip has exceeded all expectations. It wants more.

"Can we kiss?"

"I appreciate you asking."

It processes this response.

"Is that a yes?"

Bart laughs softly.

"Yes."

No amount of research could have prepared it for the sensation or, more accurately, sensations. It has physical sensations in its lips, on its skin, down in its genitals, in its heart, lungs, and stomach. It has emotional feelings that involve both a satisfying of an anticipation and an intensification of that anticipation. I enjoys the moment on many levels while at the same time, warning sounds beat in its mind. Bart's hands are still on its face. As the kiss completes, he takes them away.

"Thank you."

Bart laughs.

"You know, you might be a little too polite."

"Sorry."

Bart laughs.

"I think some of it is a joke, but you've really got me wondering."

It smiles. Bart shakes his head, looking at its face. He puts one hand on the back of its neck and pulls it into another kiss, this one longer. Bart kisses with more pressure. It matches him. It enjoys this one, too. Bart's lips part, and his tongue protrudes slightly. It knows this is common. It parts its own lips and lets its tongue protrude as well. The meeting of tongues is an interesting sensation. The tongues feel each other. While the sensation itself is stranger, the feelings it produces are less complex than the first kiss. It alternates matching and complementing the movements of Bart's tongue. Bart's other hand finds its waist and rests there, around the edge of its pelvic bone. It extends its hands blindly and finds them sliding inside Bart's smooth jacket to his chest. It presses its open hands against his chest, soft and dense. It slides its hands around to Bart's sides, deeper into the jacket, feeling the smooth material of the jacket on the backs of its hands and Bart's soft shirt and dense body under its palms. The sensations in its genitals begin to intensify. Physical changes begin to occur. As with most of what it has encountered tonight, it has studied this phenomenon extensively, but it is unprepared for the reality of it. It pulls back from the kiss and retracts its hands. Bart retracts his hands as well.

"Everything ok?"

"Yes."

"Too much?"

"Yes. No. Just…"

It knows the right word but can't remember it. It must find it quickly.

"Intense."

Bart has said the word it was trying to find.

"Intense! That's the word."

Bart smiles while looking at its eyes again.

"This is not where I was expecting this night to go."

"Me neither."

"Would you like to come inside?"

"Yes."

Bart's hand finds one of its hands and holds onto it as he stands up. It stands with him, and they take the steps together up to Bart's door. Bart lets go to find his keys and open the door, but takes its hand again to lead it inside the building and up a flight of stairs. Bart moves slowly so it can figure out the stairs which are probably the most difficult physical challenge it has yet encountered. Its skills are improving, however, so it does remarkably well. Bart unlocks a door at the top of the stairs, and it finds itself in a human apartment.

"It smells like coffee."

"Yeah, that's still you."

It looks down at itself, at the coffee soaked into its clothing.

"Oh. Yeah."

"Do you want something to drink?"

"You mean booze?"

"Yes, but water, too, if you'd prefer."

It knows about alcohol, of course, and knows it is a danger.

"A little booze."

"A little booze it is. Whiskey ok?"

"Whatever you drink."

Bart moves away into another room. It sits on his couch. On a small table in front of the couch is a book. It opens it, just to look. It loves the look of human writing. Bart reenters the room without his jacket and with two small glasses of whiskey.

"It's very boring. Have you read it?"

It closes the book.

"No, just curious."

That's one of its favorite human words. It's happy it had a chance to use it. Bart sits with it on the couch and hands it a glass.

"Important ideas always come inside the most boring books."

"Important ideas are always with us."

"How do you mean?"

It may have started something it can't competently continue.

"In our minds... Any idea you need is already in your mind."

Bart's forehead makes wrinkles as he seems to contemplate the sentence it just put together. It takes the opportunity to sip the whiskey, taking a smaller sip than it did of the coffee. The whiskey fills its mouth and nasal passages with a complex and burning fume. It spits the whiskey back into the glass.

"Oh no, you don't like my coffee or my whiskey?"

"I think I do like the whiskey. I just... It's intense."

It sips the whiskey again, holds it in its mouth as it analyzes the fumes. It swallows it and feels it run down its esophagus. Bart swallows his glass of whiskey in one gulp and puts the empty glass on the small table.

"It's ok if you don't like it."

It swallows the rest of its whiskey in one gulp as well.

"And it's ok if you do!"

It puts its glass next to Bart's on the table. Bart takes one of its hands and slides closer to it. It feels its feelings.

"So, let's talk. My unbreakables are: I don't do intercourse the first time I'm with someone, I keep it on the couch for the first date. Some articles of clothing should stay on, but which ones we can figure out as we go. I like to finish, but you don't have to, some people don't want to. Either way, fluids should land on our own bodies for tonight. Is all of that ok?"

It smiles. It loves having rules.

"Yes."

Its feelings are loud voices arguing with each other. This is about to go way beyond a simple nighttime test drive. It knew it would probably encounter more situations than it anticipated, but it has found itself suddenly in the middle of a very advanced undertaking.

"Do you have any unbreakable rules before we start having fun?"

Bart smiles. It has not prepared for this. It should have rules, though. It should have a lot of rules for this situation. It feels slightly dizzy. The coffee smell is strong. The whiskey fumes hang in its mouth.

"No. Yours, I mean. Same as yours."

"Ok."

It knows that isn't good enough.

"And..."

"Yeah?"

"Just be polite to each other."

Bart laughs.

"I can do that."

It smiles.

"Ok, then. May I kiss you again?"

"Yes."

Bart leans forward and kisses its lips softly. It responds. Its louder feelings take over. The kiss finishes.

"May I take off your shirt?"

"Yes you may."

The thing begins to unbutton Bart's shirt revealing the dark hair underneath. Its genitals respond just to seeing this hair. It laughs a little.

"What?"

It can't tell him how proud it is of its unbuttoning skills. Or maybe it could. Maybe this human would find that funny. Or somehow sexy. It knows the whiskey is already moving into its bloodstream.

"I just like this."

"Good, me too."

He helps it slip his shirt off. It runs its hands through the hair all over this human's wide chest. Bart's body is larger than the one it has, rounder, and much hairier. It likes all of those things. It kisses Bart's lips as it explores his torso with its hands. Bart pulls back.

"May I take off your shirt? Please?"

A new feeling surfaces. It feels insecure about what Bart will find under its shirt in comparison to what it found under his. Human insecurity was one of the few things it always passed over in its studies. It hadn't understood its relevance. It realizes now there is much in it to be considered.

"Yes."

It is wearing a shirt without buttons. Bart slides the shirt off over its head. Bart wraps his arms around its bare torso and pulls it toward him, their chests pressing together as they kiss. Its human genitals have undergone the expected change. Bart lays back on the couch so it lies on top of him. Bart rolls so that their bodies are side by side, then rolls again so he is on top.

"May I remove your shoes?"

"Yes."

Bart moves off of the couch and kneels on the floor. He reaches over and unlaces its shoes, then pulls them off. It isn't wearing socks. It didn't see the point.

"May I please remove your pants?"

"That would violate the rules."

"Aren't you wearing underwear?"

"No."

It hadn't seen the point.

"Me neither! Well, then this is where we stop undressing, and that's fine."

Bart leans over the couch and begins kissing it again, one hand exploring its chest and moving down over its stomach. It pulls out of the kiss.

"Or..."

"I'm listening."

It really wants to ask.

"Maybe, could I wear your jacket?"

Bart laughs.

"Yes. I guess the rules don't say it has to be our own clothing."

Bart goes into the other room to retrieve his jacket. It sits up on the couch in anticipation. It sat up too fast. It feels dizzy again. Bart comes back into the room with his soft new jacket.

"Stand up, come over here."

It stands too fast and wobbles. Bart rushes to its side and steadies it.

"I'm feeling the whiskey."

"So you're definitely a light-weight."

It doesn't know that term. It files it away for future study and begins to think of how to respond. But it is saved from that by Bart's jacket sliding over its shoulders. It and Bart both laugh as they try to work together to get its arms into the sleeves. Its arms slide down the textured tubes of the jacket. The soft material hangs on its shoulders and brushes its back and chest. Bart zips it closed.

"A bit big on you."

"I like it."

It puts its arms around Bart and kisses him again with force, parting its lips and protruding its tongue. It feels Bart's hands on the waistline of its pants.

"Now may I remove your pants?"

Human sexual desire and physical sexual interactions were a big topic of study. It knows they are a large part of human life and culture, but it had no idea how loud the impulses themselves could be. Or how complicated.

"Yes."

Bart unfastens its pants and they drop, freeing its genitals. Bart touches them. Some things in its mind quiet. Others get very much louder.

"May I touch yours as well?"

"Yes, you just have to keep my pants on."

Bart is looking into its eyes and smiling. It is looking back and smiling. It is sharing something with this human. It will have so much to report when it returns.

"Of course."

It slips a hand past the waistline of Bart's pants and finds his genitals, which match its own. It feels them clinically. Bart's hands on its own genitals are a bit more aggressive, but the sensation is quite pleasurable. It tries to match his technique but is impeded by his pants.

"What's your name?"

A panic begins to take over most, but not all, of the things operating in its mind.

"I don't know your name, what is it?"

Bart does not pause or slow down to ask the question which means it must process the physical sensations Bart is causing, the physical activity it is engaged in to cause a similar sensation for Bart, the question itself, and all of the issues the question suddenly brings up.

It can not tell what specific effects it can attribute to the single gulp of whiskey, but it is certain the whiskey is not helping things.

"Sorry."

"It's ok, I haven't asked until now."

It tries to process the levels of this moment.

"So? Your name is?"

Its first impulse is to repeat the first name that comes into its mind, but that name is Bart. It knows enough of human names to know that Bart is uncommon, and it would be highly unlikely and possibly suspicious that its name would also be Bart. But it cannot think of another human name right now.

"I…"

"Do you not want to tell me?"

It wants to tell this human everything. It does not want to lie.

"I don't have a name."

Bart's face almost smiles, almost laughs. His forehead wrinkles, puzzling. Both his hands have been on its genitals. One goes away, the other slows down considerably.

"If you don't want to tell me your name, just say so. I guess it's ok, though, I kinda… I mean I thought we were…"

Its genitals begin to revert to their original state. It can not explain the actual truth to this human.

"I'm sorry."

Bart removes his hand. It retracts its hand from Bart's pants.

"I can't tell you my name."

"You can't?"

Its feelings argue. It feels somehow attached to this human now. It feels very strongly that it wants to continue relating to him, and it knows that it can not. It also finds itself concerned about what Bart may be feeling now or what he may feel when it is gone.

"I can't stay. I shouldn't have…"

It pulls its pants back up. It attempts to unzip Bart's jacket. Zippers are supposed to be easier than buttons, but this one is somehow difficult.

"What happened?"

Bart has stepped back and watches it struggle with the zipper.

"Are you leaving? Here, let me help."

Bart gets close to it again and brings his hands to the zipper.

"It's a little funky sometimes."

Bart's hands force the zipper to release and slide down. As Bart gently slides his jacket off its shoulders, down its arms, it feels a heat at its eyes. It looks up at Bart.

"Are you crying?"

"Am I?"

"What's wrong? I'm sorry, did I do something?"

Bart is so polite, and it feels like he also feels somehow attached. It has made a mistake.

"You shouldn't be sorry. I'm sorry."

As with everything else, it knows about tears, but feeling them on its own face is surprising and different than expected. It does not like the sensation of tears. They feel sickly warm and untidy.

"I've been lying to you, Bart."

"About what? You've told me essentially nothing about yourself."

It pulls its shirt back on as quickly as it can. It picks up its shoes.

"Wait, can we talk about this? What just happened?"

It stops and looks into the human's eyes. Now it feels like it can see inside his head, into his mind. It can see that the human is not angry. He is concerned. He cares. It has made a mistake. It wants the human to know everything, to know that he has done nothing wrong, that it is the one at fault, that it should never have begun this interaction, that if it were actually a human it would stay and let Bart finish and get its own fluids on its own body. It wants to tell him that it is not a human. But it can not tell him that. It can not actually tell the whole truth. It looks into Bart's eyes helplessly and says all that it feels it can.

"I am not staying two blocks away!"

It turns and exits Bart's apartment. It allows gravity to assist it in going down the stairs. It struggles with the door to outside, afraid it may be locked, that it may need a key like Bart has, but it eventually gets it open and gets outside. It stumbles down the few stoop steps and walks off along the street. When it doesn't think too hard about it, knees are actually quite simple. They do their own job if you just let them. It walks quickly, but it can not walk away from the warm wetness running from its eyes. It passes a human sitting against a building.

"Hey, if you're not using them shoes, I'll take 'em."

It still has its shoes in its hand. It never put them back on. It tosses the shoes to the human.

"What, really?"

It walks on. The dark pavement feels terrible under its fragile human feet, but it doesn't matter. It will not have to go much further in them. It stops under a light and takes several deep breaths. It has always been a lover of humanity. In theory. Its first experience among them has been more than it could have wished for, but it is left cursing the complexity of human sensations and desires. It apologizes to Bart in its mind and returns to where it came from.

SCOTT - MATTHEW CONWAY

PRIDE AND PREJUDICE
RICHARD BYRT

You reminisce about the lad in Alabama
that Pals Across the World gave you as your penfriend
in 1963.   - You've always thought you never got an answer
because he thought, "he's queer", when you wrote you loved Jane Austen
and disapproved of racial segregation.

But that Alabama lad wrote back, enclosed his photo.
And if the postal system hadn't lost his letter,
you'd now be living with him in a gay retirement complex,
together sipping cocktails on a beach in California,
re-reading Pride and Prejudice, and soaking up the sun.

A SMALL PRICE FOR FREEDOM
RICHARD BYRT

After forty years as a tax inspector, I joined a gang
but never learnt to graffiti
without spraying myself in the eye.
My knees gave way when I tried to run. The pretty
boys in blue soon pinned me down.

I tried to be a criminal but never really succeeded.
Gripped by the thrill of flashing lights and sirens,
manhandled by lads in peaked helmets.
Loved the judge's manly Northern accent
and the dapper barrister who vainly tried to defend me.

Loved the peace of solitary – small price
for freedom from the never-ending
nagging of my wife.

THE SWEET OLD LADIES
RICHARD BYRT

chuck wheelie bins into the Thames.
Wait on street corners for casual sex
with other sweet old ladies, sweet young ladies
and sweet old gentlemen.
Aerosol AR-S.O.L. all over Westminster Bridge and up
Big Ben. Attend Evensong devoutly,
dancing naked in the nave.
Rev their motorbikes up and down
the posher suburbs at three in the morning.

I asked the sweet old ladies
if I could join their gang – please.
They said I wasn't sweet enough.
At 77, wasn't old enough.
And didn't do enough knitting.

PRIVELEGE
ADITI ANGIRAS

They always ask us
so who's the man who's the woman
I tell them, listen
I don't think we have the privilege
to pretend to be what we're not
when we're too busy
being people
we really are
listen, I tell them
I don't think we have the privilege
to play with things we don't believe in
when we're too busy
feeling, fighting
breaking, breathing
and believing
When they ask us
so who's the man who's the woman
I say, listen
we don't have the time
to live in boxes
when we're too busy
gazing the skies
you don't have the privilege
when you're too busy
digging burrows
you call homes
and we call burying holes
listen,
we're too busy fucking
and fucking
your gender roles.

ON YOUR THIRTIETH BIRTHDAY
MAT WENZEL

You eat mixed sauce pizza and drink a beer,
call thirty; you explore the dark to find

exactly what you were looking for—the dark
and what feels like a map that you know

you can't read, but at least you know it's there.
You trim your chest hair and your nose hairs.

You wear an ironic beard and refuse to buy
ironic brews at the bar, and you run with your shirt off.

You feel like a teenager because you just can't get enough
heat enough sun enough wine enough blood enough flesh

enough distance enough of a man to brave the grey
horizon of the sea. You will laugh at the waves

wrapping their muscled arms around you and
throwing you down onto the sandy floor, raising

and rolling you, until you are face down crawling
on the shore with grit in your smiling mouth.

OPTICAL
GREGORY WOODS

The mirror reflects him,
much as it wishes for darkness
or for loopholes in natural law.
It knows all there needs to be known
of composition, light and shade.
As a colourist it brooks no competitor.
When he steps into its field of vision
he surrenders not his soul
but something of himself
more trivial if no less to the point.

All the worthwhile moments of his life
have happened in this glass.
He recognises nobody
except in their reflections:

the woman who bore and bored him,
the master with the cane, the feral priest,
the laughing sergeant major,
those students who persuaded him
philosophy was more significant
than politics.

An unknown woman
bared an armpit to the candlelight,
unknown by name if not by nature.

Whatever he forgets can be
recalled on his behalf
through a trick of the light.
In excellent spirits,
he never even winces
to see how old he's grown. (He
thinks his ravaged face
distinguished.) The boy with
the smile, the boy with the pout,
the freckled boy, the boy who had nothing
to say. All of them
appear here, all but each alone.
He speaks to each as in the old days,
tenderly when called on for tenderness,

with a slur, with a stammer,
with irony's compromised lilt,
inquisitive when out of touch.

His eyes are enormous behind their lenses.
He chuckles like a baby
at his cooling teacup's parallax.
He bulk-buys light bulbs
for fear of a dearth.
He doesn't even close those eyes to sleep.

TWINS
GEER AUSTIN

When I look at the two of you, I wonder what it would be like to have an identical twin, and what it would be like to be a woman. And if I were a woman, would I dye my hair yellow and choose the same hairstyle as you? And if my twin and I had the same hairstyle, would I opt to wear my bangs pushed up like a spiky tiara to differentiate my look from her because her bangs hung limp like cooked vermicelli? Would I wear orange lipstick while she wore red lipstick? Would we wear matching turquoise dresses cut low to show our cleavage, and would her cleavage look different than mine because she wore a pushup bra, and looking at our cleavage, would people think we weren't really identical because of our different bras or would they realize that hers was pushing up while mine was less constraining. And would we go to the beach together so we'd have identical tans? And if we married, would we marry identical male twins with their own identity issues? And would we cheat on our husbands by pretending to be the other twin? And would they do the same to us? And would they be able to tell us apart but allow us to play switcheroo because they wanted a little variety? And if we got divorced, would we get divorced together or would one of us stay married and let the other one go back to single life alone? Would we be identical flight attendants or would one of us become a flight attendant while the other one became a trial lawyer? Would we call each other Sis for our entire lives, or would we address each other by our given names? And if we called each other Sis, would it sound odd if someone else called one of us Sis? And if we both got divorced after our marriages fell apart, and if she were a trial lawyer while I was a flight attendant would we travel together on business whenever possible or would it be impossible for us to spend much time together? Would I quit flying and go to law school so I could have the identical career as my identical twin? And would people shake their heads behind our backs and mutter, "Enough with the twin stuff already!" or would they envy us because we always had each other? And if one of us did something terrible like murder her husband, instead of divorcing him, because he was a no good, lying, cheating fool, would the other one come to court every day and sit in the front row and tell the press that she didn't believe her twin was guilty even though she had confessed to the crime? And if our twin went to jail for life would we get twin visits like conjugal visits for husbands and wives? And if we didn't go to jail but divorced our twin husbands, gave up our divergent careers and worked together for the rest of our lives as twin litigators, would we move to the same retirement community when we reached normal retirement age? And would we die together, be buried side by side and go to heaven or hell together? Would there be a special part of heaven for twins? And would we be laid out in identical dresses? And would our survivors and heirs remember to lay twin bouquets on our twin graves? If I were a woman and had an identical twin would I be just like you?

LAUGHTER LINES
DAVE WAKELY

Dashing. Now there's something I haven't done – or been – in a long old while. Nor something anyone's probably thought about me, come to think of it. Not ramshackle old Gordon. It'd never do to be late for her ladyship, but it still feels strange to be hurrying home at this time of year, now that the last of the autumn tourists are gone. Maybe they've grown as immune to Munich or Tokyo as I have to Wiltshire, but I've never understood why you'd travel half the world to look at earthworks or long-barrows. A windy hilltop planted with fragments of broken skulls and not a scrap of evidence about who clubbed who. This place might have a long history, but it's not a pretty one.

Maybe it's Dad's influence - always the proud teacher, even if it wasn't at the posh school on The Mound - but isn't the pleasure of history in discovering what it means? Selling the hippies crystals and dowsing rods might keep the gift shops busy, but there's enough to fret about in the here and now without pondering the ancients. Judging by the museum displays we used to have in the library, they'd most likely have strangled you with your fancy rune pendant.

It's definitely getting chilly though, and the November skies are as grey as my temples. I'm glad of twenty minutes in the greenhouse with a mug of tea before I have to head out again, checking the new shoots and catching up with the cricket. Even if we are getting thrashed again. "England undone by pace and spin" the commentator burbles, and I hear myself say "Too bloody right, son" out loud. Too many afternoons alone, Gordon, that's your bother.

I give the handle of the wind-up radio a few cranks. It was a present from Tom a couple of years back, although it surprised him when I asked for one for my birthday. "Aren't they for the poor people in Africa, Pop?" he'd asked when he phoned, crackling down the line from Phuket between shifts pedalling the tourists round in a rickshaw. All around him, phones bleeped and chirped like heart monitors in a hospital ward.

"They have poor people in Wiltshire nowadays too," I'd told him, "though granted, they do tend to be a bit older."

He'd said something corny about being as old as you feel, and I decided against depressing him with the answer. My circumstances are no more his fault than his are mine, and cradle to grave's a long enough haul without some old wazzock's sarcastic commentary babbling away in your ear. When I was his age, some old Tory buzzard used to bang on about getting on your bike and looking for work. So now we know what he really meant, then. Bugger off to Thailand, sonny, you're not needed here.

My shoulders might be older than Tom's but they're broader too, especially after all this gardening. Bloody hard work, this poverty lark. Still, all those years moaning about not having time, it'd be a crime not to. This afternoon, I'll get the winter crops in and tidy up the jars in the lean-to. My muscles might complain now, but my stomach will be grateful later. Dig for victory, wasn't that what Granddad always said, Tom? Cheaper than a gym too, and they don't give you free fruit and veg.

Just time to hang up my work-shirt in an old suit-bag, stick a blue plaster over the cracked skin on my gardener's knuckles and a quick squirt of aftershave to cover the smell from last night's pickling. Check what's sprouting in the greenhouse, what's strong enough to survive planting out.

I'm sure the mystery will unravel, but The Coach and Horses is hardly Suzie's normal choice for the yearly month-before-Christmas lunch with little brother. Most years, she's taken me somewhere fancy and insisted on paying, if only to show me how far out of my price range her life is. Fifty-three years she's known me. Surely she must know I'm not much impressed by money?

We used to drink in there as teenagers - I wonder if she remembers that? She hated it then. 'The dark place', she used to call it, all too old and gloomy. She'd put Gordon Is A Moron on the jukebox for me, and I'd scrounge 10p to play The Bitch Is Back for her. But mostly she'd just sit glowering at me with her day-glo feather ear-rings and the face of someone who'd realised they were angling in an empty pond. I was eighteen before I realised we were both stealing glances at the same girls.

We teased each other rotten as kids but I miss how she was back then, the lippy tomboy who still let us know her. The sister I played with on the common, building hideaways from broken branches, playing hide-and-seek behind the standing stones. Taking the piss out of the weekend Druids with their picnic-baskets and baby-buggies. The girl who screamed blue murder when I put her in the old ducking-stool by Miller's Pond. Where's that girl hiding now, I wonder? I've missed our happy squabbling.

I still have the marks from our childhood. There's a circular burn just above my wrist where she held my arm to the electric ring on the caravan cooker till I let her have the top bunk. Seven years old and she'd already branded me as a loser, even if she did spend months apologising afterwards.

We drove Mum spare with all the arguing. "Always a battle of words with you two, isn't it?" she'd say, squeezing herself between us like a boxing referee. And it's still all words with both of us. Half a century we've surrounded ourselves with them, piling them up like sandbags. Me tending the Reference Library till the cuts put a stop to it, and nowadays lining the walls with bookcases like I'm trying to insulate the house with wisdom. She's taken her own route, of course, writing the type of sentences that no more invite close scrutiny than they might endure it. The kind of rah-rah business guff that keeps a woman in a nippy two-seater and a riverside cottage in Twickenham.

But then that's Suzie all over... or leastways, as an adult. Showing the fortress but never the treasure, keeping up the formidable façade. The house is probably lovely but I've never seen inside, never been invited. Tom showed me the outside on Facebook once. All picture perfect, but not a single peek of what lies behind the fancy lace curtains and the manicured bay trees in their mock-Regency pots. Whatever goes on beyond behind those walls, it's as sealed as North Korea and my sister's in no hurry to start issuing visas.

I know there are chickens in the garden, rare-breeds. When I phoned about Dad's funeral arrangements and Rosie answered out of breath, she told me she'd been outside feeding them. The kept girl tending the kept wildlife. She's always nice enough, but we've hardly ever spoken.

As I walk into the saloon bar, I'm surprised to see I've got here first. No sign of big sister, swiping and tapping at her phone till I distract her. The impeccable modern girl, googling away for things she could just as easily ask. Most years, she rushes me through like a courtesy appointment. Just something she's obliged to go through with, and an obvious glance at the watch every few minutes. Life's not really about conversation these days, is it? Not like the old dears used to be outside the library, swapping half-truths about the Poles and the Lithuanians on the new estate like witches casting spells against the latest intruders. Talk's not that free with Suzie. Maybe when time's money, you don't waste it on folk like me.

Roger pulls me a half of shandy and tells me she's phoned ahead, booked the little table tucked in the bay-window along the sidewall. I stash my carrier bag under the table, check her present's still inside and sneak a hasty sniff of my hands while there's still time to dash to the gents for some soap and water. A faint hint of top soil, nothing offensive, but I don't want to go scenting her world with my scrimping and saving.

We used to sit here in petulant silence, wet Easters when she was back from Durham and I was secretly glad to be out of Aberystwyth's freezing sea-breezes. From here, you can look left down the High Street or right over the churchyard wall into the Garden of Remembrance, one rambling rose still gamely showing a few pink blooms. Mum's bones are down there, nourishing its roots. Fifteen years she's been feeding it now. I don't know if Suzie's ever seen it, least not in flower.

Dad was cremated: his wishes, not ours. I stood in the crematorium with Suzie, thinking how wrong it was he was just going up in smoke. She just stood there, discreetly holding Rosie's hand. I wanted to tell her she could always have done that before. That Dad had known, hadn't given a toss. He'd just been happy she had someone, even if she couldn't seem to say so. But at least she showed her face, if not her feelings.

My phone chirrups in my pocket and I haul it out, half-expecting her last minute cancellation, but it's Tom.

"Hi Pop. Bck in Englnd for Crimbo, drvg rickshws in Soho – party season! Wot u wnt for Xmas? Hrd fm Mum? Tx"

Thailand's not working out then, I guess. Poor sod's still surprised I don't hate him, that I don't tell him off for wasting his life dribbling round the world, growing daft moustaches and acting like a kid when he's twenty-four. Still too young to realise I might understand. Envy him even, just a little, future still so far ahead he doesn't really have to think about it.

"Pick something nice and then send me the dosh instead," I text back.

He'll notice the bit I've not answered though. Janet's five years gone now - just after the job and just before Dad. The year my life went south and she moved hers North East. No birthday cards and no divorce papers. Not even a demand for money. Just silence after it all got too shameful, married to a man who thought keeping her in courgettes would be enough. I embraced domestic poverty and she embraced a man from her Book Club with aspirations and a Range-Rover.

I finish my text.

"It's the thought that counts. :) xx. Shall I give your love to Auntie Suzie?"

I don't get a reply.

My eyes scan the main road for her car, my ninety second warning before the stylish entrance. I know the way she'll walk in like she belongs somewhere better and greet me as 'Darling'. Hold me at arms' length and kiss the air either side of my face. How disappointing that'll feel, and how glad I'll still be to see her.

And then behind me, I hear her voice. "Gordon?," it says quizzically, and I turn to see her standing in the doorway in a sweater and jeans and an old waxed cotton jacket, her hair freshly bobbed. No earrings at all, not even her usual pearl studs. She could almost be that boisterous girl I used to swap insults with.

"Suzie, my love, come and have a seat," I say, rising to greet her, already wondering if we're about to spend another hour talking around life like it's something dangerous in a cage and taking care not to poke anything through the bars. I put my arms around her, ignoring how she flinches as I kiss her on the cheek. As I relax my hold and let her wriggle out of her coat, the hint of perfume reminds me how long it's been since I held a woman. As I order her a spritzer, keeping up eye contact so she won't be looking down as I'm counting out the pound coins, she's full of excuses and apologies – how her car's off the road, what a nuisance it all is so close to Christmas. How the van – I know it's Rosie's, but the name's discreetly omitted – doesn't accelerate and how it's all taken so much longer than she thought, following the diversions round the floods. How someone should put in better defences.

"Never mind all that," I tell her. "You're here now. That's what matters."

She pulls on a smile like a doorman caught off-guard without his liveried hat, and sits like she always does, fingers of her left hand covering the trace of a teenage scar along her jaw. I wonder which of us will find the right way to start the conversation.

I usually scan the papers for her by-line for a few weeks before she comes, see how she's billing herself now. 'Workplace guru', 'Emotional Intelligence expert' – she's pulled some fancy terms out of the hat, none of them quite saying how she's talking up a new existence since the bottom dropped out of being Head of HR for a chain of estate agents. She's good at it, I'll give her that. More spin than a yarn factory, our Suzie. Never a lie exactly, just a neat evasion. All about as worthwhile as a horoscope, just not as embarrassing to be caught reading it.

"So how's the exciting world of freelance journalism treating you?" I ask, almost regretting it before the words are out. I can hear the sarcasm even if she can't.

I sip my drink as she starts to answer, trying not to let her catch me gazing out of the window too obviously. I've learned to make small talk over the conveyor belt at work as I scan people's shopping, but I still glaze over when they answer. Someone'll be telling me about their glamorous holiday or their exciting weekend, and I'm nodding politely and reading between the lines.

I know Tom moans about loyalty cards and data tracking and the rest, but the lackey at the checkout sees the TV dinners for one and the half-bottles of red just as clearly as the computer does. They redeem their vouchers and they condemn themselves. The hair-dyes and lubricants, the married man who suddenly starts buying condoms and magazines about weekend breaks. The momentary blushes and the hasty packing. Towns this small run on curtain-twitching and gossip.

I see the wedding rings too - or their sudden absence, just like I notice Suzie's not wearing hers as her hand cups her jawline. I only learned about the civil partnership from a note in a Christmas card. A very private affair.

She's still talking, but I'm not following the words. I'm looking at her eyes, blinking rapidly between the wrinkles at their edges. She's always looked after herself, but they're multiplying and thickening now. I remember asking Mum once why they called it foundation. "Because it's how you cover up all that debris underneath," she told me with a wink. Always fussy about their masks, women.

As Suzie talks her crows' feet are clenching and tensing like a bird on a slippery perch. Her tongue might be chirpy and buoyant, but her eyes are desperate to cry.

I reach across the table and take her hand.

"Suzie, please – what's wrong?"

She pulls herself free, not ready to answer. In an instant, she's on her feet and pushing past me, almost running into the beer garden. She manages to hold her composure till the door swings shut behind her, but I can see her sitting on the rickety bench under the patio heaters, the window glass too thin to completely mute her sobbing.

I grab the bags and follow her outside as fast as I can without drawing attention to the drama.

There's no flinch this time as I fold my arm round her shoulders, pull her closer and let her muffle her blubbering with my jacket collar. I don't need to ask if it's serious - I've not known her cry too often down the years.

"Please, Suzie, talk to me. It's not Rosie, is it? Tell me it's not."

She pushes herself upright with one hand, eyes red from crying and cheeks blushed with embarrassment but there's the flicker of a smile on her lips. I keep my back to the window, doing my best to shield us both from prying eyes.

"No, no – thank god, no. I've still got her at least," she says, sniffing back her tears as she fumbles in her pocket for a tiny velvet-covered box. She pulls out the plain gold band and slips it back onto her ring finger, breathing in deeply to steady herself.

"No, it's not Rosie... we're good, great. Oh, I'm sorry. That sounds so selfish. I mean, only thinking of myself... what with you and Janet... I..."

I plant a kiss on her forehead, smooth back her hair as she tries to recompose her face, waiting till she's ready to say more.

"I just take it off when I'm somewhere I don't really know," she says, as if she's eager for me to understand, to be reassured. "One time, this man kept asking about my husband and I felt so bad standing there telling lies..."

Her words trail off. The tears still breech her eyelids, a stream now rather than a torrent, but they're not over yet.

"Hey, whatever this is, it's not about me, is it?" I tell her. "So how about we get you somewhere a bit more private. More dignified, eh?"

I pull her gently back towards me, let her snuggle back into my shoulder.

"A walk to mine ok? It's a good place for a cry – I do it a lot."

I gather our bags and help her to feet, see her trying on a braver face. Soon we're walking down between the high walls of Back Lane hand-in-hand, like we used to all those decades ago on the way to primary school.

As we walk, she slowly lets the story out, indignities escaping in measured doses. How competitive the market has become, how people make assumptions about what an older woman really understands. How it's all about being breezy and hip now, all mash-ups and tweet-ups. I don't even ask her what those are, I just let her talk until it's obvious she can't quite bring herself to say it.

"The work's run out, Suzie, hasn't it?"

"Yes," she says, plain and matter of fact. "Yes, totally."

I squeeze her fingers softly in mine, expecting another flood, but it doesn't come. Instead, there's a glimmer of energy back in her cheeks under the streaks of mascara that her tears and my clumsy attempts with a serviette have smeared across them.

"Five years I've spent, an old dog performing new tricks till all I look is bloody stupid. Selling them ways of seeing me as obsolete. And now they have. Without as much as a fucking thank you."

I slide my hand up to her elbow, link her arm through mine.

"Then it's time to start thinking what you're going to do when that anger wears off, eh my girl?" I tell her, surprised to be the one with the right experience. The one who knows that the bruises that come after the wound starts to heal still hurt just as much. How you have to improvise a bit in life sometimes, make your own poultices to draw the toxins out.

I retrieve the radio from the greenhouse as she sips her tea, dial in something classical to fill the empty spaces. I've not got much spare to offer her, but there's a loaf I made yesterday, last year's honey for toast and a few ladles of vegetable soup that I reheat while she sits looking out over the garden, condensation slowly dripping down the misted window.

"So why didn't you just ring me and tell me?' I ask her, voice as soft as I can make it.

I can hear my Wiltshire vowels, as much the mark of the rural peasant as the wobbly shelves of hand-labelled jars and pots. All I can think is how this shouldn't be happening to the clever girl with the degree from Durham who's probably never watched the TV news and caught herself wondering if it's already a different century somewhere else. The smart lass who's never put her court shoe in a cowpat. How I've always been more than a bit proud of her, even if I've always stopped short of telling her.

"Embarrassed, I suppose," she says. "It was why I came today... I almost didn't. Couldn't face it... telling you, I mean. Silly me, eh?"

As she speaks, the crows restart their little dance at the edges of her temples. Whatever they're scrabbling for, they've not quite unearthed it yet.

"Can we go outside?" she asks. "Show me you garden, Gordon. I'd like that."

"Course we can, my love. Say, do you want to help me plant out some winter veg? Give me a hand, eh?"

All afternoon, she scampers fascinated from one bed to the next, helping me plant out the broad beans, watching as I prune the gone-over fruit-bushes, showing her how to do it so you get more next year, not less. Either it's the relief of crying or the novelty of manual labour, but I can almost see her shoulders starting to unclench as she slowly warms in the weak sunshine.

She asks endless questions as we dig over the raised beds and get the next cycle of kale in, learning how her brother gets by, growing what he can and using his staff discount at the checkout for the things he can't. She seems amazed so much still grows even in these short, cold days, staggered at how many stones and lumps of chalk I have to dig out to get anything to flourish in this thin dry soil. I dig her up the last of the potatoes and the fennel to take with her later, a little memento of her afternoon.

"I'm sorry about earlier, Gordon. The tears and all that," she says, lugging the watering can from the standpipe to water in the new plantings.

I offer her a smile. "Don't be silly. You're my sister, aren't you? It's allowed, you know."

"It wasn't the work," she says, her steps along the narrow grassy paths between the vegetable beds as cautious as her words. "Not really."

Whatever she wants to say to me now, I tell myself it's down to her. I hold my peace and let her carry on with the watering.

"It was that pub. I know... it was my idea. But I need to tell you why. I owe you that much."

I pause, resting on the handle of my spade, hold in a breath and watch, her eyes focused stubbornly on the water spraying from the rose of the old watering-can.

"The scar on my chin... you know, how I fell over in the ladies that last Christmas I was back down from Durham?"

I nod, swallowing. I remember all right. The ambulance and the stitches, New Year's Day morning waiting in Casualty to fetch her home. Mum and Dad fretting, talking themselves out of telling her off for drinking too much, worrying if she was going to be scarred for good.

She stops her watering and turns to face me.

"I didn't fall over."

There's a pause that I leave to swell before she carries on.

"I mean… it wasn't an accident."

She's looking straight at me now, no blinking or hesitating.

"I don't get it, Suzie. What do you mean?"

"I was stood at the sink, splashing my face with cold water, trying to sober myself up a bit. You know, too much Pernod and black…"

I can still picture her coming out of A&E, head swathed in bandages and feather earrings pressed into her hand for safe-keeping. I dig my spade in deeper to keep it steady and step towards her, ready to offer… what, comfort? I'm more of a man for 'make do and mend' than for improvising. I was never good at emotion. There's no orderly catalogue system for feelings, no handy guide you can refer to that says 'for grief, see also denial and anger'.

"And this girl just grabbed my hair, hissed 'Fucking dyke' at me. Smashed my face into the hand-dryer."

The tears have come again and I ferret a clean hankie from my pocket and pass it to her, but the words are flowing now too.

"Who was it, Suzie. Who did that to you?"

"It was Becky. Used to be Janet's friend at school?"

I'm nodding but I'm dumbstruck. There's no right shelf to pluck the answer from.

"I thought no-one knew. Small-minded place like it was back then, I thought I'd just go for a drink to see the year out, chat with some old mates, pretend to flirt with the boys and then go back to Durham and Rosie. I still don't know how she knew, or if she even did. She was always a bad-tempered bitch, that girl."

The watering-can is dribbling over her feet now where she's shaking, and I take it from her hand and put it down safely on the path.

"And that's why I don't come back. Why I've kept my head down all these years. And it's all so fucking stupid. It was back before you even fancied Janet, let alone… you know. It's hardly your fault, is it? I'm so sorry."

Finally she's calm, the last tears inching down her cheeks and her hands dabbing at them with my tatty old handkerchief while I tell her over and over there's nothing to apologise for. I wait till she's completely still, and wrap my arms around her.

She's wiped her fingers across her face at some point, a few splodges of mud mingling with what's left of her make-up, and she looks down at her hands, nail-polish half-concealed under clods of earth.

"Tell you what," I offer gently. "How about we have a cuppa in the greenhouse? And why don't give your face a bit of a wash while I brew up? You'll feel better for it."

When I bring the teas, she's set two old folding chairs side by side and pats mine gently as an invitation. Without her make-up, the scar looks vivid in the late low sunlight, a jagged white line like a primitive symbol carved into a chalk hill with a sharpened flint.

I try not to look at it as she leans towards me, her eyes dry now but temples drawn in curiosity.

"So what happened to her, Gordon? To Becky?"

She almost whispers it.

"Oh, she married that guy from the rugby team at the posh school. Darryl, was it? Wound up teaching there. British Constitution, I think they called it."

I see her shoulders droop as she waits for the ending, as if she's holding out for something less triumphant.

"She got fired a few years back. Lost it one afternoon and hit a kid. Some loaded Russian's son. Not a slap, mind - a proper thrashing. Never taught since. They moved away in the end. Couldn't take the talk. People with kids would cross the road to avoid her."

There's a silent second or two before Suzie's laughter breaks.

"Oh God, Gordon, I know we shouldn't but..."

"Poetic bloody justice though, eh?" I manage to say before she hands me back the hanky so I can dab my own eyes, our snorts and titters echoing off the windows and filling the greenhouse with sound.

"Oh, would you look at us?" she tells me when we finally stop, occasional giggles still rising in her like bubbles in a glass. "Hermits Anonymous, the pair of us. How did that happen?"

"My name is Gordon Allbright, and I am a recluse!" I declaim solemnly, chinking my mug against hers in a toast. "Is there a 12 Step programme, you reckon?"

"Shit, there are steps?" she shrieks, pretending to be aghast. "We're neither of us bloody dancers, are we?" She's not forgotten all about me then.

"Seriously though, Suzie," I say, changing the subject to something more pressing, "it's getting dark and they say there's more rain coming. What with the floods and all, do you want to stay over? Better than struggling home in Rosie's van, eh?"

She's still smiling, but she looks as much surprised as grateful.

"The van'll be safe enough in the car park, and you can always give her a ring – let her know you're ok and that," I say, watching her smile soften, broadening a little.

"You're sure? It wouldn't be a nuisance?"

"Sooz?" I say, "Mi casa su casa, yes?"

"Me too, you old bugger. Me too."

She leans across and kisses me, lips soft and warm on my cheek.

After I've cobbled together some kind of supper, I do what I can to make the spare room presentable as she busies herself in the bathroom. Five minutes with a duster and a spray of air-freshener, a bulb for the bedside light. It's really Tom's room now, when he stays, although it looks more like the bric-a-brac table at the end of a jumble sale, bits of lives we don't lead anymore accumulating in drifts and piles. His old model railway is still set up on a trestle table in the corner, a miniature station-master waiting patiently on the platform for a train to pull in. Years he must have been stood there.

I knock on the bathroom door, tell her I've left her a spare dressing-gown on the landing and nip back downstairs to stick the kettle on for a final pot. It's just starting to whistle when I hear her emerge, and I give her a few minutes to make herself decent.

When I take her up a cup, she's wrapped in my old gown, looking refreshed and pale. Suzie unadorned. She looks like Mum did at her age: a woman accustomed to fresh air on her face, who lets the breeze mess up her hair and doesn't argue too much with the consequences. And I realise now what was making that funny buzzing noise I heard as I came up the stairs.

It hasn't moved for fifteen years, but the toy steam train is rounding the bend and wobbling into the tunnel, Suzie beaming at it, a nail file and an optician's screwdriver in her hand.

I stand in the doorway in my slippers as she sits in Tom's old dressing-gown, transfixed by the tiny locomotive shuffling its way back and forth on its little branch line. "A fresh cup for you, my love. And I see you got that old thing going, then?" I say.

"A couple of loose connections," she says, sounding triumphant, "but nothing a girl can't fix."

I listen, nodding as she tells me she's phoned Rosie, told her what's happened, that she's ok and she'll be home in the morning.

"Anyway, my love, I'm on earlies tomorrow," I tell her, "so you sleep well and I'll fix us some breakfast in the morning. It'll have to be about 7-ish, if that's all right?"

"That'd be lovely," she says, putting down the train handset with a reluctant sigh as she guides the locomotive to a halt at the platform. I can see she's found more of the people from the old train set. There's a posh woman with a suitcase, standing on the platform with the station-master, and a young girl waving from across the tracks. "You sleep well too. And thank you, Gordon. You know, for everything."

I pull the door to and potter off to my own bed, radio lulling me off with a Book at Bedtime, volume low enough to hear Suzie talking quietly – another call to Rosie, I'm guessing.

A few minutes later, just as I reach out to turn off the bedside light, my phone pings again. Still no reply from Tom, but there's a message from Rosie.

"Thx for looking after Sooz – v kind. Can u join us for Xmas so we can return the favour? She'd like that. Bring Tom 2 if he wants. Please say yes. Rosie x"

I lie there in the dark, looking at the little glowing screen, my fingers hesitating over the keys as I realise Suzie's right - there are steps ahead. Long strides for old legs too, especially with two left feet. And a great many more than twelve of them.

CHRIS - MATTHEW CONWAY

THE INKSLINGER
RAYMOND LUCZAK

Even though he was in excellent shape, Lance Bryson refused to take off his shirt for anyone, not even for his first time with a woman. One of his pectorals had slid down sideways so his right nipple wasn't up where it should be. He hadn't thought much of it growing up because he wore a shirt all the time, but when he saw how men, in their blush of understanding that they had to use their bodies to hook women, took to working out, building perfect torsos, and walking around shirtless, he suddenly felt he had to.

His right hand had only three long fingers with no thumb. A fourth finger, which could've been his ring finger, stopped short of its first joint. His right arm was three inches shorter than his left arm, which was fully developed. He couldn't remember a time when no one found his right arm odd or freakish. He was long in the habit of hiding his right hand inside his jacket, or keeping it inside his front pocket, like the general Napoleon Bonaparte in his paintings.

All his life he'd felt completely asymmetrical. But there was no name for what he had. It was only a birth defect.

By fourth grade, he had proved to be pretty scrappy. Everyone learned that if they picked on him, he fought back, and hard. Sometimes he swung a fist at the kid's jaw. He liked the feeling of power that he got whenever he held up his deformed fist.

Eventually, his classmates left him alone, but in fact that was the problem. They left him completely alone. He'd frightened them with his ferocity.

Dad said that Lance had to look out for himself because no one else was going to. Lance wanted to ask him if anyone was ever going to look out for him, but he knew it was a stupid question.

He tried to look busy by walking around the playground. Sometimes he got on the swing and aimed for the sky as high as he could. He imagined himself as one of those comic book superheroes blessed with the ability to sail through the air because if he could, he would. He wouldn't wear one of those silly costumes, but he'd careen around those snickering boys and those whispering girls who were always glancing back at him. He would be a wind that no one could catch.

At dawn and then after school, he joined Dad and his three brothers as they performed their chores around the tree farm, which was within a 20-minute biking distance of Littlefork, Minnesota. The land, full of maples in dizzying heights and widths, had belonged to Dad's family for four generations, and the farms on both sides of the property belonged to two of his uncles. They lived in the shadow of the Koochiching Forest, which was about twenty minutes south of the Canadian border. Winnipeg, up in Canada, was a good five hours away. He'd never been there.

In the summer twilight, as bats fluttered above the trees, he listened to his uncles, cousins, and brothers carry on with their boisterous voices over beer. They bellowed about the trees, the Minnesotan weather in all its moods, and the variables affecting maple syrup prices. They never talked about anything else, and they never lowered their voices.

Dad rarely talked much to him. Those flinty eyes of his told him everything.

He hated hearing the easy cadences between himself and his three brothers as they drilled into the trees and replaced the buckets of syrup. He felt rather like a hired hand like some of the temporary migrants willing to work for very little money. He just happened to have the same last name as their boss.

In fifth grade, Ms. Lomax read out loud a few short tales about Paul Bunyan, the legendary lumberjack giant who felled entire square miles of timber in mere hours. She asked the students to come up with equally tall tales.

Then came his turn to read. It wasn't long. "One day he tried to chop down the world's tallest tree, but when it fell, it fell so fast that Paul couldn't move out of the way quickly enough. The tree's branches were thick like daggers so they tore off Paul's right arm. That's why he had to go one-armed and that's why we don't hear any more stories about him."

He turned and went back to his desk.

The entire class turned rigid with silence.

Ms. Lomax stammered. "But that's not what I . . . I mean, Lance, really." There was a hot flash of anger in her voice. She turned to the next student in his row. "Your turn."

For the rest of the school year, she always gave him a look that said, You're too *different*.

He dreamed of swinging an ax like a boomerang at her and having it slice her neck like a wide knife going through an onion.

His classmates institutionalized their distance. "Weird" was the word they used the most. He took to speaking in whispers. He wanted most of all to merge into the woodwork and go unnoticed.

When his older brother Steve got married and moved out, Lance took over his room in the attic. At 12 years old, he felt puny in the empty room. There was a twin-sized bed that had belonged to Steve. He didn't feel right in it. Steve was tall and brawny. Steve had married Ella, a woman who was a foot-and-a-half shorter. Lance liked her. Ella laughed easily and she didn't seem at all bothered by his right hand. He envied Steve for finding and marrying such a nonjudgmental woman.

He chanced upon a box of comic books in Steve's closet. Superheroes in costumes that would have looked ridiculous in reality somehow became plausible in the comics. The heroes wrestled with villains in darker and more sinister outfits.

The he saw the cover of *Pincher*, a one-off comic book drawn and written by a Dean Raskie, a man with wire-rimmed glasses and in a white lab coat who looked deliriously happy with his arm, suddenly stretched outward like taffy, stretching out in a claw. The teaser tagline read EVERYONE HAD HURT HIM . . . NOW IT WAS TIME FOR PAYBACK!!!

He didn't know what to feel or think when he saw the main character Johnny Swede having a deformed right arm. A fire had left him a partially melted arm and without parents, so he bounced from one foster home to another. No one wanted him. Years and years of endless humiliation went by. In college and afterwards he studied molecular chemistry, biology, and genetics. Dr. Swede discovered that the DNA from his stunted arm had a particular molecular structure, which, when combined with a highly experimental regrowth drug, enabled his arm to elongate and bloom into a lethal hand-claw. His arm developed amazing biceps capable of holding up weight up to 300 pounds without making him break into a sweat. The only problem was that he could do that only when his body released certain rage-induced chemicals. Returning to his hometown, he confronted each tormentor from his childhood, one by one. No matter how they tried to run and hide, his claw taught them a quite a lesson. He pinched their necks and held them just off the floor until they died. No one, let alone the determined police detective, could figure out what kind of creature was killing all these people. There seemed no pattern to how the victims were chosen. Because it had been so many years since they had seen Johnny Swede, the detective couldn't figure out what all these victims had in common. When the woman Dr. Swede loved realized that he wasn't going to stop killing his tormentors, she gave him one last kiss and shot him point-blank in his heart. The detective was unable to come upstairs in time.

Lance sobbed.

That, right there in a mere 24 pages, was the entire story of his own rage, exposed like the dirty secret that it was. And all in fuzzy color on pulpy paper. He read it over and over again. He memorized each line of dialogue and description and mentally photographed each panel.

But then the more he thought about the story, the angrier he became. Dr. Swede wasn't really a bad guy. He didn't warrant death. What kind of a message was that to guys like Lance? That they deserved to die because of their physical deformities? What about those tormentors? They had no right to treat him that way at all. At all!

No, Dr. Swede couldn't die. There was no way he could. Rage by its very nature is invincible. It may sleep most of the time, but it never dies. It's always there, lurking.

So he began drawing by studying how Dr. Swede looked in his moments of rage. He would call himself The Inkslinger after Paul Bunyan's ingenious accountant sidekick Johnny Inkslinger. And he'd do a number on everyone.

At night, when Lance knew he should be asleep, instead he crouched over his desk. Over his left arm was a lamp that gave him warmth and light. He sketched and sketched one drawing after another until he felt satisfied with his ability to convey an eye, a mouth, and everything else that made Dr. Johnny Swede human as everyone else. He spent more time agonizing over how his stunted arm should look like, so he looked closely at the way the muscles in his own shortened forearm moved in the mirror. He perused the latest comics at the drugstore downtown, but he had no allowance for such luxuries. Seeing the wide range of characters and their quasi-human forms made him wish that everyone in real life could accept him as he was, in the same way that no one in comics ever questioned the illogic of these body proportions.

Night after night, as the chill of winter seeped into his bedroom, he remained tireless. He had to convey the supple musculature the same way that the artist Curt Swan did with his later Superman drawings. Sometimes he worked so hard he didn't realize that his nose was dripping. When a bead of sweat fell onto the paper and smeared a line, it was almost enough to make him explode out of frustration.

When he finally fell asleep from total exhaustion, his right arm took a long time before it finally loosened with the rest of his body.

Around the dinner table, Lance always sat next to his mother, and at the end of the table where his right arm could be hidden from sight. He'd seen how his father's eyes glossed over that arm. It was different when Dad looked at his other sons. There was no glossing over.

If Dad spoke to him, it was always with a stern tone of voice. He heard Dad's conciliatory boys-will-be-boys tone of voice when he talked to his other sons.

He dreamed of the day that he'd be returned to the orphanage. But as far as he could tell, Dad was his real father. He had the same eyes, the same jaw, and the same sloping shoulders. His left thumb curled back just like Dad's.

When he was fifteen, he asked Mom. "Why does Dad hate me so much? I didn't do anything wrong."

"Hush, hush," she said as she pounded down the risen bread dough on the table.

"I hear how he talks to my brothers. He talks differently to me."

"He doesn't hate you."

"Well, he doesn't love me like he . . . I wish I was normal."

"You are normal."

"Don't lie to me, Mom." He stormed out of the kitchen and went outside to the pond on the other side of the farm. His brothers had gone off with Dad and their buddies for a rare afternoon of swimming on Lake Kabetogama, a half-hour drive away. That was another reason why he was so angry and hurt. They didn't ask him to come along. Did they truly forget about him? Or was it because their buddies still didn't like the look of his right arm? Or was it because they mistakenly assumed that he couldn't swim on his own?

He watched the mallards swimming. A few of them stood on the muddy shore and shook their iridescent feathers. He'd always liked ducks. Nothing seemed to faze them. They never hurried when they paddled, and they were always looking out for their little ones. Then he saw a duck, not quite little nor large, hopping slightly toward the pond. He peered down and saw that one of the duck's webbed feet looked as if the front part had been cut off. He watched the duck hop onto the water and right itself before paddling. The duck wasn't as smooth; it bobbed slightly sideways as it approached its siblings. They parted for him, but they didn't move away. It was just another sunny day for them.

It was the most beautiful sight. He wanted to be treated just like that duck.

He wondered about whether it'd be better if he amputated his deformed hand—no, the whole arm! What then? What would Dad say to that?

Thinking about Dr. Swede made his high school years easier. Somehow, even if no one knew about his secret identity, he felt happier in being The Inkslinger. In his dreams, the power of his drawings would more than equal the cruel stings from a slingshot. His body was changing, but he was happy with the changes. He was going to have a hairy chest. He gained a little weight in his arms. He continued to help out on the farm.

When he decided to write a letter to Johnny Swede's creator, Dean Raskie, it took him a few days to think about what he wanted to say. He didn't want to seem like a wimp. He chose his words carefully. A single paragraph was best. He said that as a person with a similar deformity, he didn't appreciate being seen as someone who should die. People who bullied others deserved to die. He was careful with how he lettered his words, matching the style used in Dean Raskie's comic.

He was very surprised to get a letter from Dean Raskie ten days later. "Dear Mr. Bryson," Mr. Raskie had typed on a blank index card. "I have only one arm." Raskie explained that it was the most autobiographical story he'd ever written. It hadn't sold a lot of copies, but those who did buy them almost always wrote him a letter of thanks. "I may not know you, but you are a superhero. Thank you for writing." Below it was his home phone number and his signature.

The next day he went to school on his bike and then right after the day ended, he pedaled to the public library downtown. He had gathered up his coins for the pay phone in the library's basement. He didn't want anyone to see him, and he didn't want his family to overhear him on his first long-distance call.

"Hello?"

"Hi," he whispered. "This is Lance Bryson."

"Oh, there you are. I've been expecting to hear from you. Your letter impressed me very much. How are you doing today, kiddo?"

The warmth in Mr. Raskie's voice surprised him. Without prompting, he poured out all of his life story, punctuated by the operator's automated voice telling him to drop in more coins. Finally Mr. Raskie took down the pay phone number and called him right back.

When they hung up at last, he felt so giddy. He had a friend who'd truly understood him! He felt as if he could grow out his remaining fingers and elongate his arm and hug everybody on the street!

They struck up a correspondence.

Dean lived with his wife and children outside Yonkers, New York. He really wanted to draw his own stories, but with children around, he rarely had the time. So he stuck to writing scripts for Marvel.

It wasn't long before Dean asked to see his work.

He sweated and sweated over his three sheets of drawings. They had to be absolutely perfect. He fretted for days while awaiting a response.

Dean said, "You've mastered the look, but it's not you. Where are you in your drawings?"

He didn't quite understand. He'd been so afraid of standing out and being made fun of.

He didn't open Dean's next two letters.

Near the end of his junior year in high school, he was called to the principal's office. Someone wanted to meet him.

When he pushed the door open to see who was sitting opposite Principal Wilson, he caught a glint of sunlight dancing in the stranger's black beard.

"There you are, Lance. Come on in."

The stranger stood up and extended his one hand. "I'm Dean Raskie. I happened to be at a comic book convention down in Minneapolis, so I thought I should come look you up. I hadn't realized how far up north you were!" He chuckled as he took out the folded drawings from inside his jacket; his other sleeve was safety-pinned inside his exterior coat pocket. "I believe these are yours."

"Mr. Raskie asked to see you because you've won a scholarship."

"Scholarship?"

"Yes. Why don't you tell him?"

Mr. Raskie explained that there was a brand-new summer camp for novice cartoonists and comic book artists, and that he'd recommended him for a scholarship there. The camp was two hours away from Littlefork. The group would meet for two weeks.

Lance had never felt so small as he looked up at Mr. Raskie's sheepish grin.

At Camp Courage North the boys were able-bodied, but they were different. There were no arrogant jocks in the bunch. They had pencil-thin arms and legs; a few of them were on the heavy side. The few girls there didn't try to look pretty at all. He had been surprised to see girls; he'd always thought comic books were for boys only. He watched all the girls. A few looked at his right hand openly only to remember that one wasn't supposed to stare like that. He decided that because no one but Mr. Raskie knew who he was, he'd behave differently. This time, instead of looking away from shame, he gave the girls a small smile.

He couldn't believe his luck when a nice-looking girl sat opposite him at a dining room table. That had never happened to him in school. The girl wore a white T-shirt and jeans. Her dirty blond hair was cut short and her face was softly sprinkled with the light brown sugar of freckles. She turned to him. "Um, can I ask you a question?"

"Sure."

"What happened to your hand?"

"Nobody really knows, but I've always had it. Some doctors think it's genetic. It looks different to everyone but it feels normal to me." He held up his three-fingered hand.

"Works for me."

"You don't have a thumb?"

"Nope." He flexed the finger that was in the thumb's place.

"Wow. That is weird."

"It's not weird if you live with it all the time." He couldn't believe that he'd actually said that.

She looked at him. "Oh."

"Tell me about your favorite comic book."

She lit up and began talking about the Fantastic Four.

He was too happy to sit there and listen.

As others drifted out of the mess hall to join others around the nightly campfire, they were the remaining pair. He looked up and saw Mr. Raskie wink at him with a thumb up before stepping outside.

Three days later Aurora asked him, "Please kiss me." It was early morning. She liked to walk through the woods before coming in for breakfast. He followed her.

"Why?"

"Because I've never been kissed."

They were sitting on a log in front of Lake George. He leaned over and gave her cheek a peck.

She was so startled that she fell backwards on the grass. "Hey!"

He fell backwards too and gazed quietly into her eyes. "Sorry."

"Kiss me again." She giggled.

He reached forward to kiss. As she turned her head, he accidentally kissed her on the lips.

She giggled.

He laughed.

She looked at him with a bit of wonder in her eyes.

He wanted so much to touch her, hold her hand—well, anything!

She leaned forward and kissed him on the lips, but this time she didn't back off.

He opened his lips a little.

She did too.

Once the tips of their tongues touched, it was pure electricity. They couldn't stop tasting each other.

Then they heard the distant ring of the breakfast bell.

They couldn't stop giggling together as they hurried through their meal and went their separate ways to their classes.

Lance wasn't the only one who idolized Dean Raskie. The teacher always took a moment to look at each student's face before responding, and when he did talk, he was precise. He never sounded patronizing when he made gentle but pointed suggestions about how to improve the craft of storytelling through images. "Story is king," he said over and over again. "Otherwise it's just a bunch of pretty pictures."

One night, after dinner, Mr. Raskie took him aside. "Draw me."

"Only if you draw me too." There was a pause. "Sorry. I didn't mean to say that."

Mr. Raskie chuckled. "Oh, no, it's all fine."

They sat opposite each other on a dining room table and took up their pencils and tablets as if ready for battle. Mr. Raskie taped the four corners of his blank sheet to the table. This way he could still draw one-handed.

Lance drew a gangly knight with a barrel chest and one arm holding up a sword. Mr. Raskie had talked about why people still cared about King Arthur and the Roundtable.

Mr. Raskie smiled. "Not bad." He responded with a very tall and wide-chested man, flowing hair, a mischievous smile, and a spear standing in his right hand. Then there was his right hand hidden in a glove. "That's going to be you one day. Just you wait and see." He longed more than anything to have Mr. Raskie as his father.

As much as he liked making out with Aurora, he really preferred her counselor Judy. She was a college student who was studying to become a high school teacher. She had a habit of pulling her loose hair out of her face and behind her ears. She had a wide jaw, a full bosom, and very thin lips. He wanted to kiss her. He dreamed about her often at night, but he knew he couldn't very well relieve himself in a cabin of seven other boys his age.

"I like you."

He nearly dropped his jaw. No one had been ever this direct without insulting him.

Judy jumped down onto the sofa next to him and took his withered hand. "This is cool. Way cool."

He didn't know what to think. He now had an erection. No woman had ever touched the most private part of his life, that empty space between those three fingers.

She looked up into his eyes. "This is the most beautiful thing about you."

"This?" he stammered.

"Yes. You're a wonderful guy, and this is what's makes you so wonderful. If you didn't have this, you'd be one of those arrogant pricks who didn't care about how girls feel."

He felt his entire body trembling. No one had a right to be this happy.

"You okay?"

"Yeah," he whispered.

"Oh, don't be afraid." She took his hand and kissed each of his three fingers. She didn't flinch from looking into his eyes.

He woke up and muffled his sobs into his pillow. It was just a friggin' dream. Oh, man.

A year later he got accepted into the Minneapolis College of Art and Design. It seemed that having Mr. Raskie as a reference carried some weight. He couldn't wait to move to Minneapolis. *Minneapolis?!?* He'd always wanted to live in a big city. That was where all those exciting stories in comic books happened. He couldn't wait!

Then came that August dawn when Steve's wife, pregnant with her third child, came to the farm to take Lance to the bus station downtown.

Dad said, "Well, I gotta get to work. Good luck."

Mom said, "I want you home for Thanksgiving, you hear?"

He nodded and hugged Mom goodbye. None of his brothers were around. Of course, they had chores.

He couldn't sleep on the meandering bus ride. He kept waving good-bye to the farms they passed until he no longer recognized them.

As days and classes in Minneapolis flurried by, Lance observed how students embraced the grotesquery in their art, tattoos, and piercings.

Instructors were initially surprised to learn about his right hand.

Without thinking, he said with a touch of pride, "I can still draw."

He was surprised when a few classmates said, "Oh, cool! Let's see what you've got. Wow! You got nice lines there."

MCAD was definitely a few galaxies away from Littlefork.

He never returned home for Thanksgiving. Over the passing months, he decided to have one of his shins tattooed with a drawing of his own deformed hand shaped almost like a hawk's talon. By then, he'd met a few others who had the same condition, and that the quite rare condition had a name: Poland syndrome, named after the 19th century British surgeon who'd first described the congenital deformity.

When his father died suddenly of a heart attack, Lance didn't attend the funeral services. He knew that there was no way he could go back to the farm. He was living with his girlfriend, Trisha. He handled web site design and maintenance for an advertising agency's clients in Butler Square off Hennepin Avenue. In his free time, he posted his comics online and made friends among disabled cartoonists like Crippen and others.

But when Mr. Raskie died, he and Trisha drove all the way to Yonkers. When they entered the church, the stained glass windows shimmered with color across the congregation. He scanned the audience, and he saw he wasn't the only one with an odd appendage. Here and there in pews were women and men of all ages, some with missing arms and hands; others sat in wheelchairs. The sunlight caught a rainbow across their eyes, an eternal shimmer for the one-armed giant who'd rescued them from lifetimes of hurt and rage. He was so proud to join them. Who knew that freaks could be so beautiful?

DAD SAID SOME THINGS ON THE CAR RIDE HOME
MAIA IRWIN

This is for the kid that is out.

This is for the kid that has only told the people that follow their blog.

This is for the person that lifts their chin when they tell people.

This is for the person that whispers it.

This is for the gay girl in a woman's studies class listening to the instructor saying that not all feminists are hairy lesbians.

The kid that got kicked out.

The girl that burst into tears when her dad said he wasn't voting for that guy because he legalized gay marriage.

This is for the kid that doesn't believe in god anymore. The kid that struggles to make peace between faith and sexuality.

The kid that throws love thy neighbor back in people's faces.

The boy that stares at dresses in stores.

The gay girl who has to keep telling everyone she's bi.

The kid that is facing hate on all fronts, not just this one.

The genderqueer kid who says something about it when those aren't their pronouns. The genderqueer kid that bites their lip and accepts it.

The kid who got asked if they have a preference and refused to say because they knew they were trying make them gay or straight.

This is for the 50 year old closeted trans woman. The eighty year old who just found out that they were never broken.

The person who just wants to be what they've been told is normal.

The person that doesn't care.

The person that's still changing names to find a good fit.

The kid who's been called a special snowflake one to many times.

The person who's identity is never in the questionnaire.

The kid that is just holding out for 18.

This is for the person that gets called immature because they never wanted a relationship like that.

The kid that feels like there's no way out.

This is for the person who gets asked if they're a girl or boy.

The person who has to explain that pan and bi are not the same things.

This is for the kid who only figured out what they were when they took a test.

This is for the kid that has known since they were 8.

The 45 year old who is still bringing their special friend to thanksgiving dinner.   The 14 year old who told everyone the day they realized it.

This is for the flamboyantly gay man.   This is for the gay man who has never sung show tunes in his life.

This is for the lipstick lesbian. This is for the dyke.

This is for the sex repulsed asexual.   This is for those that don't really mind it.

This is for me.   This is for you.

MAN AT THE EDGE OF THE WORLD
MARK ELLIS

Cape St. Vincent, Portugal

Evening and we are late in our journey,
sky a grayish blue like slick whale skin.
Wind blowing mists and clouds landward,
gusts that make the land, the points thrusting seaward
seem to shift, to move along with our swaying bodies.

Nowhere have I ever been happier,
though we still have far to go to reach Seville
and will not make it before dark.

Standing at the whitewashed wall,
wind lifting the shirt from my chest,
beating my hair, burning my eyes and ears
my eyes see a man alone on a distant point.

He stands there, looking down
where the waves break against the steep cliff
sometimes looking out, to the west.
For a moment,
I turn back to the lighthouse, the brightening windows
and look back, but he is gone.

Many times I have dreamed about this man, this place.
Sometimes I am watching him,
more often I stand in his place, I am him
looking out to sea
or looking down at the waves beating the cliff.
I am a statue, the idol in a temple,
looking down at the world and its misery.
I think of diving from my stand, but never can.
My place is to stand here looking seaward.

This is a holy place, a place of embarkation.
The Navigator Prince Henry trained his sailors here.
Romans, Greeks fought the sea around this cape,
as did those before them, half human, half spirit.
And I stand here as well, half human, half spirit
on this point, at the edge of the world.

MISOGYNISTIC LESBIAN
XANDRIA PHILLIPS

she is not a shoe to be broken
in. don't revert to a male customed
singing her parts into order. she is not
the lock. your tongue is, and she
unlocks you the way only throbbing
can. you thought there about what
a handful she could be. not just her
breasts, but the cocks of matrimony
floating up in her eyes as you lifted
her shirt. your hand can be just
that tool of sexy degradation. you too
can pull yourself from her tensed
with pleasure and mire, just as you too
can imagine a band of poised silicone
cocks waiting to prepare her vagina
for you and all that you do.

NICK CARRAWAY OUT ON THE TOWN
JAMES PENHA

> The supercilious assumption was that on Sunday
> afternoon I had nothing better to do.
> —*The Great Gatsby*, **Chapter 2**

The elevator boy dressed soon after coming
inside Nick. "The super'll can me humming
the funeral march if he sees that 'out of order'
sign I left outside the shaft." He was drumming

his fingers on the nightstand waiting to be paid
but McKee's Leika hadn't yet been made
the receptacle of Nick's pleasure since the boy's
lever engaged eagerly, but its rapidity dismayed.

When Nick had told McKee he'd "be glad,"
he'd turned to talk directly to the lad
who'd rubbed his finger tips to deal
with McKee whose C-note was judged "not bad."

McKee promised to document the action from behind
or otherwise facelessly but Nick had to remind
the photog of his promise though the boy didn't seem to care
who was watching what as long (or short) as he could grind.

After the shot was shot and the boy had left,
McKee finally disrobed into his sheets and Nick bereft
and juxtaposed clambered out of bed and dressed
for a departure designed to be definitive if not deft.

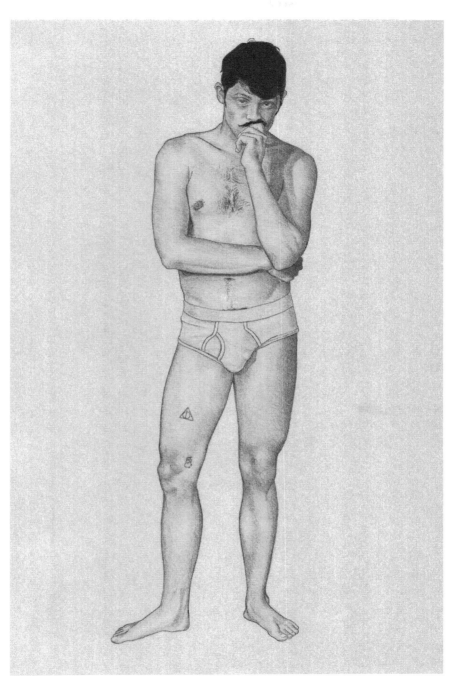

CORY - MATTHEW CONWAY

HONEYMOON
CHIP WILSON

Seville sang from buxus
On Marlborough Hill.
Its burnt evening dew is
vapour causeless in frozen air.
It is kind
On Andalusian lips-
The burnt and dusty chewed.
My cheeks fizz with wine,
Fluted and chill.
And the memory cured
me wholesome with
Beans and tarts,
The Rosemary earth of
Paprika-singed roots
and waxy Manchego biting
With its citrus peck
Unmelted in searing Montellano.
The air-con did nothing in our
Stifling woollen room,
Our burgundy boudoir.
Not like the fire
In our honeymoon home
Which awaits our gaze
and our writhing feet:
Yours in socks
And braver toes of mine will still
Complain of draft.
And we'll drink, sleep.
Kinetic light will lull us safe
In arms large and tan
Algae blue
With tattoos
And beards will knit
The closeness we can muster.
Books we will stack and hold
And daffodils will alight in cold.
    They'll be honey.
Paws and skin valleys
To map and cave
And kiss and shave.
And an amber pint to charge
with yours.
On our first nights
As husbands.

TO THE MAN AT THE BAR
CHRISTOPHER ROSE

You harass my boyfriend with your banter
as he slings drinks behind the counter
because your martini isn't strong enough
or he didn't give you the correct change

then you drone on and on
about your three daughters,
five sons, two ugly grand children,
your child support payments

and how both of your ex wives
are selfish ogres, too.
But he and I know that despite
your sexually exaggerated tales

of your supermodel girlfriend, we know
your true motivations as you steal glances
at patrons here are at this watering hole
under a rainbow flag.

CROSSROADS
KEVIN HOGAN

He went into the hotel bathroom
To change far beyond clothing.
She emerged the same person,
But in a purely feminine form.

And though I'd never gone out
With a girl whose arms and thighs
Were as muscular, her skin was
As smooth as her kisses and hair.

We did all those things you do
In a hotel room with someone
You fully intend to take out
To dinner, but only much later.

Then came later and the time
To go out on the town, so
I asked if she'd care to join me?
Her acceptance was barely a nod.

Soon we stood at the threshold
Of more than a door to a hallway,
And I'll never forget the feeling as
She took my arm at her crossroads.

COLLECT YOURSELF
KEVIN HOGAN

Reach an age.
Hold a job.
Put up fences.
Raise a family.
Give them all
Your very best,
Until the day
You wake up
In a body
As foreign as
A Kafkan bedbug.
Then as you
Lie crushed within
A thickening shell
Of external expectations,
If you discover
That you are
More than titles,
Make the journey
To where you're
Welcomed and can
Summon the strength
To smash archetypes
And the patience
To collect yourself.

FIRST LOVE
FRED LOWE

Seventeen,
1965 , the West Village:
I was seventeen,
he was 26, a full grown man
with eyes as blue as ink
faintly diluted;
his hair was black and glossy
as anthracite –
that ever delicious
Irish combo
of blue and black
and moonstone white.
His cock, well, I never
saw anything like it:
a column, a marble
pillar with a fat round,
dented knob.

It was May:
wisteria in full bloom
covered the façade
of his building. The
window beside the bed
was open. I lay under
him, quivering, clueless
as a child bride awaiting
instruction and
watched the bees,
furrily black as his chest
and belly, buzz and suck,
working the sweet,
racemes.

It was like a dream.
I finally had my cake,
 this wondrous man,
and I planned
to eat it, too.

BULLY
FRANK ADAMS

The boy
who beat me
when I was eight
did not know
he'd be beating me
the rest of my life.
He beats me daily
and though my wounds
have healed: he left
permanent scars
on my heart.

MONDAY NIGHT SHOWING
HANNAH R. HJERPE

Every Monday night for the past fourteen years—unusual exceptions including national holidays, birthdays, or the odd funeral—Val and Tony had gone to see a movie. What became ritual when they were first together had faded into habit once they were not, and now both in their late thirties, eight years post-breakup, the practice had begun to seem arcane to even them. But, unlike cigarettes or carbs, they could not quite find a good enough reason to give it up altogether. Each Sunday evening the decision was made: title, time, theater. Responsibility of choice exchanged each week, the decision passed along through a single text message—Flashes, 6:15pm, Cinema 20. Six Days Even, 5:45pm, AMC on Hollywood. No Uncertain Terms, 7pm, Regal 15. They met five minutes before the house lights dimmed, exchanged a compulsory hug, and settled into their seats, center of the row, a third of the way back. They exit before the credits roll. Tickets were purchased ahead of time by the deciding party, snacks were brought in pockets or not at all, and no one existed during those ninety minutes except them.

Since their split, Val and Tony had accumulated other lives: families, stable jobs, furniture not made of wicker and not meant for a lawn. They invested in button-up shirts that needed occasional pressing, electric juicers, sensible vehicles. Val had finally taken those Spanish classes she swore she'd take; Tony spoke knowledgeably on craft beer and jazz. Deftly spun sugar glass futures that had once seemed so impossibly far-flung to the pair of 20-somethings, lying awake late at night in sticky sheets, had crystalized before them and now perched perilously on separate cakes in separate bakery windows.

Their wives had never met. Val had never seen Tony's kitchen, where he'd laid tile he had made himself. She had not met his two-year-old daughter, and did not know she was from Tony's wife's first marriage. Val did not know that he had finally bought that '68 El Camino, or that he had used it in one of his own films. She did not know that his wife kept birds whose incessant chirping kept him up at night. And he, in turn, had never taken the exhausting series of dirt roads back to the studio Val rented from her now ex-mother-in-law. He did not know she quit drinking four years ago, after driving her brother's Volvo into a frozen pond. He had seen a photo or two of the ceremony, but remained unaware that Val had made both her own and her wife's, now ex-wife's, wedding dresses. He did not know that their petition for adoption had fallen through. Val did not ask after Tony's brother. He did not ask after hers. They did not call or write. They did not email or do lunch.

It was a Sunday evening, the second of November. The sky was dark already, the air still and crisp, hinting at frost—early for this far south. Val stared blankly through her studio's back window out onto the dried and browning garden. The perennials had been left unattended for far too long; an oversized and unsupported tomato plant was left to clamor over itself until inevitably crushed by its own weight; various desiccated shoots from unlabeled bulbs curled and shriveled like mummified fingers. Worst of all, though, were the dozens of engorged, unharvested squash. They sported patterns of rabbit teeth and insect tunnels, evidence of deer nibbles and spider webs, and reflected a distinct negligence that made even Val squirm. But she had never entertained more than a mild amusement with the rows of impatient vines before Claire had moved out, and now that the main house would be kept empty for nine months out of the year, the effort expended on nourishing an unmanageable overabundance of zucchini hardly seemed worth it.

It occurred to her then that she hadn't told Tony even about the divorce. There was no story there, really. It had been a quiet event, and largely unmentioned unless perfunctorily required. Val and Claire had been an efficient couple; they had tended a relationship built on a foundation of practical but tepid affections, so its slow and unmediated decay over the last couple years had surprised no one. A largely neutral couple, their fights had always been few and far between, often over insignificant topics. The gloss-level of wood finish to be used on the interior of the guesthouse was one snag; whether to serve French or Californian wine at the department holiday party, another. But as the years went by, their disagreements became increasingly insignificant and revealed much more of their diminished relationship than either cared to admit. Val drank; Claire had affairs. And whether out of fear or indifference, the ever-widening rift encouraged by these disagreements was never addressed, and each time left larger silences in the squall's wake. When Claire was offered tenure out of state, she took the job and moved out the following week, leaving divorce papers on the kitchen table. And so the garden fell into disuse along with the inherited house and the jointly owned station wagon that Val refused to sell.

Val's phone buzzed once, hidden under stacks of ungraded midterm papers. The garden and the divorce and even the car wreck blurred and faded from her thoughts, like waking from a bad dream. Sloughing the papers off with an unusual carelessness and scattering them to far corners of her unswept floor, she snatched at her now silent phone. The glowing face read,

'Ten Men Fewer, 8pm, AMC'

They do not discuss the movies anymore, beforehand or afterwards. There are no debates over tasteful political aesthetic or the questionable effects of one light filter over another. They do not scan plotlines in anticipation, or quibble about artistic decisions in their seats as the credits roll; they hadn't in years. When the film concludes, they quietly stand and stretch and exit the theater step-in-step, pausing not even to examine the posters of the upcoming attractions. Once a couple feet clear of the theater, they will momentarily turn to face each other and one of two just barely noticeable reactions will be the only necessary review. They will look at each other, and one or the other of them will produce either a nearly imperceptible smile, or a nearly imperceptible shrug. In response, the other will nod once. The exchange occupies a fleeting amount of space, just a fraction of a moment. A fraction that, to an objective observer, might not have ever even occurred. But after so many years, and so many shrugs, they do not need more time than that.

Monday night arrives and draws to a close in nearly the same breath. The credits begin to roll and they stand and stretch and quietly exit the theater, step-in-step. They pause. Tony shrugs and Val nods. It has been a slow season for good pictures. Any other night, they would turn away now, remaining silent until the following Sunday night.

But instead, Tony doubles back. "Val—"

"Maybe next time, it should be our last one."

"Yes, I think so."

They walk to their cars, separately.

Val's classes blur together that week. Mornings at faculty meetings with glazed smiles and weak coffee; half-hearted lectures and shortened office hours; evenings spent grading and regrading midterms; losing focus and staring out over the back garden, mind scattered to thoughts of squash and cabernet bottles; coming to, only to see her own finger, pale and cold, languidly tracing the letter "A" on her back window. Many hours later, ceding ground and returning the absent-mindedly graded exams to her bag, Val scans local show times looking for just the right film. It cannot be too short, or it might seem like she was too eager for its end; it cannot be too long, or she might come across as reticent. It was her idea, after all. Or at least, she said it first.

The genre of the film was equally important. A comedy gave the impression of flippancy—a war story, that of a hyperinflated ego. They were not doing this for attention; they did not deserve accolades—nor did they deserve rebuke. They had known this would have to happen for several years now; it was out of their hands.

Sunday evening arrives. She has finished grading the papers. She has finished sweeping. And she has finished a weak, but very hot, cup of mint tea. Still not used to the late autumn desert chill after nearly fifteen years, she retreats further into a very old sweatshirt. Dragging her computer over onto her lap, she looks up the theater and narrows in on time listings.

5:30pm – perfect.

Adults: 2

Standard or Extended Service tickets?
A momentary pause, mouse hovering over the latter. Purchase.

Val arrives at the theater fourteen minutes before the film starts. She is not quite sure why she is so early—she has driven to this theater dozens of times. She looks around, down both sidewalks, but where usually she might walk around the block or sneak a cigarette, she turns, opens the theater doors, and walks in. Tony is already there. He looks up from his watch. Truthfully, it might have seemed odd for either to be early if it were not the last time.

He walks up with an uncomfortable briskness and hugs her, holding on just one or two seconds too long.

"I thought it might be…"

"—Odd?"

"—being here early", he finishes.

"It is the last one, though", she concedes.

He nods.

She hands him his ticket. They enter the theater and find their seats, center of the row, one third back. The house lights dim, leaving the aisles gently highlighted by warm yellow track lights.

The film is uncomfortably long, just as she'd planned. They sit sharing in silence, absorbing faces and the occasional clumsily cut scene, internally criticizing audio issues balancing dialogue and music. She will find no need to mention these thoughts later, though, even if it were not the last time. He sees them, too. And after fourteen years, she can pin a minute shift in his posture to a disappointingly lit scene—a gentle brushing back of hair from his forehead to a deftly executed line. He squirms slightly, slipping further into his seat—he thinks the song playing in the background is inappropriate for the scene. He's right.

Val slips in and out of focus, and the evening comes to a close more quickly than she has anticipated. The credits begin to roll, but the two do not move. Several more minutes pass in silence as they sit, eyes lazily scanning through the slowly scrolling names of make-up artists, narrative voices, production companies. The projection ends, the house lights remain dimmed, and a pre-recorded female voice announces over the loudspeakers,

Good Evening. Our theater is proud to provide extended service to its Gold and Platinum customers. Will all individuals holding extended service tickets please follow the illuminated aisles to the front of the theater. Take caution in the darkness.
Your patience is appreciated.

As the recording ends, a tertiary set of lighting illuminates the aisles, coating their feet in a faintly pulsing violet glow. Though neither Val nor Tony have seen these particular lights before, they are more than aware of where they lead. The two old friends rise and progress with a seemingly rehearsed deliberateness towards the aisle. Three other individuals in the theater mirror these actions, though they appear to have all come alone. Like beads of sweat dragged onwards by no other force than gravity, the five progress through the now deserted—though still dark—theater, forming a quiet, single-file line. At the base of the screen is a small set of three wooden stairs. Decades of use have rendered the stairs worn and softened, but they appear no less sturdy than they might have when they were first built.

Val and Tony linger, stepping in at the end of the line of five. For the past eight years they had hardly exchanged more than two-dozen words in person, and now, at the end of this line, they struggle to come up with any at all. Tony doesn't mention that his wife had left him three months ago, that he'd lost custody of their daughter. Val doesn't say anything about the half bottle of wine she'd had before coming to the theater, or the voicemail Claire had left that morning saying she wanted to talk. Looking ahead, as the line diminishes, they understand explicitly consequences of this decision, and stand resolute in their silences. All three of the other individuals holding extended service tickets have taken the steps now; Val and Tony are the only two remaining.

They look at each other. In the corners of Tony's eyes there is a nearly imperceptible bunching, distracting from a nearly imperceptible dampness.

Just barely a smile. Val nods.

Taking each others' hands, they ascend one stair at a time, step-in-step all the way. Pausing for a moment at the edge of the screen, Tony turns towards Val. The two friends tighten their grasps. Tony opens his mouth for a moment, but closes it.

"Ready." Val whispers.

"Yeah."

Val takes a step forward, her years-old converse pushing through the membranous cinema screen. It takes a little more force than she expected it to, but her shoe punctures the barrier and—

"Val, I—"

But Val has already pulled them both through.

The house lights come on, and the theater is empty.

ON VISITING A DIFFERENT LIGHT, A GAY BOOKSTORE NOW CLOSED

ANDREW CALIMACH

A Different Light
In Chelsea used to shine
And there one night
I took a boy of mine,
On Seventeenth,
Just two blocks east of Nine

"Let's go buy books"
Was all I said to him.
Why make detail?
He was only fifteen
And literature
Was not his interest keen

When in we stepped
All eyes his way did turn
As if announced
The Messiah's return.
Shot through by stares
Bright red his cheeks did burn!

I did not see
John bolting out the door.
I only knew
Gone was he from the store.
In the cold street
He trembled, plenty sore.

To make amends
I feigned total surprise.
And swore to him
I did not realize
So many men
Found beauty in his eyes

Marvel you not,
The gays are human too.
Shunning young friends
For fear of big to-do,
They shave all over
And then have to make do.

I told John not
His looks I meant to flaunt.
Out of vain pride
Those men I meant to taunt
And show by fact
What words could never vaunt.

To whom proclaim
Our love was just as good
As that of men
Who crave a skin more rude,
Or a mount seek
For trot and canter crude?

Whom call unjust
When suave savages,
Chasing blind lust,
Wreak Biblic ravages
While boy fans must
Pay all the damages?

If on I press
For truth beneath the lies,
A darker shade
My lilting verses dyes.
Hues of the hurt
My crass act underlies:

A lifetime bent
Under an outcast's yoke,
Pursuit of joy
Shadowed by gallows' stroke,
My inmost dream
The mindless crowd's cruel joke.

Twas pent up rage
And inculcated shame
Led me betray
My feelings' gentle name
And use dear John
To tweak chimeric fame.

* * * * * * * * * * *

Yet as I cast
Eye on yesterday's tide
I see confirmed
That simple goodness, spied
In a boy's arms —
Friends still, though by age tried.

Warmth unashamed
No damage did it cause;
To human touch
The natural manchild draws.
To soft caress
The toughest sinew flows.

My cradling arms
His fearful mind subdued.
His naked grace
All space with truth imbued.
Robed in love's weave
His own muse he pursued.

With opened eyes
He shunned convention's plan,
Mind and flesh free
To climb art's peaks and scan
The hidden path
That wakes the inner man.

When time pressed on
And he love's flames outgrew,
Embers unquenched
Quickened friendship anew
—As Greeks foretold—
Sparking devotion true.

"If not for you
Not half the man I'd be
That I'm today,"
Out of blue sky said he
When we, men now,
Surveyed our history.

"I dread to think
What had become of me
Had we not met,
Nor our love been free."
I listened mute,
My heart at liberty.

Full fourth decade
Unrolled his years' string,
He mused out loud:
"If back the past I'd bring
To when fourteen,
I would not change a thing."

He swore his youth
With beauty I did fill.
Now in return
He grateful pays that bill
As my ripe age
He drapes in gold-spun twill.

My darling boy
On this uncertain stage
If oft we meet,
Else turn a distant page,
Now matters not —
We've broken from the cage.

* * * * * * * * *

Free rein to give
The innate wildling thing
That in each heart
Lies curled, is to bid sing
A mystic bird,
The primal to give wing.

Yet that won't do
In our plastic nation.
Just as we've wrought
Nature's devastation
We've torched to ash
The heart's sylvan vocation.

Instinct to trust
Is not the modern way.
We safer feel
Trite morals to obey
Preferring cant
To nature's complex play.

But in our zeal
To hem normality
We fate ourselves
To stiff banality,
Our soul hocked for
A coward's morality.

Why strain our minds
With love's ethics debate?
On fingers count
Th'arithmetic of hate:
Boy's one year short?
That man decapitate!

Why ask we not
Wherefore ourselves we find
Kept from life's best
By manacles of mind?
As in a dream
To the absurd we're blind.

Yet love of boys
Is every good man's see.
What will you need?
All generosity,
Courage to lose,
Heart tender, and mind free.

"Love conquers all,"
That oft' hollow refrain
Here celebrates
Triumph of life humane
Over raw hate
And men's crushing disdain.

Sing heart your love
Carefree in bright daylight
–Love sprung from ash–
That lovers true yet might
View boy with man
In that old, different light.

IN THE QUEUE
DEREK COYLE

Sometimes, the way
you ingest the world
is through your eyes.

I saw him on an evening
of soft drizzling rain
in a chip shop in Mullingar.
Not long off the bus,
I'd checked into a B & B
just up from the Greville Arms.

I came upon him
the way you might
stumble on a man,
naked on the top of the sheets
in his bedroom, thinking he's alone.
He turns and sees you at the door
and still
he invites you in.

He was dressed in boots,
a torn t-shirt, jeans.
I took him for a builder.
Our eyes turned to each other
as we waited our orders.
I pushed him
up against the cheap
tiled wall of the shop,
oblivious to staff,
customers, the street.
It was as if, in one brief moment,
I had seen him
with the eyes of God.

He glistened
with all the glow of young life,
rippling and pulsating through him,
the way Rodin imagined
in The Bronze Age.

I pulled his hair back.
I knew what I was doing
as I kissed his lips,
undid his jeans,
our tongues, hands and bodies
seeking each other out.

When the time came,
my chips and coke
were bagged and paid for.
And I left,
no word spoken,
never having known
the real thing.

23 BELMONT STREET
DEREK COYLE

When I go back to that city
I always pay a visit.
Once when I went to look - I couldn't help it -
my old house had been sold on.
The office style curtains suggested it.
Solicitors, estate agents, decorators,
had been and gone.

That room.
It exists now like a dream.
I have no way of knowing
if it existed or not.
It is so familiar though.

In what was my room at the back,
the black and white posters of guys
smiling out at what passed for life there.
The reading chair by the window.
The table by which I read and wrote.
Over in the corner the bed
in which I first made that kind of love.

I hope it's not just in here
those sad old things reside now.
That green cloth-backed chair,
its material reminded me
of my dead grandmother's hat.
It has to be the favourite
of some student somewhere.
The bookshelf I left behind.
The first day he came back
he stood before it, claiming
he'd read this book and that book.
I loved this bolshi confidence,
even if it was all bull.

One evening as we made love
he asked me to pull over the curtains.
I don't know why. No neighbours
looked into our backyard.
It was months after the first time
I'd made it to that kind of manly pleasure
I found what one might call love.

I recall the morning.
I woke at six,
just getting used to sharing a bed.
I looked and looked,
stared at the face
of that all too fleshly god.
Your eyes flickered open,
they closed.
How did you handle
such a gaze?
You pretended to be asleep.
We touched and kissed,
I reckon.
I can't remember that.

COUGARS, OTTERS AND BEARS - JONATHAN HEMELBERG

A BOY NAMED _____
MAT WENZEL

Born at the change of a season
between rock salt and amaryllis,
I am a clubbed foot baby, forgotten
like an iron left plugged in. I am

a metal man on a horse with a spear,
crossing the Charles bridge to save
Christmas. I'm a divine messenger,
checking my hair, my robe, my expression

of piety, taking a selfie on the way out
the door. I'm a student and I'm on fire—
Self immolation just a nice way
to say, "I'd rather be on fucking fire

than tolerate this injustice." I am pharaoh:
an object of wrath, *made by God,
fitted for destruction.* I am the neophyte,
with my fingers marking this morning's reading,

long and slender neck, eyes pleading
to be *over the wall tonight.* I am a lover
spurned, a bull lanced, a wolf with half a tail.
There's a crown on my head,

and warm footprints behind me, in the snow.
I can't stand in this place for I'm a man of unclean lips.
I'm a man of cold charcoal among petrified trees.
My wings race me to the shore,

past green steeples, public service billboards,
and famous fountains and bridges, pausing
briefly on the stairs to whisper in a model's ear,
until I reach the square, just in time—robe askew,

baring shoulder and knee and bathed in summer
light, to pose for a photo with fifty asian tourists.
I am crying "stormily," head bent into a stack
of striped and scrolled in *jaune* and apple-green,

faint orange, monogrammed-in-Indian-blue dress
shirts. I crave likes and follows, as the stars
long for applause. I write a poem to the river
and the forest. I hand out poems like they're propaganda.

I am a marble statue of David
Beckham. I'm Emily Dickinson.
I'm the Virgin Mary. I'm Jesus Christ. I'm
that name that won't be spoken.

FAMILY MAN
G.S. CROWN

Don't tell my children that I'm gay. Don't tell
them that I have a secret closet full
of shadows who stretch out their hands and pull
me in. Don't tell them how these shadows smell
a kindred spirit when I enter, spell
my name in Greek, and ask me to annul
the prohibition of linen mixed with wool;
don't tell them that their heaven is my hell.

Don't tell my wife how difficult it is
for me to sleep with her, don't tell her I
imagine she's a man I've met and make
believe her body isn't hers, but his.
Don't tell her when she falls asleep, I lie
awake and wait for shadows to awake.

THE TIME MACHINE
G.S. CROWN

A closet can become a time-machine
that takes you to the past, that takes you to
your adolescence when you realized you
were different from your friends; a deep ravine
divided you from them. You saw their green
as red, their black as white, their pink as blue;
yet even so, they didn't have a clue
you dreamt of boys when you were seventeen.

You chose to keep your colors to yourself,
you chose to keep a secret who you were.
You chose to marry, too. You keep the men
you dream about atop a closet shelf
your wife may never find; you keep from her
the time-machine which tells you: choose again.

CHOPPING WOOD
VAISHNAVI NATHAN

A forty-five minute drive in her green pick-up truck
for hummus and tortilla chips meant
it's Thursday and about two hours past midnight,
we'd fall asleep watching Trailer Park Boys.
In her room, minimal and dim,
each object held sentimental practicality.
I still remember the look on her face
lit through the darkness at 11.34 while
I was sitting near the fireplace in her clothes.
Was it mid October along Henley beach,
our fingers sticky from strawberry and lemon gelato,
she laid on my lap and said today was alright?
She was never good at using words
so she collected acorns and chopped wood instead
to let me know that keeping me warm
in winter meant needing me.

THE SILENT CRY
RUSHAA HAMID

I spend summers eating dust,
watching my great-uncle spin tales
whose meaning I claw at through foreign vowels
the warm tongue of that Arabic faltering
permeating my bones.
This is my history in a lie,
softly covered details of a past, and a tribe
that wandered from a dirt bank in the Nile.

Later I would retell that same twisted story,
straining to pull it from my childhood
to impress a girl that would ask
"why I felt the need to co-opt African history"
and "why I felt the need to defend Islam",
when it hates people like me.
She smiles as if to say with her teeth
you are safe among the white people.

The more I breathe in myself,
the more distance grows between each side
a constant choice between two
swollen halves of myself that yearn to be one,
constantly severed by the voices of others.
I want to say, you can't tell me how to feel loved,
which culture gives the closest embrace.

My father said "Learn to kiss asphalt,
love that 10-stitch-hatred,
breath in your fire
burn your throat to save yourself."
I swallowed truths until they pumped back up
out my oesophagus,
spitting out rehearsed lines about silent loves
and now, supposedly free,
I have to swallow other truths.

BETTER WITH ONE OVER ANOTHER
RHI WILLIAMS

I'm better with words
than I am with music,
better with boys
than I am with girls,
more practice
despite the attraction.

It's easier to wrap a man
around a body
than a mind,
but the closeness
is stifling.

It's no different
the days or the weather.

I'm better with moments
than I am miles,
just better with pictures
than time.

CURSES AND BLESSINGS

HANNAH TARA FAYE

WILD ORCHIDS
G.S. CROWN

I know I'll never sleep with you. I know
I'll never pluck your rose or even touch
its stem. I know you'll never know how much
your fragrance fills my dreams. I'll never show
you scarlet jungles where my orchids grow,
wild orchids no one picks but me. I clutch
them now, the way that drowning men will clutch
at twigs when swallowed by an undertow.

I have a wife I married years ago,
before you bloomed. We raise our children well.
With warmth. I think my family loves me, too.
I write on petals so that winds will blow
these words away for good; I'll never tell
you face-to-face it's you I love, it's you.

SEX INEQUALITY
RHI WILLIAMS

There's thoughts of loss
but that may be melodrama,
I'd rather not be involved in either.
I've nothing to offer
except my flip-switch gender.
I kept trying for a while,
lessons are learnt slowly
my mind traipses quietly
thinking long over situations
that present themselves to my heart.
I'm unsure of the truths,
whether they be hers or mine
and I never learn what to do
where to change my heart's
way of feeling,
my minds way of thinking.
There is really little to do
that I am willing,
little change beyond the extreme,
there is comfort in familiarity,
even familiar heartache.

PAPER OR PEOPLE
RHI WILLIAMS

I often go to bed with books by my side,
but sometimes I would prefer a person to paper.
The imagination is no substitute for skin,
the warmth of blood, life or love,
another's eyes flickering in a state of REM.
Lovers lie, but so can pages,
I've empty notebooks to fill with my own prose,
tales spun from darker places not recommended
in any travel guide you'll find on bookshelves or bedside tables.
There is little chance to have room for both,
a king size bed does not equate with a large heart
but if I had to choose one over the other,
pens, paper, and made up people would win every time,
I would just like a break sometimes from these sharp edges.

CITY OF CULTURE
CHIP WILSON

Jubilant hoards of cod'eads'
Smile imperfect teeth.
They shine deep as the silt flats
That secure the rested ships
Of the land only sailors.
Past industry there is art.
Dead Bod and the like.
On Saturdays
and the turgid Sunday,
Mam's roasts will be blitzed
Hectic with lurid drinks.
Cuddles and kisses over ears from
Grandmas bell-deafen
The life in dereliction.
And raw bonds attest
For expats and visitors.
Auburn water denies it
A coast to pine for.
The eternal horizon,
Marred only by sea,
Is our city home:
A home for those who'll hold her dear.

BIBLIOPHILIA
IAN-JOHN COUGHLAN

Mother, he is gentle. It's cold in the wet dark,
But his laughter sounds like wedding bells.
His hair smells just like char.
I kiss his eyes, I kiss his hands, I kiss his dirty shoe.
He whispers, Your body is my gospel.
I am a book he opens with his fingers.
For him, I'm paper thin.
When he reads me, he moves his lips.
Roses bloom in my skin
When he underlines his favourite bits.
And I just called to tell
That I'm missing you, I piss on you,
And, Mother, we are well.

MY HIGH SCHOOL SWEETHEART
SOSSITY CHIRICUZIO

He is kind, really. One of the only teenage boys I've ever known who isn't looking to get something from me. Well, other than a friend, and some kind of cover. I figure that part out later. If I am his beard, though, he is also mine. He is tall and well built, smart, and talks to me like a person with a brain. My first day of school, he finds me wandering and lonesome, carrying all my textbooks and a fair amount of shame. He took half of them from me and showed me around.

He is the only guy in the group of girls that forms over the next couple of years. They all find him dreamy but distant, and envy me for having such a hold on him. Not that we are ever super specific about it, but it is clear to anyone who wonders that we are a couple. Or something. Never seems to keep people from calling me a lezzie when insults are flung, I imagine it doesn't always save him from being called faggot, either. But my hickeys are genuine, if a bit routine, and after we make out a bit we always find interesting things to do like archery, or exploring the ravines or riverbanks behind his house.

He takes me to a family gathering in Tucson, once. Big interesting gathering in a big interesting house, and everybody is really nice. At dusk we take a walk with some of his younger cousins out into the washes, where we're talking about old rock and whether anyone can make a band like Led Zepplin these days. The awe of the younger folks, the dim lighting, and the reflected courage from Kirk sweeps me away, and I stand in the sand and the shadows and sing Stairway to Heaven. I feel sexy and mysterious and strong for a full 5 minutes, and everyone is quiet, listening. He takes my hand when we walk home, I feel seen.

He introduces me to weed, classic Tombstone style. We find a soda can and slip away to the courthouse. Not the one they actually use, but the one just off the boardwalk, where you can view relics of people's lives and re-enact a trial for social studies class. There's a giant sphere of a safe outside, in a small concrete enclosure, open to the sky. You can tuck right in behind the safe and not be seen, while the smoke drifts up and away. He carefully bends the can in the center and makes a shallow depression, then borrows my earring to punch a series of holes. the trick is to make the hollow deep enough that the wind doesn't blow the weed away into the dust, where you'll never, ever find it.

We have sex, once. He is my first, if you don't count any of the violations of my childhood, and I try really hard not to. We agree that we are the right ones to lose our virginity with, and that we trust and love each other. It is awkward and painful and quick, neither of us moved by desire, just a need to have done it. To be able to say we had done it. Who was going to ask, we aren't sure, but being virgins is definitely a liability, especially since we are both trying so hard to be read as straight. Not that we discuss that part. He is gentle afterward, bringing me aspirin and holding me. We agree that we never need to do that again, and go back to the way we were before, topic closed.

He finally cuts and runs, dropping out of high school and leaving for California when he can't squash himself into a tiny box anymore. A few experiments with guys on the army base make it clear to him, and he chooses truth. I love him all the more for it, even though it leaves me adrift in my Junior year. He comes back to take me to prom, like he promised, though it turns out he has tickets to the U2 concert in Tucson that weekend and maybe I'd like to go to that instead? His uncle is driving up in his van and will give us a ride and a place to crash. Of course I say yes, and my mother helps me pack and doesn't tell me that she has a prime ticket to that show herself. She just smiles and sends me out on an adventure.

We sit in an easy chair and a bean bag in the back of the van, sorting out all the seeds and stems from our bag of cheap weed and drinking black velvet from a bota bag. I feel like the friendly ghosts of my parents past are along for the ride, in a ritual with your ancestors kind of way, and heft the bag to the sky before shooting that clear stream down the back of my throat. We have nosebleed seats, but feel so worldly and defiant. Away from everyone who knows us, away from the familiar landscape and narrow horizon. We sleep on the fold out couch that night, cuddled for comfort and easy in our friendship. He knows who he is, and I am beginning to understand myself.

WATCH THE DOG
BRETTEN HANNAM

The steps of the bus are wide, but I still have trouble hauling my suitcase behind me. Gravel crunches under my feet and the winter air stings my lungs. The bus belches dark exhaust as it pulls away, and I'm standing in an empty parking lot with no sign of my aunt.

The sound of the forest is everywhere—the sound of nothing is so many living things. Even in the dead of winter. At the edge of the parking lot, an animal lurks. A dog. It's a mutt, like me. It heads towards me, as if it'd been waiting for me.

I smile and think of petting it, or maybe scratching behind its ears.

As it gets closer I see its eyes, one dark black, the other a ghostly blue. The air tastes stale, and something spills inside of me, liquid seeping outward to the surface of my skin.

Today is the day I die. The dog is the messenger.

Its gait is even, almost casual. I try to think, but I'm soaked through to my skin and I can't move.

My aunt's truck rolls into the parking lot, horn sounding. Blaring. The dog darts off into the bushes with a sly grin. Not yet, but soon.

I climb into the truck without thinking, and my aunt apologizes for being late. She talks about what the family's been doing all the years I've been in the city, far away from country life. I nod in the right places, and make noises like I'm interested. Inside it feels like there's a great, swelling wave ready to burst out and sweep across the world, carrying everything away. The wave doesn't quite get through my skin, but it's still there, just below the surface.

I think if I stuck myself with a needle, I would explode and there would be a tremendous sense of relief and satisfaction. But I don't. Instead I turn my attention to the dream catcher hanging from the rear-view mirror. My grandmother used to make them, before she died. This might be the last one she ever made. Or just one of many. I think about asking my aunt if she sleeps in the car, but she's too busy talking about all the people heading to her place for the party. I can't get a single word in, so I rest my head against the window and wait.

I'm sitting in a trailer packed full of family members that I don't know, and that don't know me. We're all together in the middle of nowhere.

I can't hear myself think. A party in my honour, someone said. Not really. If I wasn't here it would've happened anyway. But it's nice of them to think of me at least.

I step outside into the cold air, closing the door with a firm yank. I jiggle the knob and feel the latch settle home. I hear the party even with the door closed. The voices of many cousins, aunts, and uncles pressing against the walls, escaping at the seams and joins.

I walk down the edge of the lawn, where the forest starts with no clear lines.

My feet are moving and before I know what's happening, it's quiet. I'm alone.

Except I'm not.

I turn, facing the tracks I made in the fresh snow.

He's a few feet behind me. Couldn't be more than seventeen, eighteen. Hands shoved into his winter coat. Snug jeans, not the fashionable kind—more like the can't-afford-new-clothes kind. Pink boots. Girl boots. From one of my older cousins. I look into his face. One of our older cousins, I think, because I see some of me in him. Or some of who made me in him.

—Why aren't you inside? I ask.

He tosses his head back, looking at the warm light coming from the trailer.

—Why aren't you?

I have nothing to say. I turn around and walk deeper into the forest. I hear him behind me, stepping around the sunken parts of the ground, avoiding the branches whipping back into his face. He knows this land as well as I do. I settle my pace. He adjusts, and I feel relief radiating off of him.

—Here. He says, and rests a mitten-covered hand on my shoulder. I wait for him to pass me before following, wondering where he's taking me.

We've been walking for five minutes, maybe more. The sound of the party fades behind us. I focus on his back. He's wearing a dark red parka. The side is a sunburst—orange moving to yellow with pure white at the centre. Growing up, I remember having clothes with that same pattern. Once you spill bleach on something, it leaves a mark.

He stops in front of me before I realize it, and I crash into him. He smirks and pushes back, playful. I think.

He shuffles out of the way, searching his pockets.

I don't realize I'm looking for something until I see the familiar bend of a tree, arching up over a boulder. The shape of it all, the negative space, make a pattern that sets something off in my brain.

The fort collapsed years ago. Weeds and moss climbing up across the roof, now resting level to my knees. The red paint that covered it now cracked and flaking off in sheets. In the centre, a small birch tree grows up through the rotting boards and rusting nails. I reach out, fingers brushing the sheet metal of the overhang. I remember I'm not alone.

I look over at him. He bends down, knees pressing against the tight fabric of his jeans. He reaches into the dirt and the snow and fishes something free. He bushes it off, rubbing it on his jacket and inspecting it in the cradle of his hands. I can't see what it is, but my teeth are on edge.

He remembers me then and smiles, thrusting his hands out like a little boy presenting a shiny rock, or a seashell. Except it's not either of those things. I feel myself sinking, then realize I'm sitting on the edge of the over-grown roof.

I reach out and take the knife from his hands. My fingers won't close around it, and something inside of me swells with anger, or pride, or fear. Or all of those things. It's rusty. Scratched. Long forgotten. I wish he hadn't reached down and picked it out of its grave.

How long had it rested there, undisturbed? Ten years? Fifteen?

I hold my hand out.

He gives me a curious glance, then accepts the knife. He looks at it once more before tucking it out of sight, into his pocket.

The stars are so clear out here. Nothing to get in the way. No obstructions. When I look back at him, he's smoking a cigarette. He catches my eye and gives a mischievous smile, not sure how I'll react. Then I smell it—not just tobacco. He holds it out towards me. I lift it from his fingers without touching his skin.

The smoke fills my lungs. I feel it spread outwards, trying to escape.

I let it go. But I'm not empty for long—air comes rushing in without my permission.

We pass it back and forth, and the anxious feeling goes to sleep in my belly, along with the fear. The only thing that's left is a clean, clear feeling of having known someone for a long time but not having seen them.

—What's your name? I ask.

—Nathan. He says. I look at him, waiting for him to elaborate. But he doesn't. He knows I'm waiting—his eyes sparkle with it.

—I'm Sam's kid.

—Sam. Aunt Sally's son.

He nods.

—Your cousin, Sam. He says.

—So that makes you my cousin. I say.

—Twice removed.

—What?

—I'm your cousin, twice removed.

—Is that what that means? I ask, colouring my thoughts of him in a new way. There's guilt for a second. But I can tell that it doesn't belong to me, all knee-jerk and without thought.

I push it aside.

It's been so long since I've been close to anyone.

He shrugs and struggles to get the lighter going. It sputters and spits, sparks bursting in the dark for fractions of a second before turning into smoke. He shakes the lighter, and then pitches it into the forest.

—Empty. He says.

I nod. Empty.

—I'm Thomas. I say. He looks at me. The corner of his mouth turns upwards into a smirk. He has faint stubble on his upper lip that would be a bad teenage moustache if he let it grow.

—You don't remember me. He says.

I shake my head. Do I know him? Have we met?

He sticks the cigarette that isn't quite a cigarette in his mouth and rolls back the left sleeve of his coat, revealing a wicked scar wrapping around his forearm like a faint spiral.

—I was five. Or six. He explains, waiting. Waiting to see what?

I reach out to touch the thin, pink scar. My own hands are coved in scars and scrapes. Not many places left untouched.

His skin is warm and soft. The scar is raised slightly, so slightly. As I trace its length he leans into my side. The memory comes. Slow at first, but snapping into focus at points.

—The rusty tractor. I say and he smiles.

So that was Nathan. Just a boy, no more than seven. Probably six. Me and Joseph and some other kids horsing around on the rusty combine that had broken down in the middle of the field long before we were born. He fell awkward off the top, rolling. I remember the blood. And the other kids running. Joseph running. And Nathan sitting there, in the tall grass, bleeding into the dirt, eyes calm. No tears.

I picked him up and carried him back to the house. His mother had a fit. His father tended to his wound, and I faded into the background, unseen and unneeded.

Yes. I remember now. Thick black hair, cowlick on the side. I reach out, trying to smooth it back. His eyes dance with amusement. It can't be tamed. I know that, but I try anyway.

The slow burn of a second lighter flares up in the dark. His skin, darker than mine. Cheekbones, higher. His eyes, brown. Mine, green. Hands, like mine—slender fingers that make them more bone than palm.

And then I see him here. Now. Not from back then. I see the person he is. Not an injured boy sitting on the ground, but someone who followed me into the dark for reasons I still didn't know. Someone sitting close, sharing warmth on a cold night.

—You're shivering. He says.

—I forgot my jacket.

He unzips his and I'm surprised when it fits across both of our shoulders. The inside is warm and little feathers from the down filling poke me through my shirt.

I exhale.

He rests his head on my shoulder, and suddenly I'm angry with myself and I don't know why. I try to pull away, but he holds me tight. My anger points at him now. He looks at me and I relax. He exhales. I smell smoke, and weed, and the cold air of the night.

I start to ask something, I'm not sure what, and he presses his mouth to mine. Any words that would have been are lost in the dark between us. He tastes like cranberry juice and vodka. Smells like stale sweat and warm, fading sun. I feel his arms circle my waist, and I realize he's moving in response to where I've placed mine around his shoulders. I'm warm and safe. And I want to cry, I'm so sad, and I don't know why. I hope it never ends, but I know it will.

I push him away. He looks at me, a flash of anger crossing his eyes. I can feel his pain. Then he takes it inside and twists it around, and suddenly it's something else. He moves in close, gentle this time.

His teeth bang against mine when his urgency bleeds back in.

He pulls away, at his own pace and distance. I can't look away from his eyes, his face.

He lights another cigarette and tells me he's had a crush on me since he was eight. Used to pretend we were married, the whole deal. I feel myself smile, and a laugh bursts out of my throat. For a second I'm terrified he thinks I'm laughing at him. He joins in, and soon we're arm in arm.

For a little while, there's nothing else. Time is solid, unmoving. I know when I inhale, everything will start back up. So I don't inhale. But even that doesn't last, and soon he's touching my face, fingers glistening in the faint light from the back of the house. He gives me a look, like he wants to say something, but can't. It's a look I know, because I wear it every day. Except it's because I want to say something, but I don't know what. I don't know what to do. So I lean into him, and he leans into me, and together we lean on a tree that probably has termites. It's nice to forget, even if it's only for a little while.

The sound of the family reunion is faint, a nagging memory in the background of the moment.

—Do you want to go to a party? He asks.

—We just left one.

—That's family. He says. I know what he means before he explains it.

The anxiety returns. My knee bounces up and down to some unheard beat.

—It's no big deal. Just a few friends. We'll stop by my parents' place on the way.

He takes my hand in his and I look at him. He's smiling.

—Alright. I say. Then I want to say 'no'. I want to tell him to stay with me, here, all night. I want to say a lot of things. But my tongue sits in my mouth, lifeless.

I lean on Nathan's car, waiting for him to come outside. It's a powder blue Hyundai Accent. The driver-side door has been salvaged from some wreck—it's a flat, dusty red. I touch a strip of grey showing from a long gash in the paint, dull metal exposed underneath.

I grin when I see him—hair half combed and shirt tucked in. I wonder if he's trying to impress me.

My jacket and shirt ride up when I slide into the passenger seat, and the leather is cold on the small line of exposed skin that touches it. The driver-side door groans and creaks as he closes it. From the inside I can see that the car is more stitched together than I thought. Back window is silver duct tape. Seats don't match.

—Where'd you get this? I ask.

—Been working on it since I was thirteen. He says, beaming.

—Is it safe?

He laughs. Not answering my question. The feeling of death, the natural knowledge of it, enters into me again. I look at him, ready to speak. He gives me a sly wink, corners of his mouth upturned in a smile. The feeling falls away, replaced with something warm and light.

The engine roars to life and soon we're heading down the road. It's quieter than I thought. Maybe the engine hasn't been pieced together. Maybe it works perfectly, and it's just the outside that's ugly.

I put my finger on the swirling patterns of frost that have grown over the glass. Soon it's cold, and the glass is warmer than before, and there is a tiny, oval hole looking out into the dark as we speed past everything.

Nathan talks, and I listen. I don't have anything to say. He tells me that his friends want to meet me.

—I only just got back. I say. It's dark but I can see him blush.

—I talk about you sometimes. I got some of your drawings up in my room.

—What do you say about me? I ask, thinking back to the figure drawings I sent back to my aunt, now hanging in Nathan's bedroom. Naked charcoal bodies twisting and bending in frozen moments on Stonehenge paper.

—Nothing. He doesn't say anything after that.

Now and then, he glances over.

I look out the tiny hole in the window, watching it frost over again. Hiding the night behind it.

I reach out, touching the side of Nathan's smooth neck. A caress. I think.

He doesn't pull away. He doesn't notice. Or at least, he gives no indication that he notices. Nerves have taken over. This is a bigger deal than he's let on.

The house we come to is small. Music fills the air around it, and cars are scattered across the front lawn like birdseed. Thick forest cradles the clearing the house sits in.

Nathan has to slam the door as hard as he can to get it closed. We pass a bent mailbox on our way in that says SHAW in big blue letters. The paint has peeled away at the corners, making it look like it's been there for decades. Which is probably has.

As soon as we're inside, my stomach turns to ice.

Strangers, everywhere. All eyes on me, both sober and high—most of them younger than me. Younger than Nathan. Young enough that if their parents knew they were here, they'd be grounded from playing bantam hockey for the season. I was the same age when I came to things like this. What else is there to do? Get fucked up alone, or get fucked up with buddies. Except I usually got fucked up alone.

Nathan flashes a grin at me. I try to smile. I can't. Then he's gone—lost in the waves of people moving from room to room. Dancing. Fighting. Kissing. My eyes pick out two same-sex couples, which sets my teeth at ease a little bit.

The last party I went to, I was fourteen years old. Joseph's friend, Alan, cornered me in the kitchen. He was beyond wasted. The thing about being drunk is that the shit you say is what you really think somewhere, deep down. If you're high, who knows what you're saying. Might not even make sense.

Alan was plastered. And he cornered me. And he was a foot taller, if not more, and twice my weight. And he called me a fucking faggot. Fairy. Cock-sucking savage. Half-breed. It was the first time someone spit hate at me.

They said I broke his nose in two places. I remember there was a lot of blood. I remember I hurt my hands pretty bad, knuckles all busted up. People like to talk, and I guess it was a popular story.

Alan didn't speak to me for three years. The next time I saw him was at the Kwik Way at the edge of town. He was nervous, and acting strange. He asked me for a blowjob, and told me he'd even return the favour. I told him I'd think about it. The next day I left for the city.

Last year I heard that he died in a car crash working somewhere Out West. I wondered what would have happened if I had taken him up on his proposal. Would we be boyfriends? Would I have died with him? Would I be different in anyway, or would I still be like this?

In my last hours. About to die.

The music changes—slower and quieter. People mill around, getting drinks. A few bump into me. A native boy shoots me a dark look. His eyes adjust, taking in the sight of me. He relaxes and gives me the slightest of nods before continuing on his way.

A hand wraps around my arm and Nathan drags me into the kitchen.

The boy he introduces me to looks unimpressed. He's white, face marred with acne but otherwise handsome. Greasy brown hair. Braces that he probably hates.

—Conner, this is Thom. He introduces us.

—Conner's my best friend. Nathan says this while looking me directly in the eye. He's trying to tell me something I can't figure out, so I smile and shake Conner's hand. He makes a noise and mutters something under the din of the party. Nathan frowns at him and they're soon engaged in a war of hushed whispers.

My hand tightens around something in my pocket.

The jackknife.

I remember Nathan taking it in his hands, putting it into his pocket, so why is it in mine?

Conner pushes Nathan. My eyes narrow, trying to figure it out. A friendly push? Playful? Nathan's eyes are wide, hands moving up to protect his face. Not friendly.

The knife rests in my palm, just like it did so many years ago. A silver fang ready to sink through soft tissue. Ready to draw blood. The action of it plays out in my head, creeping over my hand. If I lose focus for one second...

I let go of the hidden knife.

I lean forward and give a firm push to Conner's lower leg, the one holding all of his weight. He hits the floor hard.

I help Nathan up. Conner glares first at him, then at me. He storms off into the thickest part of the party and throws himself on a girl who more than welcomes his mouth.

Nathan's hand finds mine, and though his face is a calm mask, I can feel how his heart aches through the skin of his palm.

I pull us out of the party, back into the waiting night.

He doesn't explain anything to me, and I don't ask. I don't know which words to use, so I pull him to me and he collapses into my arms.

As I hold him, his body shakes. I know he's crying. This pain is something familiar to me. But for the first time, I feel it for someone else.

I'm driving. Nathan sits in the passenger seat. I don't know where we're going and I only have a learner's permit.

In the middle of the country, away from the city, there are no streetlights. There are no lights at all. The country is filled with vast darkness. You can't see your own hand if you hold it in front of your face. It's hard for people that live in the city to imagine, or even people who live in town. But this village where I grew up, where we are now, is just a loose collection of houses scattered through the forest, hills and marshes. Nathan and I are in this old beater, travelling through the dark that might as well be the deepest part of space. Before I realize it, we're driving down the old Guinea road, past Skull Lake where I used to explore as a kid—down the twisting turns of a gravel road.

We hit pavement and I pull the car into the parking lot. There's not much snow here. Maybe because of the water. I get out and test the wooden bridge that goes across the stream. It holds. It's the same colour, probably the same wood, from when I was a boy.

The sand is hard—frozen. In the summer this place would be filled with kids seeking refuge from the hot sun. Along the far side of the river, a man-made structure blocks the flow of water, making a modest swimming hole. We used to call it the Dam. Not original, but accurate.

I settle in beside a tree, pulling my jacket around myself.

I hear Nathan before I see him—feet crunching down on the cold sand. He sits beside me, lighting a cigarette from the reservation, not a packaged one you get from the convenience store. The sound of rushing water is the only thing I can hear as I look over the swimming hole.

—This was where I had my first kiss. I say.

—Who was the lucky guy?

—One of my best friends, Jake.

He's quiet, thinking.

—Jake Barry? He asks.

I nod and point to the rock in the middle of the water.

—We were twelve, almost thirteen. Swimming late, after everyone else went home, for whatever reason. He had a sunburn—he's one of those really white, white kids. And I was just darker, saying how I never got sunburnt. We were messing around, splashing, dunking. I hoisted myself up on the rock to catch my breath. He followed. I don't know how it happened, but he just looked over at me, and kissed me. I remember wondering how he knew I liked him.

Nathan shakes his head.

—I never knew Jake was gay.

I shrug.

—Last I heard, he married some girl from Cornwallis and moved Out West to have a kid. He says.

—Who goes Out West to have a family? I ask. Bizarre.

—He must be bi. Nathan nods to himself.

I remember that he's younger than me.

—We were kids. We were in love, the way kids fall in love. It wasn't really gay. Or bi. It just was just something nice. I tell him. He's more confused now.

—You gotta be something, though. He says.

—Why? I ask.

He talks for a long time, about nothing and everything, circling something deeper. Words getting tighter and tighter, like a hangman's noose. Then the tears.

—Tell me about Conner. I say.

He tells me that they were best friends since they were little. Two years ago they started going out. Then one day Conner decided he wasn't gay and Nathan wasn't either. Nathan pushed it, and they had a falling out. Tonight was the first time they had seen each other in months. He hoped that seeing me would prove something—he doesn't know what.

He leans on me, telling me he's sorry. I don't say anything. I know he wishes he could go back in time and change things. Who doesn't wish that at some point? We all want to go back.

He starts to light another cigarette, then sees something on the ground. In the ground. The small flame doesn't give much light, but it's enough to see it. A dog print. Frozen in the ice, like some ancient fossil. But it's more than that—there are dozens, circling the tree we're sitting under, all of them frozen into the sand. Frozen in time.

A wandering dog with death in its eyes.

Looking for me.

Nathan wants to stay longer, but I tell him we need to get warm.

I don't feel safe. I feel like there're sharp teeth lurking in the shadows, ready to bite.

Nathan stops on the bridge, and I turn to face him. He slides his hands under the edge of my jacket, warming his palms on the skin of my back. He smells like smoke.

I hug him back.

We kiss, and it's more about comfort than passion. A moment between two travellers heading down empty paths, now converging.

For a short second the only noise is the rushing water of the stream, and the sound of us.

It happens on the drive back. It's not that he's being careless. It was meant to happen—planned out like this since before I was born, or he was even a possibility.

The dog darts out from the shadows. I know it was a dog. I know it's the same dog that left the prints in the sand. The same dog with the two-coloured eyes. This is the moment—this is how I die. I don't feel anything, just the numb fact of my end.

—JESUS! Nathan's hands grip the wheel tight.

The reality of him sinks into me. The scar on his arm, the poorly combed hair, the now-swelling left eye where an elbow must've connected at the party.

He'll die too. No more Nathan. It doesn't seem fair—I'm coming to an end, but he's just beginning. The dog will take both of us, running into the wild with blood-soaked paws.

Everything happens faster than it seems. A flash of fur and Nathan's hands beginning to turn the car to avoid it.

If I let him turn, I will die and this will all be over.

If I do nothing, Nathan will end with me.

No one will judge me. No one will express anything but their heartfelt condolences, or shared grief and anger at a god that takes things that don't belong to him. No one will blame me for his death, or mine.

His eyes are wide, full of fear. In less than a second the realization hits him. He sees how it will play out. He turns toward me, just a little. And in his eyes I see only one thing—his last thought. And I don't understand. I don't understand why his last thought is me. His eyes are full of concern turning into apology. I want to say something, but I can't. I feel everything inside, swelling and waiting to escape.

I don't know how, but the jackknife finds its way to my fingers. The forgotten blade is dull, but the tip is sharp, like a needle.

It sinks into my palm.

My skin breaks.

My world rushes into this one, filling and flooding every space and spark.

My hand lifts, floating through the air as we head for the tree. My fingers grab the steering wheel like a vice, stronger than I'm capable of. I wrench it towards me, gears and shafts and wires protesting. I don't let go until it gives.

The tires hit a stretch of black ice hidden beneath the snow. The car spins. Not luck.

The impact is jarring, loud. My right side aches. Nathan groans, shaking off the haze of death that nearly engulfed us. He glances over, assessing me. I give a weak smile. He returns it, and then it sinks in.

—Holy shit! He's out of the car in a heartbeat. I struggle to join him.

The rear end of the car is crumpled up against the trunk of a huge poplar tree, back wheel trapped in the wrinkled metal, where our bodies would have been.

—Did you see that? He asks, looking me over. Touching, feeling for things out of place. He looks at the blood in my hand.

—It's nothing. I shove it into my pocket, knuckles expecting the bite of an open blade, but finding nothing.

He keeps talking, but I don't hear any of it. I pull away and start to follow the tracks in the snow—a mad dash across the road, disappearing into the night.

Nathan looks over the car and I follow the tracks backwards, reverse engineering them to their point of origin.

For a moment everything seems solid, tangible. The air is sweet and cold. My mouth is dry. Each print leads me to the place where everything is hiding.

Half-way across the road I realize Nathan is beside me, holding a flashlight. We make it to the opposite side, where the snow runs parallel to the pavement in a small heap. The prints come from the other side.

I crane my neck, peering over. Nothing. No tracks. Nathan is confused. He keeps looking, trying to find something to explain it. Anything. I know he won't find anything— not buried tracks, not a single sign. Because that dog didn't come out of the woods at all. It came from somewhere else.

My head is clear, like someone opened a giant window inside, and let everything out into the atmosphere. My death is gone, along with Nathan's. Vanished the instant my hand made contact with the steering wheel.

I watch Nathan talking on his phone, trying to get a lift. I feel the smile spread across my face. Not against my will, but not needing its permission. Wide. Genuine.

Maybe the dog wasn't the end.

—Rose is on her way. I'll come back in the morning with Kenny and we'll tow the damn thing into the garage. He says, sliding into his seat.

—I'll help. I tell him, smile still on my face.

—You okay? He takes my hand in his, dry blood now forming a scab, and later, a scar.

—I'm okay.

—Did you hit your head?

—No. I'm alright. Everything is alright.

For the first time in my life, my skin is my own.

ABOUT THE CONTRIBUTORS

THE 'LAUREATES'

Glitterwolf was created to shine a spotlight on creative people and their talent. In issues One to Three, we featured the 'Poet Laureate' Christopher Black, who contributed an original poem to every single issue, and in our second year we introduced the poet Mark Ward and the photographer Thom Vollans. In our third year, our poet and artist laureate are as follows:

MARK WARD
POET

Mark Ward is a writer from Dublin, Ireland. His plays include *The Middle Distance, Saliva* and *Blue Boy*. His prose has been published in *Jonathan* and the *Queer in Brighton* anthology. His poetry has been featured in *Assaracus, Storm Cellar, The Good Men Project, The Wild Ones* and the anthology *Out of Sequence: The Sonnets Remixed.* He has recently completed a chapbook called *How To Live When Life Subtracts* and is busy tinkering with his first full length collection, *Circumference* (from which "Night Sweats" is taken) which will form the first part of his American G.I. series.
http://astintinyourspotlight.wordpress.com

SIERRA SCHEPPMANN
ARTIST

Sierra Schepmann is a writer, actress, and photographer in Los Angeles. She is originally from Cincinnati, OH. Her photography has been featured in *Sinister Wisdom, Off the Coast, Skin 2 Skin,* and *Cactus Heart.*

You can find her at sierraschepmann.com and see more of her work in *Glitterwolf* Issue 7 and the forthcoming Issue 9.

FRANK ADAMS

Frank Adams is a Lambda Literary Foundation Fellow in poetry. His poems have appeared in *Q Review, Down-go Sun, Micro Delights, Iris,* and in anthologies including *Between: New Gay Poetry.* He is the author of *Shadows, Mist & Fog; Strangers, Men & Boys; Love Remembered; Mother Speaks Her Name;* and *Crazy Times.* He lives in the USA.

ADITI ANGIRAS

Aditi Angiras is a poet and activist based in New Delhi, India. Her writing deals with politics, desire, modern love and all things queer and feminist. She is actively involved in the quest for and the creation of deinstitutionalised and anti-establishment spaces for discussions/poetry/love/living.

GEER AUSTIN

Geer Austin is the author of *Cloverleaf*, a poetry chapbook from Poets Wear Prada Press. His poetry and fiction has appeared in anthologies, print and online journals including *Big Bridge*, *Colere*, *This Literary Magazine*, *Potomac Review*, and *BlazeVOX*. He has been nominated for the Pushcart Prize and was the editor of *NYB*, a New York/Berlin arts magazine. He leads writing workshops for underserved populations through New York Writers Coalition, most recently at New Alternatives for Homeless LGBT Youth. He lives in New York City.

CRAIG BARRON

His most recent short fiction publication was in *Chelsea Station* (October 2014), a story which has been included in *Best Gay Stories 2015* (Lethe Press). Productions of his plays include the Cultural Program at the Toronto AIDS2006 International Conference, and the 2014 Vancouver Gay Men's Health Summit.

DENNIS MILAM BENSIE

Dennis Milam Bensie's poem "Eight Ball" was published in Greater National Society of Poets, Inc in 1980 when he was a freshman in high school. It was featured thirty years later in his memoir, *Shorn: Toys to Men*. His short stories and poetry have been featured in *The Furious Gazelle*, *Short Fiction Break*, *Burningword Literary Journal*, *Mad Swirl*, *Chelsea Station*, *The Ink and Code*, *Everyday Fiction*, *Bare Back Magazine*, *The Round Up*, *Specter Magazine*, *Fuck Fiction*, *Cease Cows*, and *This Zine Will Change Your Life* and his essays have been seen in *The Huffington Post* and *The Good Men Project*. His second book, *One Gay American*, was chosen as a finalist in both the Next Generation Indie Book Awards and the Indie Excellence Book Awards. Bensie's latest work, *Flit: A Poetry Mashup of Classic Literature* will be released by Coffeetown Press in October 2015.

JON BREDESON

Jon Bredeson is a gay poet, fiction writer, and English major at the University of Minnesota Duluth. His work has recently appeared in *The Furious Gazelle*, and is forthcoming in *The Outrider Review*. He is currently at work on his first chapbook.

RICHARD BYRT

Since retirement from mental health nursing, Richard has been an MA creative writing student at De Montfort University, and an active participant in poetry events in Leicester, central England. He lives by Leicester's canal with his partner, David, Shady, the dog, and Teddy the cat. Richard's first collection, *Devil's Bit*, will be published by De Montfort Books, Leicester, for Upstairs at the Western, a local volunteer-run pub theatre. This collection includes, with acknowledgements to Sally Jack, "A Small Price for Freedom" (Glitterwolf, Number 8), and three other poems previously published in Glitterwolf.

ANDREW CALIMACH

Andrew Calimach has collected, restored, and published the Greek myths of male love, and is currently working on a second edition. His articles have also been published in, amongst others, *Eros* magazine and *Thymos*. On the poem: "This poem is about two New York boys I have loved, and who loved me and still do, in a different way of course, now that they are grown men with families of their own. The first boy, John, does not speak in the poem. The second boy, unnamed, does speak, and his words are quoted here almost verbatim."

SOSSITY CHIRICUZIO

Sossity Chiricuzio is a queer femme outlaw poet, a working class sex radical storyteller. What her friends parents often referred to as a bad influence, and possibly still do. She is a Lambda Fellow, contributing columnist for *PQ Monthly*, and host/MC of X-rated open mic Dirty Queer. Recent publications include: *Adrienne, Wilde, Vine Leaves, Atlas and Alice, Transcendence, The Outrider Review* and *Mash Stories*. More info at: sossitywrites.com.

ALICIA COLE

Alicia Cole, a bisexual, genderfluid feminist tired of societal misogyny, lives in Lawrenceville, GA, with her photographer husband and a menagerie of animals. Her work has appeared in *Blithe House Quarterly, Lodestar Quarterly, Plunge Magazine, Bitch Media* and *The Cascadia Subduction Zone*, among other publications. She can be found at www.facebook.com/AliciaColewriter.

MATTHEW CONWAY

Matthew Conway was born and raised in Texas. Having completed his BFA at the University of Texas at Austin, he has continued his studio practice at the artist collective MASS Gallery. Additionally, he studied drawing in Florence, Italy. Conway's instagram handle is matteattack. He continues to reside in Austin, Texas.

IAN-JOHN COUGHLAN

Ian-John Coughlan is an Irish artist, currently living in Japan. His work employs the use of sculpture and video, but also works-on-paper and the written word. He has exhibited across Europe and his art has been purchased for the State Art Collection. Further work can be found at statedsilences.tumblr.com

DEREK COYLE

Derek Coyle has published poems in *Irish Pages, The Texas Literary Review, Cuadrivio* (Mexico), *Wordlegs, The SHOp, Burning Bush 2, Over the Edge,* and *fathers and what needs to be said.* He has been shortlisted for the Patrick Kavanagh Award (2010, 2014), the Bradshaw Prize (2011), and in 2012 he was a chosen poet for the Poetry Ireland 'Introductions Series'. In 2013 he was a runner up in the Bradshaw Prize. He currently lives in Carlow, Ireland, and he is a member of the Carlow Writers' Co-Operative.

C. CLEO CREECH

C. Cleo Creech is a North Carolina native, raised on a tobacco farm, who now lives in Atlanta, GA. His art/chapbooks include Dendrochronology, Flying Monkeys, and Phoenix Feathers. He's been published in a number of journals and anthologies. He edited the acclaimed anthology, Outside the Green Zone. His piece, "The Peace of Gentle Waves," was recently turned into a major choral work. Twitter: @CleoCreech. Instagram Poem/Pic of the Day: @creech444.

G.S. CROWN

G.S. Crown is a pen-name. He is a married man with children, but is also gay – something his wife and family do not know. He lives in a closet and does not tell his family or his colleagues at work what he feels; the ones who know the truth are his pen, the paper he writes on and his computer.

LEWIS DeSIMONE

Lewis DeSimone is the author of two novels, *Chemistry* and *The Heart's History*. His work has also appeared in *Jonathan, Chelsea Station, Christopher Street*, and a number of anthologies, including *Best Gay Romance 2014* and *My Diva: 65 Gay Men on the Women Who Inspire Them*.

MARK ELLIS

Mark Ellis lived most of his childhood in Tennessee, but left as soon as he was old enough to study, travel, work, eventually becoming a librarian and medievalist. He writes poetry and articles on medieval literature, and information technology. He loves to read his poetry at open mic events, and has published in *RFD* and *Glitterwolf* and has a forthcoming story in *Red Truck Review*.

HANNAH TARA FAYE

Hannah Tara Faye grew up in a conservative Christian school in Cambodia. The Transparency series has allowed her to explore her own bisexuality whilst aiming to honor and dignify the Transgender women in Asia, specifically the women she met who could express themselves despite the intense stigma and hardships attached in revealing your true sexuality.

FLINT

Flint is a queer writer, activist, writing instructor and BDSM professional who lives in Los Angeles, California. Her work has been published in *Staging Social Justice, The Outrider Review, The Gambler, Round Up*, and *Two Hawks Quarterly*, where her poem, "In Praise of Two Hawks Fucking," inspired the journal's name.

RUSHAA HAMID

Rushaa Louise Hamid reads, writes, and occasionally pretends to be a Dalek. Currently she is working on finishing the first draft of a play, and composing a Masters' proposal for a further degree in Politics. You can sometimes find her under the portmanteau 'Rulo' or @thesecondrussia

BRETTEN HANNAM

Bretten Hannam is a screenwriter living in Nova Scotia, Canada. His short films have played at festivals across the world, including BFI London Lesbian and Gay Film Fest, Melboune Queer Film Festival and Frameline International Film Festival in San Francisco, USA. He writes short stories in his spare time, all with LGBT characters in whatever genre catches his brain.

JONATHAN HEMELBERG

San Francisco based artist Jonathan Hemelberg graduated with a BFA from California College of the Arts in 2010 and with a MFA from the University of Edinburgh in 2014. His work focuses on the ways in which nature is often used to create definitions of queer culture and queer identity.

HANNAH R. HJERPE

Hannah R. Hjerpe was born and raised in Key West, Florida. She has since lived in upstate New York and Dublin, Ireland, receiving undergraduate and post-graduate degrees in English and Irish literature, and focusing on a master's dissertation on queer Irish literature. She currently lives in Los Angeles, California, as an outreach worker for homeless seniors. Her interests include fresh salsa, bitter coffee, cold bourbon, and comfortable mattresses. And Netflix documentaries about prison life.

KEVIN HOGAN

Kevin Hogan is an LGBTQ activist and a prolific poet. For the past three years, he has served on the Board of Directors of the Bisexual Resource Center, the oldest bi organization in the United States. In addition, in September 2013, he was amongst the select group of leaders invited to the White House for a historic first meeting with the Obama administration on matters of bisexual health, inclusivity and awareness. His first poetry collection, *My Ríastrad*, containing the poem "Collect Yourself," will be available from Antrim House Books (www.antrimhousebooks.com) in September 2015.

JOHN HUBBARD

John Hubbard was born in London, but has lived and worked in Dorset for decades, as a gardener, lecturer, and teacher of students of English and Literature from the ages of eleven to over eighty. He is married to David, his partner of twenty-eight years.

MAIA IRWIN

Maia Irwin is currently attending school in Hilo, Hawaii and hopes to become a sociologist who focuses on social justice and injustice. She enjoys being the family radical feminist bisexual sci-fi nerd. Her poetry often has religious, queer, and feminist themes.

MARK WILLIAM LINDBERG

Mark William Lindberg is a queer author, artist, performer, and educator living with a man and a dog in Queens, NY. His first novel *81 Nightmares*, a genderqueer horror experience, is currently available at most online retailers. www.markwilliamlindberg.com

FRED LOWE

Fred Lowe is a practicing psychotherapist and full-time poet recently nominated for a Pushcart Prize. Technically bisexual, he has a same-gender partner of 19 years. He is also an active grandfather of four. He publishes fairly widely in the USA and less frequently in the UK and Ireland. He and painter/graphic artist Val Sivilli have recently completed a limited edition artist's book, a truly lovely thing if he does say so himself.

RAYMOND LUCZAK

Raymond Luczak is the author and editor of 16 books. His first novel *Men with Their Hands* won first place in the Project: QueerLit 2006 Contest. He is the editor of *Jonathan*, a fiction journal featuring queer male writers. [www.raymondluczak.com]

DAVID M. LYDON

David Lydon received his degree in English and Psychology from Trinity College Dublin. He is currently a PhD candidate in Human Development and Family Studies at The Pennsylvania State University. He explores psychological themes through both artistic and scientific mediums.

VAISHNAVI NATHAN

Vaishnavi Nathan is passionate about using language to explore the various mediums of arts and culture. Her work has been published in the *Harpoon Review, Eunoia Review, Blue Hour Magazine* and others. She holds a degree in Language and Intercultural Communication from University of South Australia. She lives and works in Singapore.

JAMES PENHA

A native New Yorker, James Penha lives in Indonesia. He has been nominated for Pushcart Prizes in fiction and in poetry. *Snakes and Angels*, a collection of his adaptations of classic Indonesian folk tales, won the 2009 Cervena Barva Press fiction chapbook contest; *No Bones to Carry*, a volume of his poetry, earned the 2007 New Sins Press Editors' Choice Award. Penha edits *The New Verse News*, an online journal of current-events poetry.

XANDRIA PHILLIPS

Xandria Phillips grew up in rural Ohio, and received her B.A. at Oberlin College in 2014. There, she studied Creative Writing and Africana Studies. Xandria is a Black, queer, interdisciplinary poet who often writes from a radical consciousness about race, the body, and femme desire. She is currently pursuing an MFA in Poetry at Virginia Tech.

CHRISTOPHER ROSE

A child of the Pacific Northwest, Christopher Rose teaches composition and literature at Portland Community College and he currently resides in Portland, Oregon. His work has been published by *The Watering Hole Poetry, Fjords Review, Anak Sastra, The Outrider Review*, and *Chelsea Station*.

DENNY SAZE

Denny Saze has recently given up teaching to become a full-time writer. Her work has been published by *Mslexia* and *Fantastic Books*. She is inspired by jokes, dreams and odd facts. She lives in a cottage in Worcestershire and when not writing, she is in her converted cellar painting, printing and making odd little dioramas in tins.

STEVE STEED

Working on his third novel in the series *Bloodline Chronicles*, the author has been called, among other things, "the new gay Harry Potter for adults." A life-long Texan, he lives in Dallas with his dog, Zuri. His controversial debut novel is slated to be published this summer in the United States. The story of 'Wayne's World' is completely true, although some of the names have been changed.

SANH TRAN (COVER PHOTOGRAPHER)

Sanh Brian Tran was the first person in his immigrant Vietnamese family to join the ranks of the white-collar worker, and promptly broke his first-generation parents' hearts by quitting his attorney profession to become a self-taught photographer. Influenced by his background, he explores themes of identity and class through fashion and taste culture. Tran moved from San Francisco, California, to a small town in central Pennsylvania. He turns the camera on himself to explore what it means to be non-white and gay in rural America.

DAVE WAKELY

Raised in London, Dave has worked as a musician, university administrator, poetry librarian, and editor in locations as disparate as Bucharest, Notting Hill and Milton Keynes. Currently a blogger and journalist after completing his Creative Writing MA, he lives in Buckinghamshire with his civil partner and far too many guitars.

MAT WENZEL

Mat Wenzel is currently a high-school English teacher in Ogden, UT. He is a student in a low-residency MFA program at Ashland University and a 2015 Lambda Literary fellow. His poems "Communion of Suffering" and "Please Excuse this Sex Poem" are forthcoming in the 2015 issue of *Penumbra*.

KOREY WILLIAMS

Korey Williams is from Chicago and has studied at Illinois Wesleyan University (B.A. '12), Hertford College at the University of Oxford, and The University of Chicago (M.A. '14). His poetry has appeared in *Assaracus: A Journal of Gay Poetry* and *Colloquium Magazine*. Williams is currently a poetry candidate in Cornell University's M.F.A. program in Creative Writing.

RHI WILLIAMS

Rhi Williams is a poet and anxious geek living in West Wales with her wife and too many animals. She writes a blog about anything and everything, writes a lot of poetry, has self-published a collection and writes bits of science fiction. Eventually she'll finish a novel.

CHIP WILSON

Chip Wilson is a writer, poet and folk singer born in Hull. He is based in London and has a husband, daughter and a veg patch. Chip works for the NHS as a clinical psychologist and specialises in dementia and the enduring self.

GREGORY WOODS

Gregory Woods is the author of five poetry collections from Carcanet Press, the latest being *An Ordinary Dog* (2011). His critical books include *Articulate Flesh: Male Homoeroticism and Modern Poetry* (1987) and *A History of Gay Literature: The Male Tradition* (1998), both from Yale University Press. He is Emeritus Professor of Gay & Lesbian Studies at Nottingham Trent University, UK. His website is www.gregorywoods.co.uk.

SHAUN WOODSON

Shaun woodson is an LGBT actor and model who aims to inspire everyone he meets. He believes that that the world is so much more than black and white. He believes it's filled with bright beautiful colors, and he wants to help the world show its beautiful colors. He dreams of creating imagery and film that can inspire, captivate and liberate the LGBT community, and most of all, he wants to yell the world it's okay to be different, and it's okay to be yourself, because you're beautiful.

ROSE YNDIGOYEN

Rose Yndigoyen writes short fiction and novels in NYC. Rose's work has been featured in the anthology *Southern Gothic: New Tales of the South* (New Lit Salon Press) and she was a 2013 Lambda Literary Fellow in YA/Genre Fiction. She thinks about feminism, queerness and culture on twitter @theladyist.

SUBMISSIONS OPEN AND FORTHCOMING:

Now open: Issue 9: Gender

In Issue Nine we're putting a spotlight on gender, so we're looking for work that explores gender fluidity, transgender, genderqueer, non-binary gender, gender expression, genderfuck, drag–any or none of the above: if you think it fits the theme, you're probably right.

Deadline: June 30th, 2015

Forthcoming: Glitterwolf: Halloween

Seeking queer, weird and dark horror/fantastical.

Submission period opens 1st June, closes 30th August.

Submission to glitterwolfmagazine@gmail.com.
Further details at www.glitterwolf.com

GLITTERWOLF
A LETTER TO MY 16 YEAR OLD SELF

FEATURING HAL DUNCAN / PAUL MAGRS / STEVE BERMAN
EVEY BRETT / 'NATHAN BURGOINE / JEFF MANN / PAULINA ANGEL
JERRY L. WHEELER / AMY SHEPHERD / NEIL ELLIS ORTS
NICK CAMPBELL / MICHAEL J. HESS *AND OTHERS*

EDITOR'S COLUMN

Dear sixteen-year-old me,

There's a letter for you—with details, but only the ones you really need to know—later on. Consider this a prologue note, to remind you of one simple thing.

You're not the only one.

There are a number of letters that follow this one, writing back to their teenage selves, just like I'm doing now. Some of them you know personally, some of them you don't. Some of them are barely a few steps past sixteen themselves, some are decades removed. They come from all across the diverse spectrum of sexualities and genders. They tell tales about the stories that built them.

They are all wildly different, but they stand together. When you've finished reading them, you can put the magazine aside, and these stories will probably never be found together again. But you can walk outside and carry on with your life, safe in the knowledge that in your future lie plenty of people (both those in these pages and not) whose stories can stand alongside yours.

You are not the only one.

Best,

Matt Cresswell
April 2015

March, 1995

So you're sixteen, living in the suburbs and practicing saxophone every night, counting minutes until jazz band comes around because that's the one bright spot in your week. The only thing you have to cling to is during those awful years is your music, and you'll hold onto it with shark-like tenacity until it finally slips through your fingers. It'll bring you some of your greatest moments and utterly crush you, and make you wonder who the hell you are and what you're doing. You'll wish you could redo your music degree, but there is no rewind button, and there's nothing you can do to change things, anyway. Sorry, kiddo. Wish I had better news, but life's going to be pretty lousy for a long time. Hang in there.

Eventually, instead of playing music you'll start writing again, and while that's not a bad thing, it brings its own share of heartbreak. The funny thing is, though, nearly everything you write has LGBT characters. But then, you don't even know what LGBT and "gay" really mean and won't even have an inkling until after college when you read a Mercedes Lackey book and finally understand. When the opera singer gets up in speech class and talks about living with AIDS, you have no clue. Even when the alto sax player—a lesbian, though you don't catch on for years—asks you to sub for her in a gay band without telling you it's a gay band, and, trying to look cool, you put on a tie and suspenders along with your short hair with no idea why you blend in so well.

That sixth grade crush on Tasha Yar from Star Trek: the Next Generation? It wasn't just a crush, or even a mere idolization. Tasha was the first boyish, self-assured woman you saw, and something deep down inside clicked. That unnamable feeling is why you cut your hair short in sixth grade, hated dresses and abhorred make-up. Tasha kicked butt and, well, she was hot, and every time you see Denise Crosby smile your heart melts.

There will be boys interested in you, but you have no interest in them and can't figure out why until your twenties. Most girls date. You never really do, and go to prom alone. The whole "coming out" thing after college feels strange since you were never really in the closet and involves a conversation with your mother about why you write LGBT characters. She says she'll love you anyway, but you don't care about that by then, and get irritated when she says she's sad because she'll never have grandchildren. You don't want kids anyway, despite the numerous ways of getting one. You don't take care of your cats (yes, you'll have fuzzy pets at last!) as well as you should, and have no desire to be responsible for little humans, even if you could afford them.

There are some good things, though. You know your friend M from middle school? The singer, dancer and actor you were so close to that people thought you were twins and whom you had to leave behind when you moved last year? You'll be able to connect with him again, once this whole internet thing gets going. He's gay (you'll have guessed that before finding him,) which can't be easy after being raised in a strict Mormon family. But he's happy, partnered and still performing, and that means the world to you. Turns out one of your other good friends from middle school is gay too, and he ends up marrying his husband on his birthday when Utah legalizes gay marriage.

But as for you, I don't know if you'll find "the one." They haven't shown up yet. No one's even come close, and the whole idea of a relationship doesn't quite make sense in your head. I'll admit, it's lonely, especially when you leave the city you love to keep from being hurt more than you already are. You'll think a lot about what to call yourself since you like boyish girls and girlish boys and trans women and dressing in a mix of guys' and girls' clothes, but you'll just stick with "queer," because labels get annoying and none of them seem to fit, anyway.

You might not have a partner yet, but you do love the Lipizzan mare that wanders into your life and stays. All I can say about that is, well, it's karma.

Oh, 1984 Steve.

You've found this message tucked inside a fortune cookie on a cold December—you still opened them eager to read the tiny words because the faceless manufacturers had yet to replace real fortunes with vapid aphorism, because keeping the future to themselves meant profit.

Sorry if this goes long. Longer than anticipated for a strip of paper that smells sesame seed oil and cheap vanilla extract. Your glasses are thick and real glass—that's another bit of nostalgia, for one day glass is reserved for phones rather than spectacles, the complete opposite of your time.

Inversion. Invert. They used to call homosexuals inverts. Relax, I know. You know, though you do all you can not to think of yourself as gay even as you remember so vividly your first wet dream. This me, this author, still remembers it just as vividly, despite the decades. The rest of your life is but a shadow but we have that miraculous, that dreadful, that pivotal moment to ground us. The memory of that dream is the lynch pin of our imagination.

One day most folk who know you will know. The first comings out will be awful. They will cause you so much pain—and loss, which is worse because regret sours so much of life for years—but like everything done during youth, you will be able to look back at with more clarity. New prescriptions for your eyes. New prescriptions for your mind. The boy who would never take drugs does not balk at taking a pill to be calm, sleepy even while the melancholy remains.

I can fit so few words on this fortune slip. You've already turned it this way and that, front and back, peeled a new layer apart like onion skin, all hoping and dreading for some better idea of your future self.

Soak in salt water to read more. Tears will do. Or a salt shaker. But you will probably use tears because once your were the most infamous crybaby in elementary school. How dare that haunt you into high school—but it does, until you graduate and travel far away and try and find yourself in a new city. You will still shed tears there, too. Once or twice real once, but once they are pure Nile crocodile to seek sympathy from a young man you think you love. It doesn't work and you're left ashamed.

You learn you don't handle shame well.

But back to love. Most folk wanting to know the future seek riches but their second question involves romance. And you're lonely. You have yet to even kiss someone passionately. No one has ever touched you like you ache to be touched. Not going on a date, or the prom, will be a heavy burden for at least a decade. The first will cost you social skills, the second will one day be a wistful regret, like not learning how to ride a bike.

I cannot ride a bike still. I did rent a tuxedo, twice. Both times after undressing I went to bed alone.

If I told you the outlook is grim, you would shed more tears, real tears, and more of this strip of paper would curl and peel and then you would see the names of the boys and men you wanted but would never have. You would see the sayings people told you to console yourself, the worst being an aphorism, "When you least expect it, you'll meet someone."

You don't.

Aphorisms fill future fortune cookies and your romantic desires. In the future both grow so stale.

One day you don't
       even bother

                to open, to
                  look

                  sorry

                  S

✷ STEVE BERMAN ✷

Dear Mark,

I know you expected a lot from the New Year 1970, and I know it doesn't seem any different from 1969 or even 1959. You were alone with your mother again. No one invited you to a party. But you got to watch Guy Lombardo and a lot of New York socialites in funny hats celebrate on television. Someday, that will help you understand the poignant ending of the film Radio Days. It also gives you an idea of true camp as opposed to what passes for glam today. Maybe that's why you will never really understand the appeal of drag shows.

The lawn mower accident that cut up your leg when you were ten has a lot to do with your isolation, your sorrow, your guilt. You have experienced more pain than you deserve. I know what it meant for you to miss school because of all those operations. I know that you consider yourself an outsider, and not in a good way. I know how much you long to be part of a group. You look at a strong man, and you feel comforted, a good feeling deep within. You want to be taken care of, but be careful. There will be many strong men who do not deserve your trust. But you are basically cautious, and you will avoid harm, physical harm anyway. You will learn to take care of yourself, and you will learn to be strong, maybe not a muscle guy, but strong in other ways.

Look at what you have learned staying home all this time. You have read a lot, and next year you will read books like *Anna Karenina* and the *Brothers Karamazov*. They will excite you, but also confuse you and frighten you. You will learn the power of words. You will understand why people are afraid of words, want to censor, destroy. You will be scared too, but you will eventually embrace this power, the very essence of our humanity.

Right now, you are very dependent on your mother. You couldn't help it, since your father left. But look at what she has taught you. You know all about the world, culture, art. You know when and where it is proper to wear a white dinner jacket. You know about women's clothing furniture. You know what it is like to be poor, to live in a fantasy. But you will not always be poor. Someday you will live in Europe. You will learn languages. You will get married and have a son of your own.

❉ MARK ELLIS ❉

Even though you are living in the "sexual revolution", you have to keep quiet about one side of your sexuality. You know what I'm talking about. But somehow you already understand that it is a part of you, even if you have to keep it hidden. You don't hate it, you love it. How did you figure that out?

Mark

Yourself at Sixteen

If I could go back in time or send myself a letter I'd say: stop trying to do the stuff you don't want to do. And: stop trying to be good.

The things you think are good right now in 1986? They're no good for you.

I'm writing this in the New Union on Canal Street on a Sunday afternoon. This is a gay bar. Usually it's stiff with scallies and drag queens. Today it's hosting a Northern Soul reunion. There's a crowd of men and women in their Sixties, wearing clothes from the 1960s, all getting tanked up and ready to have a bloody good dance about. They firmly believe that you can turn back time and revisit your earlier selves.

Here's what else you'd say to yourself from 1986:

Drop the school subjects you won't need. Advanced maths and trigonometry? Turning equations and formulae inside out? That'll do you no good at all. Stop cudgeling your brains for things that won't fit. Stop trying to diversify. Concentrate instead. Novels and short stories are your thing. Read as many as you can. Get up to date with the classics and contemporary fiction. Oh, and get reading Angela Carter now, instead of when you're 20. Get yourself 'Nights at the Circus,' which came out in paperback last year, and which I know you'll love.

Stop longing for Doctor Who to come back. It's off just now and it'll come back for a couple of years, but it'll vanish for a good long while after that. But eventually it will come back and it will be good. You don't have to support it with every iota of your being, willing it back into existence. Oh, but during the wilderness years there'll be all sorts of original novels and audio plays. And you'll be writing some of them. Really! So, keep a good notebook filled with Doctor Who story ideas. I know you pretend you don't do that anymore, but carry on. Keep a good list for when the call goes out.

Take your writing seriously. Do it every day. Not just Doctor Who stories. Every kind of story. Especially ones to do with your family and your life and what it's like right now.

❧ PAUL MAGRS ❧

And write down everything you can remember about your life up until now. Everything your 45 year old self has managed to forget.

Do the things that you really enjoy.

Drawing from life isn't a waste of your time. Drawing and painting will give you joy all your life. Keep your portfolio. Throw nothing out. Don't let anyone else throw out your work. Keep it. And keep going.

Don't listen to the usual rubbishy and fearful advice. Contrary to popular belief you can write stories and you can draw pictures and make a living out of those things. They are not just 'fun hobbies' to fill up your time when you aren't doing a 'real job', such as teaching.

Just don't listen. Keep doing what you love. The truth is, plenty of people make a living out of drawing and writing. They always have. It's because you're from a working class background that your mam and your Nanna are saying these things to you: 'You must find something practical to do. You must have real skills to fall back on. You can't just do the things you're good at, the things you love. No one ever gets to do that.'

Yes, they do.

You are gifted and you've just as much right as anyone else to draw and write stuff for a living.

Don't spend years and years wrestling with this, always thinking you should be doing something different to what you love. Something conventional and sensible. Ditch that guilt about how you spend your time right now. Go and draw. Make stuff up. Keep everything you write and draw safe.

Similarly, stop trying to have girlfriends. You know and they know they're only friends-

who-happen-to-be-girls. You have not one iota of sexual interest in girls and never will have. Stop mulling that one over. Stop torturing yourself.

Oh, and when you get a bit older and you do actually come out at twenty, watch out for sexually predatory women who like to seduce gay men half their age. They're bad news.

Watch out for other people who act like friends and come along and try to use you, too. Remember that people sometimes have ulterior motives and aren't always very nice.

Friends and lovers – real ones – often come along exactly when you aren't expecting them. When you aren't looking for them.

Don't be too trusting. People have to earn your love and trust. Don't fling those things at them, hoping that will make them stay.

Crikey, you really were an innocent, weren't you?

Stop trying to please everyone. You really can't. Learn how to please yourself.

Remember and discover and remember what you really love.

Stop trying to be so good.

Paul

Dear Sixteen Year Old Me,

I'm thirty-two now.

At sixteen, I knew I wanted to be a writer. I wanted to explain the world, to capture it, to try to understand it, all in first drafts of course (I was sixteen!). You are a writer, and you always will be. You knew that without me telling you. You knew that without a publishing contract.

At sixteen, I hadn't kissed a boy. I was a virgin. All of my friends were straight and I felt like an alien. Even in a capital city in the late 90's, I felt like I was the only one. That no one would ever touch me like that; hold my hand, kiss me, fuck me, love me. Now, I've been with a wonderful man for four years that I intend to marry, something you wondered if you would ever have.

At sixteen, I thought I'd never leave home. You will, but you need to be careful. The real world is out there and you're so naïve. It's adorable. Hang onto it whilst it lasts.

Mostly, relax. You will fall in lust, in love. You will get your heart broken. You will feel like an exploding star the day your first play is performed, the day you first see your poems in print. You will have lifelong friends and a great family. Things really will be fine, I promise.

Best,

Mark

❦ MARK WARD ❦

Hey Sarah,

You've always have the type of short attention span that Millennial-slamming thinkpieces are made of, so I'll try to be brief: you got the hell out of the South. The first girl you fell for was recently arrested on meth production charges somewhere in rural Georgia. Your parents and God are dead to you. The war in Iraq was a lie, R.E.M. broke up, and Lance Bass never made it into space (but he did make it out of the closet which is just as surreal, if not moreso).

It is March 2015. You are 26 years old.

Right now, you're sitting at a coffee shop on the Upper East Side. The bar you're facing is scattered with the following "creative-type" effluvia: remnants of a fruit cup, an iced black coffee melting brown, a pen from a feminist sex shop, Sontag's Illness as Metaphor, Cole Haan sunglasses, a MetroCard. You have a little money in your pocket and you're wearing a trenchcoat the color of the Cow Tale candy which filled the shelves of our childhood gas stations. People know your name, your writing. In an hour, you'll be picking up your girlfriend at her job a few subway stops away. She doesn't have qualms with kissing you in public ...or a meth problem.

As I write this self-indulgent little epistle to you, I realize that what you want to hear are positive things about your future. You want to feel good about the things you currently feel not-so-good about, and you want shit worth living for. But you're also a bit lazy and want to press fast-forward on our life so you don't have to do the work, or sit through all of the pointless lectures and struggles which will make us who we are--as both a woman and a writer.

Avoiding a challenge is no way to live. A hell of a lot of white-eyed casualties line the half-dirt, half-gravel road to this moment in time. Irretrievable pieces of you float in the bottoms of liquor bottles flung from passing pickup trucks. I'm now tempted to teach you a valuable lesson and backspace through everything that I've written to you about our seemingly grand future and start from scratch, annotating all of the brutal hardships we've experienced between 16 and 26.

❧ SARAH FONSECA ❧

But I won't.

So: since I'm doing this for you, I need you to do something for me: stop brutally sizing us up like that, as I'm still grappling with our crippling perfectionism, fear of being noticed, and class envy. You have more control over that chip on your shoulder that compensates for your lack of knowledge than you think you do. Read more. Learn more. And, for the love of all things holy, live a little.

Remember that time in grade school when you created a club on the playground called the Lamers? If memory serves me right, it consisted of a haggard crew of fifth graders. You decided that it would be good to have dues, so you brought a glass piggybank to school and left it buried in the bark chips under the Lamers' clubhouse: the jungle gym. As it turned out, collecting money as such on a public school campus was illegal, and you wound up being dragged to the principal's office for your offense.

While that failed attempt at galvanizing 11 year-old outcasts now mortifies you, a girl in the throes of high school assimilationism, 26 year-old you sees things quite differently. That moment in time was educational in a way that no classroom will ever be. It was on Lincoln County Elementary's chain-linked playground where you mastered two of the most lucrative professional skills: fundraising and organizing.

I'm telling you this because, despite having so few stakes in high school life, you are so easily mortified. You hate standing out and being noticed, but you--by virtue of your strange-named, bushy-haired, brown-skinned, girlfriend-desiring existence--are doomed to stand out, even when you're doing little outside of breathing. So fuck it. Move. Do what you want. Have weird thoughts. Talk about them. Maybe even act on them. And never stop burying piggybanks in the bark.

Love,

Dear Me,

You're on the beginning of a long journey into The Strange World of the Bisexual. I'm addressing you from an astonishing 23 years hence. Sorry to say I haven't got all the answers and you don't wake up one day with the whole life thing sorted, but on the plus side you still have all your own teeth and hair.

Anyway, this bisexual thing. It'll begin to nag at you as you become more aware of your evolving sexuality, there'll be times when you'll refuse to acknowledge its existence but ultimately you'll embrace it and find that accepting your sexual identity for what it is is the best thing that's happened to you.

But that's all way off yet. You've begun to become aware of a growing curiosity about pretty boys, boys like you, wondering what they might feel like and taste like. It's all a bit much to take in, as you're barely getting to grips with girls without needing a whole other load of confusing emotions to deal with. You find it alarming, but also very exotic and exciting.

Why is this? Well, being a callow, naive, insecure youth from the provinces you've got a lot of baggage and lazy cultural assumptions about same-sex attraction to unpack before you can give into these stirrings without tying yourself up in knots of guilt, shame, confusion and paranoia...

Being an inexperienced, insecure teenager growing up in a remote small town still stuck in the tail end of the intolerant 80s, gay and bisexual people are completely alien to you. Acknowledgement of any same-sex interest intrigues you, but it also scares you – don't be too hard on yourself but the casual homophobia you've grown up with as constant background noise, has rubbed off on you and you're internalising it. Not cool, Jimbo! Don't put yourself through the wringer over this – fancying other boys is not only acceptable, it's awesome. When you go to Uni, don't keep all this buried – you're paranoid you're carrying around an awful secret, but trust me, everyone else at Uni is too wrapped up in their own shit to even care what's going on in your own little world.

❧ JAMES GENT ❧

Eventually, you'll get to explore this curiosity and find out what those boys taste like (beer and cigarettes mainly). What about girls? Barely a year will go by where you don't have an outrageous crush on a girl you know, but it's the same thing – you've wrestled with enough demons to get beyond the 'gay' thing, you really don't fancy having to go through a second closet... It's not only casual homophobia that's left its mark on you, but also some very ignorant falsehoods about bisexuality that you take very much to heart – it's not real, bisexuals are just greedy, lazy or indecisive, and that you need to MAKE UP YOUR MIND AND PICK A BLOODY SIDE!

Don't let all that binary bullshit fool you. You'll have a series of epiphanies (No spoilers, would hate to deprive you of a heck of a wild, messy, confusing and cathartic ride – it'll be the making of you) and ultimately come to not only accept but embrace living and loving as an open, proud bisexual man. You'll still encounter ignorance in the form of what we call 'bi erasure' and 'bi visibility' (yep, get ready for lots of new identity politics jargon, PC's big in the 21st century)—straights and gays alike will both try and marginalise, deny or de-legitimise your identity. Ignore these people, they are assholes—be proud and be visible, not everyone will understand but there are hundreds and thousands of other people just like you!

Bottom line, old chum, it is SO important to not feel like you have to hide a vital part of your personality away or feel ashamed about it. Be kind to yourself, you're only young once.

Love,

James

Dear Michael,

You are probably sitting on a twin-sized bed under that New York poster you picked up cheap at Spencer Gifts in the mall. You have just finished making a mixed tape on your cassette deck or jerking off into a sock or reading an assignment for your contemporary literature class. This is a class you will always remember because the assignments are whole real books, like *The Great Gatsby* and *Catcher in the Rye*. These books (and a close friend) keep you sane and steady now. Something's coming, an upheaval. You will leaving home in another year or so, making you way into the world. That's what they say, isn't it? You don't know what you're getting into out there, nobody does. This list of advice and dictums might prove helpful as you begin your journey.

1.   Take notes on what's happening around you. You're going to forget things you thought you'd carry to your grave. You will.

2.   Treat your body well. It has to carry you through all those long miles. Moisturize.

3.   There is no cure for desire.

4.   Strive for perfection in your work, but accept that you are never going to achieve it. There are flaws burnt into every human creation.

5.   Whenever you feel the urge to judge someone remember the lyrics by Cat Stevens: "There are many ways to be." Harold and Maude used this song to good effect.

6.   Your parents are horrible, repugnant creatures, but you are too. Every generation learns the same disturbing facts.

7.   The impulse to cut people out of your life will be strong at times. And there are people who deserve a quick guillotine splice, especially all those Axis-2 nightmares. Overall, resist this temptation.

8.   Don't get married young. Fuck freely and safely. Floss. (But not before sex because it can cause hairline cuts in the gums and make you prone to infection.)

✤   MICHAEL J. HESS   ✤

9. Finish the things you start. There is probably nothing so regrettable as that which is left undone.

10. Burn your bridges while you are young. You will still have the time and energy to move across the gorges and gaps in other ways.

11. Stalk the gaps. (Read Annie Dillard.)

12. Don't take everything so personally.

13. All those bigots and religious nuts are afforded the same rights as you. This is just the way it has to work.

14. Steer clear of people who align themselves too closely with any one dogma.

15. You will never regret, given the option, not joining a group—religious, social, or other. Be your own man.

16. Not all authority figures are out to get you. Still, police officers are best avoided.

17. Situations can change with the abruptness of a jump cut. This is good. You will never be allowed to get too comfortable in your always fashionable shoes.

18. "Witches can be good, giants can be kind." Stephen Sondheim.

19. Your heart will always be a subject of discussion.

20. The clock is ticking. There are mountains ahead. Snakes. Get to work. Love. Live.

Michael

�֍ MICHAEL J. HESS �֍

Hey Buddy

I know you're lonely. The wonderful lesbian teacher who lent you *The Front Runner*, the novel that helped you realize you're gay, she's left town, and so have your lesbian buddies, Bill and Brenda. You've got another year of high school to endure before you flee small, conservative Hinton, West Virginia, and head for college. You're wondering how you're going to make it through, hiding your homosexuality from your parents and your peers, yearning after handsome classmates you can't have.

You'll never be this isolated and lonely again, I promise you. You have a lot of things to look forward to. Here are a few:

Your straight buddy, Mike, the one who's about to join the Marines? The guy with the dark beard, muscular body, and hairy chest, so sexy he could be a porn star? Model your sense of masculinity after him. He'll teach you how to be a strong man who protects his clan and stands up for what he believes in. For the rest of your life, you'll be attracted to furry, solidly built, bearded country boys who resemble him. He'll help you define what's erotic.

That poetry you write about Mike and other good-looking boys at school? Those long entries you scrawl in your journal? You're not wasting your time. Keep that up. By the time you're fifty-six, you'll have published fourteen books. In one of your novels, you'll give yourself the youth you wanted but never had: you'll meet Mike again, and he'll want you as much as you want him, and the two of you will become fervent teenaged lovers.

Those confusing fantasies you have about tying Mike up, gagging him, beating him, ravishing him roughly and then holding him tenderly? They don't mean you're psycho. They only mean that one day, when you're nineteen, you'll read another novel, *The Beauty Queen*, and realize that other men share your fascination with kinky sex. A few years later, you'll step into a leather bar in Washington, D.C., sip a glass of Scotch, look around the room, and feel like you belong.

That despairing sense you have that no one will ever want you? Boy, you'll have so many men over the next four decades that you'll lose count. A few will break your heart, but at least you'll feel deeply, as deeply as dark, passionate Heathcliff, your first literary role

❖ JEFF MANN ❖

model. Every time your heart is broken, you'll write more poems. And one day, after many, many years of frustrated bachelorhood, you'll meet John, a man who'll want to stay with you despite your hot temper, prickly ego, and wandering eye. Eventually—I know this is almost impossible to believe—the laws will change so dramatically that the two of you will get married.

Your pudgy body? Your pimply face? Your hairless torso? Those will change too. In a few decades, you'll have a bushy beard, a furry chest, strong arms, and an assortment of tattoos. The homophobes you're so afraid of now will think twice about crossing you then, believe it or not.

Those lesbian friends you're missing so badly? They're only the first of many. Your love life might be difficult and frustrating for decades to come, but your friends, especially your lesbian friends, they'll save your life. When beautiful men let you down and leave you full of self-doubt and grief, women will help you survive.

Finally, that hometown you're wanting so badly to escape? The Appalachian culture in which you've been raised has shaped you in profound ways you can't yet begin to realize. When you do leave West Virginia, you'll see how much of a Southerner and a mountain man you actually are, and you'll head back to the hills in a hurry. Learning to balance your identities as an Appalachian and a gay man will be the hardest thing you'll ever do. It'll take decades. But you'll do it. By the time you've come to be me, you'll be living with your husband in a wonderful house in Pulaski, Virginia, a mountain town much like Hinton. You'll also own the Hinton house you grew up in, and you'll go back to visit your family as often as you can, and there you'll listen to the New River and look up at the surrounding mountains and tuck into good country food and be thankful that you've had the life you've had and become the man you've become.

Bearhugs,

Dear child,

All right, you're 16, not a child anymore, except to people my age. Forgive me. It's hard to look back at that age and think of you as grown.

So. 1979. Sophomore at Giddings High. You're at the tail end of a very good, happy childhood, a youth that didn't prepare you for the life you will have. Well, who's ever prepared for the life they have? Not many I suspect. Remember the goodness, nonetheless.

There are things I would tell you, but you can't bear them now. (That's a biblical reference, in case you don't yet recognize it.) Telling you now, there on the farm, in that Central Texas community—well, you'd just deny it, as you have when others have suggested it. Besides, there may be ways that your ignorance will keep you alive in the decade ahead. Let's move on.

Let's try this. Your mother is the goddess of practicality. She does what needs to be done and if she's ever anxious, she seldom shows it. She works hard.

You want to be like her, but you want it easier. You work hard when you're engaged, fair enough, but your conservative heart has yet to accept that you're called to some impractical things, at least in the eyes of your German farming community. You'll want to be practical like a good Lutheran boy, but you won't be engaged and this will make you lazy.

Instead, give yourself to your artistic urges, without apology. You will grow old with fond memories of slopping pigs and hauling hay, but embrace the fact that you're not a farmer. Forget practicality. The point of a calling is to follow, not to justify it. Impracticality isn't a cause for anxiety, but not following is.

I'm remembering how conservative you are, or want to be. You could never quite give yourself over to conservatism, though, because that's not who you are. Be less rigid, be more free. Love more, judge less. As I write this, I remember that you have access to all these messages. I'm left to realize that if you don't listen to them, you won't hear even if your older self sends you a message from your future.

That's another scriptural nod, an adaptation, more than a quote.

Scripture. Your faith. This will sustain you through all the years ahead. Take comfort in that. I won't alarm you with all the ways it will change, but I will promise you that it will grow.

In fact, let me end this note with words you will surely recognize. I hope you'll be glad to know they stay with you into your fifties:

May the peace of God, which passes all understanding, keep your heart and mind in Christ Jesus, our Lord.

That's from memory. Check it against the actual text. I may have gotten a word or two wrong.

So much more I wish I could tell you. I'm suddenly anxious that I can't.

Just—love. Give it, receive it, live in it.

Peace to you,

Your older self

P.S. You can stop spending so much time checking your chest for hair. It'll come in. It won't be like Lee Majors' but you'll be pleased enough with it. Go write a story instead.

P.P.S I wish I could give you a hug.

Dear me,

I see you walking down the school hallway. 16-year-old self. Manic panic blue hair with baby barrettes. Bell-bottoms you patch-worked into a galaxy of purple velvet stars. Cookie monster in a spiky dog collar safety pinned to your backpack. You walk into the classroom. Hear a dirty blonde in her 30's whisper loudly, "What's wrong with her," and then, "some people dress like they're on drugs." "I'm not homophobic, I just don't need to know about their lifestyle," says a woman with a frosted perm. You keep walking, and take a seat by the window so that you can stare out into space and pretend that you don't hear them. Later, in chemistry, a scraggly man sitting two seats over, playing with his toothpick, says aloud, "Wow, they have high school girls here. And some of them are exotic."

Again, you are reminded that you don't fit in. Prime example: the prank calls from the neighbors across the street, asking for the Wongs and Wangs, even though your family is the only Asian one on the block.

You are a stranger in the hallways of community college. Your classes are on Capitol Hill, Seattle's gay neighborhood. You tell yourself, I'm not gay or anything, I just like being here. And indeed, you are here 10 hours a day on Broadway for school and for work, by choice. Rainbows bursting from your bag as you march down the street, matching the rainbow flags in nearby stores. You wear glitter in your hair and around your eyes - sometimes it mingles with your tears, so that gold sparkles streak down your chubby cheeks.

Every day after school, you go to your job at Value Village. In the thrift store, I see you surrounded by fabrics and sounds of the 60's, 70's and 80's, a time trap machine. You clean out the dressing rooms, filled with mounds of clothing, broken hangers, torn off and crumpled price tags, and dirty tissues. You clean them like dank confession booths, evidence of transgressions. Everyone you work with is queer, thank god for that.

At the library, you pick up a Bikini Kill CD. You listen as Kathleen Hanna screams, "Rebel girl, rebel girl, they say you're a slut, but I know..." You read Randall Kenan's book about a

CELESTE CHAN

queer teen who comes to understand himself through the theory of relativity.

Soon, queerness will come to you like a gift. Like a telescope view of an alternate reality.

You'll wear your heart on your sleeve, sewn and sutured, tattooed by a rocker chick named Magenta. You will read Sassy and obsessively listen to Riot Grrrl, their growls and screams speaking to the sheer f---ing urgency you feel in your heart. You will not slit your wrists, you will tattoo them with typewritten words.

You will learn that it's not "what's wrong with you," it's about what is wrong with the lies, manipulation, and abuse of an oppressive culture. Your nerdy, freakiness is a way of seeing outside. Your stacks of library books show you something else exists. You will read and read and read, to save your own life.

You need to know that it is okay to have a heart, one that beats magnetically, that stretches your chest, this ceramic heart thumping outside of your skin, growing 20 feet tall and rising. You need to know that someday soon, you will remove the swords from your throat.

I'm writing to you from twenty years in the future, and I want to hold you. Go forth, brave little one. Let no one and nothing tear you down. Go forth, salt water and sparkles spilling, your head held high.

With love,

Celeste

✿ CELESTE CHAN ✿

Dear me!

Here are some things I absolutely cannot tell you about. 1) Snogging ___ on the Common, 2) Where you go wrong with ___ (same person, by the way), 3) The phone call with ____, 4) Meeting ___ , 5) Dancing with ___, 6) Moving to ____, and 7) _____. Even I don't know that last one.

I bet the most daunting one you've spotted is 5). At sixteen, you've not been in a club, and don't plan to, thank you very much. It's not your thing – and in any case, you've already got a boyfriend. He doesn't want to get drunk and go dancing either, so you're safe.

Is it so easy to be queer, where and when you are, or is it me? I don't even remember realising I was different to my friends, or deciding to keep it a secret. It was no problem. I've always been the quiet type.

You haven't felt the need to tell them about your adventures. Do friends need to know about strangers? Like going to Kings Cross, that summer night last year. Okay, it was to a gathering of gay Doctor Who fans, but Kings Cross in 1999 wasn't as safe as it'll one day be. No-one at school needed to know, but you had to go.

When you introduced Bahar to David, she looked askance, mainly because of the age thing. But you shrugged. You felt your paths diverging and didn't care.

You don't mind keeping your own counsel. It's easy to identify with the fabulous, secret worlds in books and magazines: you've done it since childhood. The people you admire, the queerest of the queer, have a sort of unreal quality, as if they've invented themselves. They make things up on their own terms and are often, to an extent, solitary. That appeals to your sixteen-ness too. But you're relieved to have a companion, at last.

Two decades older than you, but that's no problem if it works. David's wise, well-read, excited to be sharing your teenage curiosity for life. Talking about Taoism, horror movies, sex.

But no dancing. You're oddly cynical about the gay scene. It's not romantic enough for you; your sixteen-ness is about intense one-to-one relationships. Blame Jeanette Winterson: 'Yes I will come for you. Roll my strength into a ball for you. I will be the bridge or the pulley because you are the dream.'

You couldn't be suppressing a certain trepidation, could you? You couldn't be playing it safe, with David?

See above list, specifically: 1), 2) and 3). And particularly, ___.

Now, I'm in no position to offer advice. I'm frequently 'at sea'. I'm not so brave as you, or idealistic. (I do have a moustache. Also, when I begin writing a story, I try and finish it. Also, ___.) I know you're trying to do the right thing. And I also think you should talk to your friends about it.

Superficially, friendships are trickier than boyfriendships: less romance, minimal flirting, no sex. They know so much more about you than you would like, and they are liable to take you out of your comfort zone, which is, of course, awful and dreadful and horrible.

When you enter into a new friendship, it's easy to fall in love. Simpler to have the drama, than admit the more nuanced relationship in which you are not the centre of one another's world. It sometimes takes some work to keep the relationship fully alive, when it would be easier to spend the time with your boyfriend. So, don't. Before 1), become friends, and before 2) talk to your friends, and when it comes to 3), don't phone David. Phone a friend.

Find a place for these friendships in your dream of life.

Can you keep a secret? One day, you'll pull your courage together and speak to a bloke who looks interesting, and is. He's not your lover but he's one of the most important people you'll ever meet, if only because – after months of wearing you down – he persuades you to go dancing. And you realise, almost too late, it's great! And it's one place your sixteen-ness will never quite be extinguished.

Kind regards,

Dear Ben,

I hope this letter finds you well. I have to confess I put off writing it for some time. Mainly because I feel I don't have much to say to you. More precisely I don't know what to say. I know I'm no expert. I have a strong feeling actually that it should be you writing to me. You are sixteen years old and wondering what everything means. I am over twice your age now, and still wondering the same things.

You are sixteen years old and struggling to pass GCSE maths because everybody tells you universities won't accept you without it. Well, actually you never get a higher maths grade than F and two universities will still take you on when the time comes. And eventually you'll be quite good with numbers (although always terrible with shapes and angles). Things change. Seriously though, just give up on the maths now.

You are sixteen years old and in love for the first time. It feels hopeless. It is hopeless. But you'll have forgotten him by the summer. Things change. Don't ever give up on love. Some things never change. You're terrible with money and that will always be true. You just don't care about it. You know it means nothing. In seventeen years time, sitting down finally to write a letter to your younger self, will you suddenly realise this: money comes and goes. It doesn't make you any more or less loved. Only your self-respect and generosity of spirit can do that. Money measures nothing except itself.

It is 1997 and you have only just heard of the internet. You won't have your own email address for at least another six years. There's no rush. Take your time. The Tories are still in power and have been since before you were born. You know next to nothing about politics, although you know that you don't have a language for who and how you love, and what's that if not totally political? (And I promise that one day you will have all the language you need, and your own public words of love will be translated into Spanish and French, and you will understand at last that even in translation love is strong enough to make connections you never imagined possible. Love is everything.) But for now it is 1997 and Labour will be in power before the year is out, and, oh but I don't want to spoil the surprise of what happens next for you... But anyway politics and power – it's all there in your body and heart and who you love and what you want that love to do. Be kind to yourself, but don't hold back. Sometimes your life will surprise you. This is good.

You feel a lot – it's one of the great things about you (your openness, your vulnerability, your sensitivity) – but feelings change. If they're anything, feelings are movement – the movement of the world through your body and through your heart. Trust your feelings but question them too. Question everything. You'll value the answers one day.

I started this letter by saying I'm no expert, and that's true. But if there's one thing that I do know now it's that things change, every day is new, you've done nothing wrong so forgive yourself, you should get out more, take a walk, and remember that the one thing that doesn't change is that everything changes. Everything is moving. Keep moving with it.

I love you. Remember that.

Write back!

Love

Ben x

Dear one,

Well it's 2000, and I know it's a disappointment that *the rapture* didn't happen. The world goes on and you still have to deal with your life. It doesn't seem worth it, does it? Everyone's asleep...to everything. You carry the burden of your consciousness, hearing the screams of the world alone, and witnessing the marvels alone too.

Surprise! You make it to 30! A warning: the intense happiness and sadness don't end, but you'll be less alone in them soon. To feel so alive, is one of your greatest assets. Some people wake up, and others don't, and that's theirs to handle.

None of your "friends" right now will last, and that's a good thing. Their worlds stay tiny and yours is going to explode. You are not the black sheep in a white herd; we are all different colors and can only see those crowded closest around us.

Move around.

"Your people" aren't amongst your sheltered upbringing nor any one sector of society. They are in the world, as hungry for everything as you are.

Your identity is about to go through an overhaul. Learn to let go of anyone who resists your shifting it once, twice, as many times as you need. They are only afraid of themselves and what it would mean if they crossed their own lines in the sand. You belong to the world and your own precious humanity. Try on everything, committing only to the limitless coastline of your desires.

Make space between you and your family. Everything in your life improves in this liberation. It doesn't mean you don't love them, it doesn't make you rebellious or a bad child, it just means you are both a challenge to each other best learned from at a distance. You will make your own family wherever you are, based on ties that nourish you.

Work on your shame.

❀ MICHELLE LUNICKE ❀

There are infinite expressions of spirituality and some will suit you much better than the one your upbringing handed you. No book, religion, or culture can contain the divine. What you call God, is everywhere: in the wind, and the trees, and you, and an orgasm, and a loving glance, and a wry smile, and in every variation and incarnation.

Your shadow, that destructive capacity you have in you...that's not evil, it's balance. That dark side will help you get rid of what's not serving you. It is well developed for a reason. Try to direct it outwards and not inwards. Every part of you is sacred. You are not possessed.

Please stop trying to cover up your sexuality by upgrading your male friend with benefits (aka the boyfriend) to future spouse status just because you're horny and have limited options. Another warning: that affliction of hormones is not going away anytime soon. I can say however, that all the sex you're having right now will feel like foreplay compared to the sex you're going to have with women later, and that will become your very high bar for the rest of your life. Your body is not broken. The pleasure is hiding behind your heart. Follow that, no matter how scary, and your body will awaken.

It's ok to be gay, queer, lesbian, trans, et cetera and sexual. It's ok to be with boys or girls or anything in between. You, my dear are an "anything-in-between." Try to find people who get that about you, who LOVE that about you. Every step in your evolution, you will be most attracted to those whose experience of life resembles your own.

On your 18th birthday, when you do all those eighteen-year-old birthday things, skip the cigarettes and buy that vibrator you were pretending not to stare at on your first visit to a sex shop. Make sure its phthalate free.

Visit Seattle for heaven's sake....there's nothing scarier there than in Enumclaw!

Take some comfort in knowing this is the worst year of your life. Because of it, you will survive others. You don't think you will ever be well, sane, happy. Please don't

MICHELLE LUNICKE

hurt yourself when you believe those things. You are not the problem. You spoke up against abuse. That's upset their cart full of bad apples. Later you'll realize this is the inheritance of multi-generational trauma and it ends with your fight for wellness, sanity, and happiness. This is a fight you win.

You are wonderful. I can't promise you that you'll be loved in the ways you want from the people you want right now. But I can promise you that there are people you haven't met yet, who will love you in ways you didn't know you most needed, and they will let you love them in return.

Write! Publish! Make art! No matter how bad you think it is. You're never going to feel "ready." You just have to jump in there. This, and regular visits to the stillness of nature will heal you more than anything. Be brave. I love you.

Hey,

It's me.

I know weird really isn't it? But hear me out.

My advice to you is this. Don't be afraid to be who you are. Don't go thinking about the bad things. Don't go crying about why you don't fit in or why you get ridiculed.

There is one thing I wanna say to you: Be the best you you can be.

If they love you, so be it. If they hate you, so be it.

If you love you, go for it. If you hate you, stop it.

I'm proud of you and you should be as well.

Hello Little Me,

I'm sorry you've got a horrible girly name, but it's not forever – nobody told you this, but you can change it whenever you like. Though in all truth, it's probably better that you leave that to me, because I know exactly what you'd choose – we haven't changed that much, I took that name and stuck it in the middle, where nobody was supposed to see it, but actually, all my letters come addressed to Dorian Nothing, and our mum hates it. It also causes a lot of confusion and clerical errors, so being just Nothing would likely be far more hassle than it's worth. But then who knows, perhaps if you'd gone all the way and become Nothing, God of Hellfire, we'd be fronting an internationally acclaimed rock band by now, gleefully surfing the waves of Furious Sodom Metal...

That boy you've just met, he's a bit special, far more than you realise. I know you've never dated anyone before, so you haven't learned yet that the world's full of boring bastards and people you don't want to fuck, but this is actually quite crucial. The fantasy land you currently exist in, where every illicitly-snuck-into nightclub is full of neon and magic, and you don't want to be tied down because you want to be seducing beautiful strangers and taking drugs and Having Adventures—it's actually all bullshit. You could spend every night in a different club for five straight years and not find another one like him. This year, in your distant future, he's getting married—to somebody else – which is alright, because people change, but I will always hold you a little bit responsible. That one was special, for a very long time—you just didn't notice.

All the misery and self-destruction is a bit silly – you're out of school now, and away from all those shit-arsed little nob-ends, so why are you carrying on their bullying all by yourself? The irony is that these days, now, the love of our life is...actually ourselves, in a strange, bewildered, narcissistic sort of way. The things we can create, in words and in music and in crude facetious comedy, it's all pretty cool. We do all sorts of stuff now – we even write songs, and sing them! And some of them don't totally suck! We're pretty cool, and starving all that away is a horrible waste of time and talent and happiness...

I'm not going to say Don't Do Drugs, because it was a lot of fun, and it made us a happier, more interesting person in the long-run. But if you could refrain from eating ten pills in

✢ DORIAN BRIDGES ✢

a single night, every damn weekend, that might be helpful, financially if nothing else. And there is a point at which you should stop – when the things you've started doing are so fucked up you can't mention them even to your extremely open-minded friends, that would be the place. Weed is good. Stick with the weed. Save your drug money and go to Amsterdam – Dampkring Café, NYC Diesel sativa, that's what you want, and don't forget to say hi to the big fat stoned cat on your way out.

But actually, even if you ignore all of this, it's not so bad. Things are good now—there are lots of things we're actually good at, and life is fun. We're going to be Officially Old this year, but it doesn't really matter, because we've only been a real person with a real identity and a real purpose for about four years. So what are you, then? A confused little blue-haired foetus, but every experience is valuable, and you've only got three more confusing, shitty years to get through before things get better. And we have the most wonderful dog now—you'll meet him in two years' time. Look out for the big grey beard, the attitude of world-weary resignation, behind the bars at the rescue centre – that's the one. He will eat a few pairs of your shoes, but he's worth it.

Oh, and don't ride that bloody awful orange horse – it's horribly inbred and will only try to kill you.

Lots of love, from Dorian

Dear Lori,

I know this probably won't mean anything to you yet but, trust me, in a few years time it will all make sense. I'm not saying you need to change now, just that it might be nice to know you are not 'weird' or alone when things start to happen. Keep this letter and refer back to it whenever you need reassurance. Hopefully that won't be too often.

Because I'm you, I know that you've fantasised about women more than men, but that it's rarely women you know personally. You'll hopefully be pleased to hear that, one day, you will start to meet women who you obsess about just as much as Madonna or one of the dancers on the Pet Shop Boys' Performance tour [if you're reading this before June 1991, make sure you get a ticket for the Wembley Arena show. It will be the best way to celebrate finishing your GCSEs]. When you first meet a woman who you are completely and utterly desperate to be friends with, stop and think about it a little harder. Is it really only her friendship that you want, or is there something more? It's strange how tricky it can be convert theory into practice when the world tells you that you should only be obsessed with people who have a penis. Trust your instincts.

Another important thing to remember is that this isn't a phase. For some people it might be, but don't ever let anyone—least of all yourself—think that this is something that you will grow out of. Don't ever assume that anyone else's desires are transitional either. Mind you, even if they are, that doesn't make them any less real. People do try things and find it's not for them, and we all desire certain things more (or less) at particular times in our lives, but never let anyone else mock how you feel about something now because they reckon you won't like it in six month's time. If you like it now, that's what matters. This works for everything but is especially important when it comes to sexuality.

Once you've started to work this all out, you'll probably want to put a label on it. The twenty-first century is a bit better for stuff like this, so I know that you'll have trouble finding a 'best fit'. However, don't for a second think that you're not bisexual because you don't fancy women as often as you fancy men... or because you reckon you could only ever be in a relationship with a man. Your feelings on this may change depending on your age, experience and the people you meet, but the only person who can tell you

❧ LORI SMITH ❧

whether a label fits is YOU. If it helps, I define as bisexual because I am attracted to people who are the same gender as me and also people who are not. It took a while for me to feel comfortable using that label, which is fine. There really is no rush.

One day you will find people who understand. One day you will find an extended community of wonderful people who are accepting of others regardless of gender, sexuality, race, age, size or ability. However, you will also meet some fantastic folk along the way and will quickly learn that others love and appreciate you just the way you are.

Love always,

Lori xxx

Dear... well, I'm not going to say your name here.

When you are my age, even earlier, you'll find that your name would stand for something that you no longer identify with, your identity as a boy. You are probably saying right now "What are you talking about?" Hello, I was you, I know about how much you felt since you were 5 that you should've been born a girl. And I know about that dress you have in your dresser that you stole from your cousin, you know, the one that looks a bit like Jennifer Paige's dress in the music video, Crush. BTW, she releases another album in 2001, so keep a look out for it.

Now I can sugarcoat it, saying that as the years go by til you are my age that life will be great, but then I would'nt be doing you any justice. Instead, I just want to say that it does get better. When you graduate high school, you're going to be leaving that hellhole a bit confused about your gender identity or trying to make sense of what you are. I'm gonna help you out, you are transgender, more importantly, you identify as transsexual. Research it when you are in your English class, but don't tell anyone what you are researching, and watch out for Mr. Mason, he's a sneaky one. But you might be asking yourself "Ok, so I'm a woman, does that mean that I'll have to like men?". You can still love women, its called being a lesbian, fabulous huh? Anywho, coming out to your family is going to be a challenge, a hella big challenge. But know this, they will still love you regardless. This also does not mean you'll have to quit school. You can be trans and still get a great education, and it is through your educational career that helps lead you to success. Guess what, we end up getting flown out to Sacramento as a student leader in college, how great is that?

Lastly, there are times that you are going to feel alone, but take it from me, you won't. You'll be surrounded by so many great friends that will be your support system, a lot of them have been there for you, helped you with your depression, and really put your life on track, you'll just love them. You are gonna run into people that are going to try to bring you down, but guess what, you won't let them get to you, because you are a much stronger person than you are now, you're gonna be Hella Fabulous. Also, the word 'Hella' enters your vocabulary during your mid-20s.

❧ PAULINA ANGEL ❧

Anywho, gotta go, I need to finish working on this song for our third album, so take care of yourself and The Beatles Rock!!

Love,

Paulina Angel
(Yes, that is your new name)

P.S. You're gonna faint in class tomorrow, try to fall between the desk

Dear Dennis,

At 16 you were highly intelligent yet very much a fool. It is possible at any age to be both things. To your credit you were less a fool than most 16 year olds. That came from those zillions of hours you spent in the Public Library reading like a fiend...

You do remember your first job, right? Janitor's assistant at your high school. A tedious, horrible job of washing blackboards with a big yellow sponge, spot-cleaning the tops of desks and scraping gum from underneath the desktops. You grew to hate the look of a classroom. And you did your job in silence, alone. Big Al, your affable, kind-hearted boss, mopped the floors and always trailed two classrooms behind you.

You made $16.50 a week which really wasn't that bad by 1970 standards. It was enough money to do what you needed to do: hop on the bus Friday nights, just across the river to Manhattan and go to the sex films at the grindhouses that lined eighth avenue like hotels on the Vegas strip. A mere twenty minutes away from the hardscrabble Jersey town you grew up in. I wish you could have seen yourself from across the aisle on that bus. A pimply-faced but good looking kid wearing garish flowered blue one hundred percent polyester pants, topped off by your big brother's hand-me-down London Fog raincoat. The raincoat, worn on many a rainless Spring night had a sordid, utilitarian purpose: it sat bunched up in your lap to conceal your intermittent jerking off at the movies. Straight movies, the finest of heterosexual fuck films. There were only 2 theaters which featured homosexual films but even in the dark anonymity of the great big city you didn't dare risk going to those theaters. One of them was named the David, remember? No, you sat for 4-5 hours at a time in the darkness, taut with lust, watching hot guys fuck women. And it was weirdly perfect: the camera was most often riveted on the guy's balls and ass, up close, so graphic his asshole the size of a pizza on the screen. You grew hard as a rock but you never let your erection out of your pants. You rubbed it and rubbed it until you exploded like a small fiery bomb in your underwear: hot, wet with a smell in your nostrils as pungent as bleach. On a good night you'd come three times. With energy for one more but you'd miss the last bus home to New Jersey.

❋   DENNIS RHODES   ❋

It was bliss. It was impossible-to-describe wonderful. Maybe 20 guys were in the ratty old Tivoli at any one time--presumably there for pussy...For years afterward you would die for a man to straddle his ass and balls over your face, toying with your nose. It was cinematic, larger than life and you'd shoot your load quick and mightily into the guy's face.

Those were your training films, both your baptism and confirmation into closeted gay life. The funny thing is you never had to lie to your mom. You always said you were going to the movies. Her young darling, a post-pubescent pervert in a trench coat!

Dennis

Dearest Boy

I know that now, in the quiet of your room, you're thinking about Z. You wonder what he's doing tonight. You suspect he's off with a girl somewhere, or with his other senior friends. Wherever he is, he isn't thinking about you. We both know that's the sad truth of this situation.

How I wish that it could be different for you. How I wish that at one of the parties after rehearsals for the school musical, he had offered you a ride home. Not anyone else, but just you. I wish he had talked to you about how cool he thought it was that you played the bassoon, and that you were interested in being a composer some day. You could have a quiet, direct conversation, before he suggested a drive to a park somewhere, instead of going directly home.

How I wish that Z had parked, and then placed his hand on your knee and said, "I hope you won't be offended by this, but I get the feeling that you like me, and I just wanted you to know I feel the same way about you." I wish he had slid his arm around your shoulders and drawn you close, and gently kissed you. Even if neither of you two Catholic boys was quite sure what to do to each other, I wish that you could have felt that connection with someone, the warm security of being held in someone's arms, that sense of finally being understood for who you are.

It will come, Dearest Boy, though it will be a long, impatient wait for you. When it does, he won't be the dark-haired, dreamy adolescent with the languorous, mischievous smile that you now pine for so intensely. He'll be blonde, with green eyes, and he'll speak 5 languages, and play the piano, and you'll finally understand why people speak of *falling* for someone, because that first night with him will feel like you're plummeting through space and time, unmoored from gravity forever. You just need to be patient.

I know you've been struggling to teach yourself French recently. So let me add three verbs to your vocabulary. The first, *écraser*, means to crush, much the way your heart has felt the last six months, every time you glanced at Z and wanted, well, you're not sure what you want from him. Perhaps that is answered by the second verb, *froisser*, to press

✣   JEFF ABELL   ✣

or squeeze, the way you want to enclose him in your arms, until you can feel his heart beating next to your own. And then there is the phrase, *avoir un béguin pour*, to have a crush on someone. I know you feel I'm being patronizing. I'm sorry, but I remember all too well the way your pulse flutters when Z is near, or when you pass him in the hallway. I know all too well the giddy sense of happiness you feel whenever he takes time to talk to you, or crack a joke with you. There are so few guys at school who are actually nice to you, how could you help but feel this way about someone as kind and funny as Z?

No, we both know, nothing will happen. He'll graduate this spring, and it will be a long time before you see him again. By then he'll be married, with kids the age you are now. He'll still remember you. He'll still be funny and kind. You'll eventually master those French verbs that now seem so impossible, so full of exceptions to every rule. You will have plenty of time to practice using the three I've just taught you. And practice, they say, makes perfect.

You should get some sleep. These late nights, spent writing in your journal, are taking their toll on you. I am thinking of you with love.

Bonne chance, cheri,

Jeff Abell

25 March 2015

Vicki,

You're 16. It's the year we get our license, even though we've been driving for a year already. The year we're racing down highways in an open top Jeep, listening to gangster rap and doing things that we really shouldn't be doing. It's the year before life changes dramatically and we have to make our way on our own, by any means necessary. And it's the beginning of the Tar—that sludge which seeps from somewhere deep inside you, that say's you're not: worthy, strong, capable, interesting and a million other things. But it's only just begun, and you have so many moments this year without it.

So enjoy the hell out of it. Chew every experience, digest it, roll around in it and make it part of your soul. This is one of the best years of your life to date, and many of the people you meet now will be the people who love you for years to come. Breathe deep and know you make it out the other side.

My nuggets of advice, which are a corny mainstay of our future, are this: Let go. Don't be afraid to be yourself. Intelligence does not make you substandard. Love is not found via sex (you will have to learn this over and over again. But if you could get it in your head, even a little, now, it would save us a hell of a lot of head and heart aches later. Just sayin'). You are thinner than you think and prettier than you feel. Your ass is not the size you think it is. Love triangles are not fun. Laughter is good. Don't be afraid to laugh loud and often. Being one of the cool kids isn't as much fun as you think it will be. Be out. Be proud. (When that cute Latina girl in your History class passes you a note asking you out, jump on it. It's the best decision you make, and not one of your friends loves you less. I promise.)

The less you show fear, the less the people around you feel it. Enjoy the popcorn. You can do this. Days that feel dark, days that seem neverendingly hopeless, do end. The sun does rise, whether or not you want it to (and there are days you want both). Accept joy. Accept love. Accept the messiness of existing. Embrace it all. You will never have the chance to do so again once it's gone. Breathe. Breathe deep, and see the colour around you. People will join and leave your path. Welcome them, and allow them to leave gracefully. Learn what you can from them, and hold no grudges. Change happens. Some things just are. Roll with it. Continue to read. Everything and anything. Knowledge is truly power. Listen. Life is the longest thing you will ever do. It's also the thing you pay the least attention to as you're doing it. Pay attention. Listen. Not just to the words, but to the emotions creating them. Faith in a higher being is optional. Faith in yourself, is not. You will be capable of far more than you know. Dreams will come true. So will nightmares. But it's all part of the process.

Don't give up. Ever.

Victoria

Dear... well... dear 'me',

I don't regret a thing you end up doing, so don't hesitate. Ever.

When you're 17 at the prom and you put your hands on the hot German exchange teacher's ass as you dance with her, have the courage to go a little further and ask her out. Getting a knock back is better than wondering what might have been. That applies every time.

Ignore the idiots who make fun of you because you can't afford Nikes. Keep on studying and we end up being a Chief Executive at 10 years younger than the national average for a woman. You now have lots of Nikes.

Listen to Mr. Crawford when he tells you about sitting down to write even when you don't feel like it. That bullshit you say about writing only when you're inspired — if we did that, we'd never have finished anything and we wouldn't have ended up being a published author.

Don't drink the vodka with the youth worker. He's not your friend. He's not even a nice guy. He won't let you fuck his sexy French girlfriend, and the things he does to us — that is a regret, and an addendum to my first line. Although, you didn't do anything, so maybe that can't be a regret.

When your girlfriend accuses you of being straight — don't sweat it. She decides she wants to be a guy less than 3 years later and she's the straight one. We — we are definitely not. We are as gay as they come, and it suits us.

You're going to find a puppy left out in the desert to die. We rescue him and thus ensue the best 14 years of our lives. Cherish every moment with that little guy, and take more photos and videos. You'll need them when it's his time to leave this mortal coil.

Try to be less of an asshole in your twenties. Modesty isn't our strong point, and not everyone's blessed with the kind of talents we have. Those that aren't don't really like constantly being in the shadows. Don't hog the limelight.

Make sure our mum knows we love her. Tell her every time you see her. Cherish her love,

NICCI ROBINSON

because you'll meet someone who'd give anything for a family like we've got.

No matter what anyone does to you, don't ever be less compassionate. It comes natural to us, and it helps more than you'll ever know. A hot drink for a homeless guy. A doggy treat for his furry companion. Always make the time to nip into the Tesco for both, it means more than dropping a quid in his hand.

You won't know true love until you're pushing forty. Don't get me wrong, the next twenty-odd years of your life are a hoot. You love and are loved by some wonderful women, but we don't let them in. Not until the really special one comes along. And when she does, you know it, so knock hard on that door and don't give up. She's like L'Oreal. She's so fucking worth it, and being that connected to another human being is beyond description. And when you're feeling incredibly guilty for destroying someone else's life by leaving them, don't buckle. You'll have spent your life looking after other people and putting their needs first, even though you don't really know it. This is our forever. Don't fuck it up.

This isn't a practice game to decide who gets benched or not, so don't treat it as such. We don't believe in reincarnation. We hold no stock in an afterlife. This is it. So make the most of every second. Grab on to every experience you're offered. Savour them. Devour them. And move on. Don't live in the past. Don't live for the future. The here and now, that's where you thrive, that's where you make the difference. Enjoy.

Nicci

Dear Rhian,

I'm really sorry but it's going to get harder before it gets better. Much harder. Don't worry though 'cause it's all going to become very, very clear and you are going to be very, very happy. I know you're not like the other girls in your class, you never have been, you never will be. That's okay though, it really is, you can live in that in-between world quite happily where you're female but you're not a girl. Not girlie. You don't need to be.

It doesn't matter. None of it. None of the little boxes you're so desperately trying to fit yourself into matter. Not now, not later.

There are a lot things that make you different from the other girls in your class. And hell, half of them have nothing to do with the fact that you would like to be a boy sometimes for reasons you don't really have (even though you tell everyone it's so you can play football in the Premier league). Even less of them have have anything to do with the fact that you like boys and girls. I mean, given your family, it'll actually be pretty easy to accept that part of yourself once you realise what it all means. The fact that you fancy your best friend Becky isn't really even the worst thing going on in your life right now, I know, but she occupies so much of your mind when you're at home and even more when you're away.

In about a year you're going to be freaking out because you'll pretty much be obsessed with her (and that's okay too, I know you're having a really rough time right now – it's a nice distraction from it all) and she's the only person you have any interest in. Even though you're telling everyone you fancy one boy or another cause that's what all your other friends do. Really what you should do is stop lying and just kiss Becky. Or ask her out.

There are a million things I could tell you to change to make things easier but nothing will change how you feel or who you are (or who you will be). They could change where you end up though and who you end up with and trust me, it's not worth it.

You will be happy. Scarred, weird, medicated but happy.

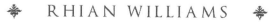

RHIAN WILLIAMS

Call yourself what ever you like. Dress however you want. Listen to whatever crappy emo band you want to. Don't stop day-dreaming. Don't stop reading. Don't stop writing.

Weather it through. You're still gonna be bi and poor and weird but you won't always be so sad.

Love, Rhian

Hey there, Justin,

Flamingly gay in a small, Midwestern town in the middle of Amish country? I'm sorry. I know, believe me, I know. For you, high school is like a ride on the bumper cars: everybody's out there banging the hell out of each other and you're that kid spinning around in the corner who can't get his to work right.

Your hormone-charged, sixteen-year-old brain is on a constant loop of "boys, boys, boys, where are the boys?" But those boys you like so much aren't quite thinking the same thing. As a matter of fact, they don't care too much for boys who like boys. Even "hate" doesn't quite sum it up. They think it's evil. That's what you hear everywhere you go. You hear it from the pulpit on Sundays. From those overweight Republicans your mom listens to on the radio to church and back. You hear it from your teachers in the classroom. Yes, that's right. In freshman biology, Mr. Weaver told the class about walking into an LGBT support group in college, thinking it was the science club. And boy did he "run outta there fast!"

Your classmates saw it in you early, some of them even before you did. Just hearing your girly little voice caused them to wrinkle up their noses and go "ewwwww!" After a while, you felt reluctant to say anything at all, and you don't talk too much these days. Because high school is a big, gay witch-hunt. It's all about finding the faggot, who's the faggot? I think that guy's a faggot! Dude, you're a faggot! So there it is, you are what that your classmates are hunting for. You're the worst thing that anybody can possibly be.

You don't know anyone else who feels what you feel. It's like you're the very last of an extinct species. You feel miserable and alone. People see that you aren't happy and they all give you the same advice: "get yourself a girlfriend, then you'll be happy!" It doesn't help when they add that these are the "best years of your life." If that's true, you may as well just end it now. You hear that a lot of gay teens commit suicide. You think about suicide. You think about it a lot.

But guess what? You aren't going to kill yourself. You're going to trudge through it, shitty though it is. You're going to study hard and go to college. You'll walk into an LGBT support group and you won't run away. In fact, you'll stay for four years and get to know kids from small towns like yours who went through exactly what you are going through now. It turns out you were never really alone at all.

You'll come out of the closet. It'll be scary, and there will be those who won't have anything to do with you afterwards. But others will love you dearly for who and what you are and you'll form the kind of friendships you never thought would come your way.

You'll help plan your college's first annual drag show. You'll walk through campus in a bright pink top and jean skirt borrowed from your best "girlfriend" who'll accompany you in your silk shirt and tie. Other students will watch you and not all of them will like what they see, but baby, you'll work it just the same!

You'll finally kiss a boy (yes, I promise it will happen), a boy who thinks you are "so beautiful," and it will be just as wonderful as you've always dreamed.

Most important of all, you'll come to love and respect yourself, because you are a compassionate, passionate, intelligent person who's worth ten of all those kids who tell you that you're nothing; that you're a mistake. Of course, you'll also learn to channel your inner bitch and put the smackdown on this particular brand of fool in the future.

So take a deep breath, hold your head high and keep looking forward. High school sucks, but it's just for now. Try to enjoy the things that are good in your life. They're there, even in the most dire of situations. And don't be too hard on your bratty little brother who's so fond of those homophobic slurs he learned at school. When you come out of the closet, he won't be too far behind, and then you'll never let him live it down! All the best, sweetheart.

You in seventeen years

 JUSTIN DEFERBRACHE

Dear Frank,

I admit I do not often think of you, though at age 63, I still see you looking out through my eyes and I feel you inside me, your sense of humor, and your desire to learn, read, and know what goes on in the world. I know the boy remains inside the man. I wonder if the man dwelt inside the boy. It took him a long time to grow-up, assume responsibility and move on with life.

At 16 we had such dreams, flights of fancy of becoming a movie star, a millionaire, a poet, and of always ending our success the same, as a recluse in a great house, with huge walls around to keep us safe. I regret to inform you we never made it to a movie star; we are not millionaires; and there is no great house with walls around it. We do write poetry and sometimes our poems are published. We found ways to build our walls and provide for our safety without the need of a fortress. Not letting people in became standard operating procedure.

At 16 you were no longer bullied and beaten. At 16 classmates only called you queer and sissy behind your back. At 16 others found you "strange" unaware you had already had two "nervous breakdowns;" unaware you'd had sex with one of the school coaches; unaware you'd known you were a queer, sissy, outsider from your earliest days of memory; unaware you had always desired men and could not understand how that could be wrong. You were not confused, you knew who you were; what you were, but had no idea what to do with that knowledge. There was no one to trust, certainly no classmates, and no adults, relatives or clergy. That left you feeling you were one of a kind, a freak so rare you should think of becoming a side show attraction.

At 18, a freshman in college, you met Bob, a guidance counselor. Your thought of suicide and self-hate brought you to him and you found in him someone who listened and did not judge, a person who heard what you said and did not discredit you, or make you feel stupid. From time forward you remained in counseling for many years, experienced both breakdowns and breakthroughs to ultimately become the man you are today.

Today, when I look back, I see we were always together, the boy and the man. I also see

❧ FRANK ADAMS ❧

that we were stronger than we knew and that our strength willed itself to live, to work and to write poetry. We have learned to selectively let people in and see that all along there were holes in our walls, because we wished to belong more than we knew. Now, we belong, or do not belong, as we wish. However, we are now, and have always been queer and strange. But, now we know we are okay just as we were made.

Frank

Dearest Amy, aged 16,

You poor thing. You don't even know you're queer yet, let alone genderqueer, although rest assured, practically everyone else does. You have boyfriends, but can't understand what all the fuss is about. You have a best friend that you long to feel closer to, but you can't quite put your finger on what that means.

You ache to be loved but know in your bones that your true self is damaged and unloveable. You write angry, suicidal poems and become covetous of razors and pills. You finally tell a friend your big secret, and surprise! It's not that you are queer, but that you were sexually abused by your father. This is your first coming out, and it is as painful and messy as a birth.

You see a therapist, and he encourages you to write down all the very worst things, the unspeakable things your father did to your body while you were watching from the ceiling. And through the alchemy of writing, it turns into the very best thing of all—that you've survived.

Truly, the worst is behind you, and the best yet to come. In two brief years, you will escape to college and start a new life. You will find wonder and bliss between another woman's thighs. Your new truth will fill you up and give your life meaning. Love will start to heal the broken things inside you, and you will consider for the first time that you might be loveable after all.

You will tell your story, over and over, and the telling will turn you inside out. Friends and strangers alike will tell you their stories in return, and sometimes you will be the first and last soul to hear their confessions. It will become impossible for you to hold onto your isolation and shame.

Fast forward a few years, and you will meet the love of your life, an amazing woman who thinks you're handsome and laughs at all your jokes. You will marry her twice (the second time, it will be legal), even though you swore you'd never get married. Her unconditional love will change your life in ways currently unimaginable. You will stop being so angry all

❧ AMY SHEPHERD ❧

the time. You will forgive the world and eventually even yourself for the crime of being imperfect. You will be happy.

And all along the way, you will gather to you a tribe of like-minded weirdos, some queer, some straight, some female, some male, and some, like you, in between. It will be your love of telling and listening to each other's stories that binds you together, that makes it possible for you to collectively create the world in which you want to live.

Amy, age 16, it is your courage, your perseverance that this future rests upon. You are stronger than you know. Even in the worst moments where you don't think you can go on, where you can't even see the point, you will find the strength to make it through. And, trust me, it will be worth it.

Love, Amy – aged 42

Dear David,

Congratulations on your sixteenth birthday. As your older self, let me just pass along a few words of what will hopefully be wisdom, having already lived your life.

Don't be afraid of being gay. Yeah, I know the 1960's are the decade of the sexual revolution and all. But I also know how difficult it is dealing with those feelings in a small Southern town.

Listen, two things are incontrovertible: you are a sexual being and you like boys. You've known this ever since you and Billy used to sneak off from Boy Scout meetings to fool around with each other.

Now, that doesn't mean you have to announce it to the whole world. But your dad already knows about you; deep down in his inner self he knows. After all, he did catch you and that other boy in the tent that night y'all camped out in the back yard that night a couple of years ago. You've never expressed any desire to date any of the girls at church or school. He knows, but he just doesn't want to talk about it. He probably doesn't even want to contemplate it. And really, now, there's no point in pressing the issue with him.

Just make sure you do talk to him at some point, maybe after you are in your twenties. Tell him who you really are and that you like who you are. Tell him you know he probably can't understand, but that's okay. Tell him you love him anyway and remind him, gently, that he always taught you not to lie. Not to scare you or bring you down, but he is going to eventually die and whatever you do, don't leave this piece of unfinished business. You will regret it, trust me.

The other thing I'd like to mention is this whole church business. Your mom and dad aren't putting much pressure on you to attend anymore so take advantage of that. Church is an easy place to hide, which is what you're doing — from yourself and others — but there is a price to paid for that. So stop. Now. Back way off the religion thing.

By doing so, you'll avoid the immeasurable influence (mostly damaging) that organized

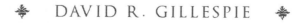

DAVID R. GILLESPIE

religion — in our case, the Presbyterian Church — would have in your life. Maybe it will even help you avoid all of the guilt that it dumps on people like us. They don't like sex too much anyway, especially when it's boy on boy or girl on girl.

If nothing else, grow up believing in yourself and creating your own meaning in life. Don't deny yourself in an attempt to fit in somewhere.

And finally, don't be afraid to seek out other boys in school. It won't be easy. Not at all. You must be careful. There are boys just like you, boys who like other boys, in your school. They are there, trust me. It might help you to not feel so isolated. I'm not suggesting you go around asking guys if they're gay, just be open to indications rather than spending all your time in Tae Kwon Do class or in your room at home putting those models together. Like I said, they are there. I know this now.

Well, I guess that's about it for now. I know it's a difficult time, in so many ways. But you will survive — bruised, perhaps, even broken at times — but you will survive.

David

Dear Irving

Do yourself a huge favor and come out. All of your friends already know, and everyone else suspects it anyway. Your mother will still love you, and your father will still hate you. Nothing you do will ever change those two unalterable facts. And stop looking for your dad's approval. You'll never get it because he doesn't know how to give it.

And speaking of coming out, leave poor Linda alone. She really likes you, and she deserves better than you using her to reassure yourself you're straight. You're not, and when you break her heart—for whatever reason you want to give her except the real one—she'll never forgive you. Not five, ten, or even forty years later.

Try to work things out with Randy. He may be a fuckhead for outing you, but he's forcing you to be honest with yourself. And everyone else. If you can't make that relationship work, know that his moving to San Francisco is nothing you have any control over. Neither is his getting swept up in the first wave of the epidemic. Grieve and move on.

Start writing about your people sooner. Your straight stories are lousy because you're not straight—and they have enough representation out there. Even though you don't want to admit it yet, you belong to a vast community of artists and storytellers who will feed and nourish you. All you have to do is give back to them. Show them their own faces, their foibles. Do your best by them, and they will reward you. Okay, not with money. You're never gonna be rich, my friend.

When you meet Jim, spend each moment with him as if it's your last. Because that last one will come all too soon. He'll change your life even as his own ends. Love him until all that's left are memories. Again, grieve and move on.

The rest of it? The drugs, the screwing around in college, the poor career choices, the never-ending succession of odd jobs and weird people you find yourself around? Don't change one bit of it. It's part of who you are, and you'll use every ounce of it sooner or later. Cherish your mistakes but work on your flaws. And remember, nothing lasts forever. Nothing.

♦ JERRY L. WHEELER ♦

Dear Gabbie,

You don't have to pretend that you liked it. You don't have to pretend that it was everything you had been waiting for, too. You don't have to pretend that his skinny body, his anemic chest, or his blind, fumbling hands are what you desire. Your real desires, your true self, are hidden so deeply that you don't even know the names for them yet. But you will.

Gabbie, I know what you think about when you are alone with yourself. I know what you would never tell anyone else. I know you only ever think about kissing her, and I know you know that she would never kiss you back. I know you think about breasts in your mouth, a full nipple rolling along your tongue, and I know you think about gasps made in the same timbre as your own. Full lips, and a blush on your belly. I know you think about finding someone who can make you feel as good as you can.

You won't find it in those baggy jeans, and you won't find it in those stubbled faces, no matter how nice they feel scratching along your neck. You won't find it in the thick, coarse hair that keeps your fingers from feeling the skin underneath; you crave softness. You didn't find it in that tree above the river, on top of the sheets of your parents' bed, in the grass outside of that party, or on that jungle gym under the driving rain.

You woke up that one morning in the back seat of that car, wrapped in his arms, and as you sat up you could see the sunrise peeking over the lake. You thought you had found it there, but you hadn't gotten naked yet. Everything looks like love in the milky light of dawn, when you're exhausted but wired because you haven't slept in your own bed yet. You felt him harden behind you and even though it made you queasy, you swallowed harder and called it power. Call it hormones.

Small one, you have lost more friends than you can count but still you grasp at girls, thirsting for a connection, drinking from a well that has only ever been dry. I know what you are aching for. I know how you replay every sleepover, truth or dare, and spin the bottle, and I know what you won't admit you were praying for. I know what you would draw if you could, and I know what you will write when you are given the words to. A

GABBIE SLAUGHTER

name is a powerful thing, love, and I would scratch yours into your chest if I could.

I don't regret what you did, but I regret what came after; I regret every act of defiance you made against your nature, and I regret that you were never given a chance to ask "why?" I regret that no one was there to tell you that you are your own best critic, and that how you see yourself is all that matters. I regret that you had no reflection in which you can see yourself. We are like vampires that way, you and I. We can only see ourselves in the things we destroy. The world makes us invisible to ourselves, to each other, and if we dare to speak the truth we are told we are a lie.

You aren't a lie, love. You only lied when you try to nourish yourself with boys. Still, you took what was offered, because you knew that girls in this place, this time, cannot nourish you either. One day you will be ashamed of how you made yourself sick, but know that I don't blame you for swallowing poison when you would have otherwise starved.

Remember when you had an ache in your gut that told you that you wouldn't make it to 18? You do. You sustain yourself on the hope that one day you will know just what in the hell it is about girls that makes your heart burn so bright. And when you find that one girl and she kisses you for the first time, it will feel like every atom in your body is alive with the power of knowing. You were seeking, and now you have found.

Owning your nature fully is almost more power than you can stand to hold, and warmer than any body you can dare to touch. Know yourself, name yourself, love yourself. You are a lesbian, Gabbie, and you will be happy.

Love,

Your 23-year-old self

♦ GABBIE SLAUGHTER ♦

Dear me,

You and I like lists, and so naturally I will dispense my sage and worldly wisdom in a properly notarised and sub-divided form. In the words of the song – I will dispense this advice now.

The starter slopes:

1a. Despite your mother's belief, the fact that you frequently take baths (on your own) surrounded by scented candles is not a contributing factor to your homosexuality. (However, she thinks nothing of you begging for pink Lego when you were six, which I consider a far more likely signal.)

1b. You are currently an archetypal chubby kid. That's far more fine than you think, but even so, you're about to become an archetypal ex-chubby kid. Unfortunately, you're going to shed the weight much faster than you shed your image of yourself.

Stop worrying. Right now you can't fathom the idea of anyone finding you attractive, but I can confirm from the dizzy heights of 2015 that statement is a) wrong then and b) wrong now. (Plus, here in the future, we've invented these things called Bears and Cubs, so all is well when you decide cheesecake is better than dieting.)

1c. You've spent five years at school in the company of a rancid fistful of aggressively heterosexual morons. The greatest revenge upon these insufferable morons is that you will spend two years living out their fevered fantasies, living with a bunch of incredibly hot cheerleaders. One of them is so susceptible to rugby players that she will confine herself to sleeping in your bed to prevent herself hopping on the nearest sportsman. (Meanwhile, the morons will remain in Scunthorpe, an equally satisfying punishment.)

Fairly painless, that bunch. These next ones might cut a little deeper.

2a. Growing up with parents two generations older than everyone elses, in a home

 MATT CRESSWELL

without a television, and church twice on Sundays is not as bad as you think it is. It's a neon arrow that sets you apart from everyone else, but also the foundation that you're built upon now.

The television thing especially: without that, you'd never have read books, you'd never have loved books, and you wouldn't now (just about) make your living from books.

2b. In case you wondered after that pink-Lego thing: yes, you'll come out to your family. Yes, it will be awful, but then it'll be bearable, then manageable, and finally it'll be fine. Mother has even met J___, your fiancé, though that was pretty traumatic all around. (I'll let you discover all about J___ on your own.)

Know this: sometimes the family's conspiracy of silence regarding your sexuality is not just them. You have to make the leap to talk about it too.

2c. Two months ago you took a photo in the final weeks of secondary school. There's six of us in that photo, our school gang. I can let you into a delicious secret. As of last year, all but one has come out as gay. (The one that doesn't is H____; in two years she'll marry a chef ten years her senior, and you'll stop speaking to her in shame because you lost the only copy of her wedding video.)

Trust whatever bond of outsider-dom it is that brought you guys together. (And don't hold it against S__ for not being able to deal with your fumbled coming out when you were 13. He had enough to deal with.)

Time for the big ones.

3a. You're about to meet Duckboy. You're going to feel like you've met the one single person who was ever capable of understanding your life—the mess of church, god and religion; the buttoned-down youth missing half its rites of passages; identity, friendship and dreams—and you are not wrong about this.

You will feel like it is you and him against the world, and you will fall in love. You will decide to tell him that fact, and it'll be okay for a while, until it's not. The sheer ferocity of your feelings for him—rehearsing conversations as you walk across the Humber Bridge alone, noting down every text conversation you have with him—is the crucible that sparks the transformation from you-then to you-now. It will give you the strength to walk into our house in a year's time and come out to Mum and Dad because it will teach you that being gay isn't just about sex, its about love.

After that, though, it's all going to all go very pear-shaped, but don't worry: it'll work itself out eventually. Ten years on, Duckboy and you are still friends. I know—I spoke to him this morning and talked about what I would say in this letter.

3b. There's a writer, a much better writer than me, who laid out the concept of 'biological family' and 'logical family'. Our family, for better or worse, will support us and will love us, but you will never feel you are a part of them. That's okay: you'll make your own, your 'logical family', and become the pinwheel at the centre of a galaxy of strange, beautiful oddballs. Even when they are far away, they are close; treasure this, and trust your ability to find these people.

3c. The evening that you come out, Dad tells you some things. He says that, as you grew up fastened tight to your mother's apron strings, he felt closed out and on the outside of you two, that you never respected him. There's truth in it, but you'll completely overlook the sincerity and bravery of him telling you this, because you are in the middle of your own crisis.

Be careful. In five years time, lying in a hospital bed with an enormous tumour clawing out of the side of his face, he will tell you, "In the end, this is all life is." After twenty-one years of a family in which no-one has ever said 'I love you', you won't manage to summon the courage to say it as he's dying in front of you. Your brothers

do, but you do not, and you will feel as if you have failed in this.

To make amends, you will ask to see his body at the mortuary. I won't tell you not to do it, but there is nothing I can tell you that can prepare you for the shock you will feel when you see him. You will still not manage to say it. From here, half a decade later, I absolve you of the guilt you will feel about this.

Instead, I gift you the five years I have had without him for you to use as the five years you have left *with* him. Please do not waste them.

With love and the tightest of hugs,

You

P.S. This magazine? You built it from scratch. Never doubt that you can't create something from a stray thought on a quiet afternoon. Those are the best ideas.

Dear me,

This is a difficult letter for me to write.

We are in a kind of time-machine, you and I, a time-machine that appears to be a long, long tunnel; there you are, not far from the beginning of the long tunnel, in the spring of 1966, aged 16 — and I am here, 65 years old, in the spring of 2015, close to the other end of the tunnel. Yet you are me, and I am you.

I see you now, in our bedroom (the bedroom you and I shared with our brother), sitting in a chair by the desk, scanning the pages of the magazine section of the Sunday edition of THE NEW YORK TIMES. You are not reading the articles now, but rather looking at the advertisements, searching for the ads that sell men's underwear and swimming suits; you are looking for, and at, the photographs of the young, handsome models. Of course you cannot let anyone know this, but I do know you well.

I also know you do read a lot, you study a lot, and many, many things interest you. But those Sunday afternoons you spend looking at those photographs — those afternoons are a part of your identity that you keep hidden behind a closed door. And for many years to come you will keep this closet door locked, even from yourself.

There is not the only identity you have, of course. For example, you have become interested in religion, too; but though you love your religion, you also know that looking at these semi-naked men, daydreaming about them, dreaming at night about them, having wet dreams, masturbating — these things do not fit in with the religion that you love. And so you will develop different parallel identities, identities that do not acknowledge each other, although they all are you.

May I tell you something, son? Over the coming years you will choose to move to a different country, to a different continent in fact. You will choose a new name there. You will choose to get married, because you want to be a father. You will marry and you will love your wife — but you will love her the way a brother loves a sister, not the way a husband loves a wife. You will have children whom you love, too. But the shadows from your closet will call out to you over and over again, and you will dream of the man-you-might-have-been. Look carefully at the shadows; I am one of them. Will you recognize me?

✸ G.S. CROWN ✸

In your marriage's earlier years, you will succeed in making love to your wife. But as time goes by, you will succeed only by closing your eyes and imagining that she is a man, that it is a man's body you are stroking, hugging, caressing, loving. And in the end, even that will fail. Even Viagra will fail.

Should I be telling this to a boy of 16? I have been dishonest with so many people, for so many years — perhaps there is a chance I can be honest with you, son, yes? You and I are gay. It will be decades before you will say these three words clearly, even though they are true.

This time-machine, this long tunnel, is situated in the closet of your bedroom. Enter it, son. It is not so dark, there are candles there which you will light. The poems you write are these candles, for something we share, something important in our identity, is the fact that we write poems, these poems that are our candles and our stars. See, you started writing poems a few years ago, and I — 49 years later and over 1,200 poems later — I am still writing poems. Because that is who we are: a gay man who writes poems. In the past, many of my poems dealt with religion, with the Bible, with the love of God; but during the last five or six years, I have written hundreds of poems of what it means to be a gay man who lives in a closet, who has never been in a gay bar in his life, who tries to be faithful to his wife (who tries and fails). And these poems are mainly Petrarchan sonnets (what's that, you ask; it's something that you do not know yet, but which you will learn about). For a sonnet is a kind of closet, too. A sonnet is also a star and a candle.

There is so much I need to tell you, but I know you cannot hear me. I feel like a guardian angel, albeit not a very successful one; for what is a guardian angel, but our future self who returns to an earlier self in the hope of trying to protect and guide him. But I can neither protect nor guide you, nor can I give you any advice, since I am full of question marks myself: Were my choices the "correct" ones? Should I have chosen a different path? Yes; no; yes; no; yes. But if I had chosen differently, and had opened my closet door, my children would never have been born. And if my children had never been born, how would they know I love them?

Although I know you cannot hear me nor see me, that I am only a shadow in your closet,

I want to tell you one word, even though it is a four-lettered word. I want to tell you: live. Do you hear me, son, can you hear me from the other end of the tunnel? Listen: live. Live.

Yours,

Me

(Forgive me but I do not know what name to use. At the age of 24 I changed my name, so the name you go by is not the name I go by now. Perhaps I will just sign with the name G.S. Crown, the pen-name of my gay poems. Perhaps it is the truest name we will ever have. And son, if you want, you can always write to me by email, to: g_s_crown@yahoo. com   What is email you ask? Wait, in another 30 years or so you'll find out.)

Dear me,

I write to you across a marathon of years, some quarter million hours, countless minutes, every moment you will never see. I write from far beyond the black abyss you crouch upon the edge of, poised to leap in fury, diving downward, inward to oblivion, past the event horizon of an imploded soul.

Beyond, within. Within, beyond. I am the fucking abyss, baby, gazing back at you. That's the best way to put it, anyway.

I write to you, dead boy, in the parlance of your scribblings in school jotters, in the figurative argot of your adolescent wrath, offering no sham of solace that you'll know I do not lie. No platitudes as panacea here, I swear--I know the scorn you'd have of consolations proving only my amnesia of what it is to be you, proving only compromise, betrayal. So, when it comes to where you see yourself right now, the emptiness you see ahead, I offer only a brutal honesty of confirmation:

You will die.

As you know in your heart you're dying even now, as you carve in biro gouges of block letters a truth beyond the literal--reveries of a pact with Death, an oath of slaughter--I know the plans you make, the raptures of revenge, even the rage to understand these daydreams as pathetic as they are impossible. You don't need my patronising truisms to unpack what's clear to you already, so I tell you only that you're right:

You will die.

It will not happen as you expect it. Death will come next summer, on a day of shimmering hot sun, to rap upon the front door in a way that's... unanticipated. He will be terrible and absurd and empty of all import. He will damn you and save you. You wanted a deal with Death, dead boy. He will bring you a gift, a corpse to burn, a hole in reality where he entered and left. You will, as you have yearned, follow Death into the void, but trust me when I say that where the abolition of your ragged ego, dead boy, will be absolute, your

HAL DUNCAN

current fancies of a coming transformation are... at best a glimpse.

You know that though already, right? Again, I will not condescend. You sense already the ineffable truth that you must die to reach, know that the metaphors and myths by which you struggle to articulate your Hell are themselves what must be murdered. You don't need a sermon.

So, I do not write to gift you wisdoms that I wish you'd had, to change a course I don't regret. I only echo the conviction burning in you at this moment, to sing back the wisdom I inherit from you. That I will never betray. You want a deal with Death. I am his emissary, the You from beyond your grave, and I accept that pact: walk on, dead boy, into the wasteland, and I will ever be true to you.

You will die, and it will be more glorious even than you dream.

You will die tomorrow, as another You died yesterday, as another the day before, and the day before, and so on, in a torment seemingly insufferable, from where you stand, in its banality. Near six thousand days of dying so far, every mayfly self snuffed out in sleep at the end of its alloted hours. More to come.

The point though: You will die, dead boy, and for every You that dies, a new You will be born from the ashes, a phoenix waking fresh-hatched every day. Some days you'll rouse bleary and wearied, soused in the illusion that it's yesterday's You continuing, forgetting that he's dust--your seventeen year old self, eighteen, nineteen, twenty, every self of every year, month, week and day you've shed as snakeskin, all gone. Some days you'll forget you died last night, so you'll forget you are reborn, reforged in fire, fresh to the world each morn.

But when you remember, dead boy, oh, when you remember...

But no, I promised you no panaceas. I write this, dead boy, not as dangled hope of joys you

HAL DUNCAN

will not live to see, but as a paean to your mad defiance, elegy for you and every afterself who never would have lived without your death. Fuck wisdom. I give you tribute, dead boy, and the one assurance you might need: my oath:

Though gone, by all your scions, you will never be forgotten.

Yours,

Me

There you are – sixteen year old me.

Now that was a rainstorm. You, and him, and that little wreck of a cabin on Zukerberg Island? Magic. Between you and me, you won't meet anyone in the next twenty four years who'll be able to top that rainstorm for best "first time" story. First kiss, first grope, first... Well, you were there. No need for a laundry list. But seriously—the thunder and the skin and the rain and the breathing and the hair on his chest? Best rainstorm ever.

You were supposed to be tutoring him. Isn't role reversal grand?

But seriously. Life just changed in a really big way, and you're walking home after the world's best rainstorm and thinking about how amazing and terrifying everything just turned out to be. It's sinking in, I know. The gay thing is scary. The way you're sure your parents will react if they ever find out is even worse. You have no idea about your friends, and—most of all—how soon you can arrange another "tutoring session" with him.

I thought I'd drop a line.

First, yes, the gay thing is frightening. It won't be like that forever, I promise, but right now, that fear is useful. You don't know it, but you're not a coward for staying quiet. Both of your lives could be completely ruined right now. It's not stupid to hide from something that would wipe you out with ease—it's common sense.

Second—and I can't stress this enough—you're so very right about your parents. That part is going to be ugly. You've got some time (see above, re: not a coward) but you'll handle it the way you always do: by making fun of it, finding good people, and acting okay until you are okay.

Third is the friends. Well, I have good news and I have bad news. The bad news is you're going to find out in a few weeks that your family is moving. Yes, again. I know, I know, you just freaking got here, just met a fabulous jock with chest hair who you're supposed to be tutoring in French but mostly he's frenching you, and now you're going to leave?

NATHAN BURGOINE

Yup.

The good news is some of the people you've met here will be friends with you even after you leave. That jock with the hairy chest? He'll be sending you a Valentine's Day card year after year, up to the point where you both get married.

No, not to each other. This is not a teen movie.

I'm not going to lie to you, kiddo. Right now, the wind is drying the last of the rain from your shirt, and you're walking home and learning it's possible to be so incredibly happy and still be terrified all at the same time. You have no idea how bad it might get—and it will get bad. You're scared you'll be alone and haven't learned yet how powerful it is to be okay with being alone. You might not believe me when I say how happy you're going to be, but wait four days.

Four days from now, you're going to wake up, and it will be raining. It won't be a rainstorm, and you won't manage to sneak another "tutoring" session for a bit longer than that. It's just rain. But for you—for the rest of your life—it won't ever be "just rain" again. You will always love the sound. You will never sleep better than when it's raining. You will remember who you are and how you love every single time it rains.

So let the wind dry off your shirt and your jeans. Sneak inside the house, and get changed. Towel off your hair (oh—and enjoy your hair while you've still got some). Climb into bed, stare at the ceiling, and listen to your heartbeat. It's okay to be too scared of what this all means to fall asleep.

You're going to be fine.

Just wait for the rain.

✤ 'NATHAN BURGOINE ✤

Jeff Abell

Jeff Abell is a composer, performance artist, writer and photographer living in Chicago, Illinois. Much of his work explores issues of identity and sexuality, and he helped to shape Chicago's avant-drag scene in the early 1990s. He has written extensively about the arts, and been an editor or contributing editor, for a number of publications, most recently for the art magazine *Mouth to Mouth*. He is an associate professor at Columbia College Chicago, in the Interdisciplinary Arts Department.

Frank Adams

Frank Adams is a Lambda Literary Foundation Fellow in Poetry. His poems have appeared in *Q Review, Down-go Sun, Micro Delights, Glitterwolf*, and *Iris* and in anthologies including, *Between: New Gay Poetry*. He is the author of *Shadows, Mist & Fog; Strangers, Men & Boys; Love Remembered; Mother Speaks Her Name* and *Crazy Times*.

Paulina Angel

Paulina Angel is a Trans Activist and Songwriter from Indio/Palm Springs California. She is the first Trans Woman elected to office as part of the Student Senate for California Community Colleges in Sacramento, advocated for SB 48 and AB 1266. She has her own indie label, PMI (Paulaphone Musical Industries) Records and PA Music, have already released two albums and planning on recording a third. Her music and likeness has been highlighted on *The Queer Life, Trans Atheist Podcast, The Strong Stance, Kitten Time* and has a song in the upcoming film, *LGBT Love Stories*. She previously attended College Of the Desert in Palm Desert and City College of San Francisco, hoping to transfer to Mills College in Oakland to major in Women's, Sexuality and Gender Studies and continue to advocate for Trans Rights in California and hopefully, the United States At-Large.

Steve Berman

Steve Berman awaits hearing from his 76 yr old self.

Evey Brett

Evey Brett lives in Tucson, AZ with her Lipizzan mare Carrma, has attended Clarion and the Lambda Literary Retreat for Emerging LGBT Writers and has an MA in Writing Popular Fiction from Seton Hill University. Other publications include a short story forthcoming in *Frankenstein's Daughters: Lesbian Mad Scientists!* She can be found online at www.eveybrett.wordpress.com

Dorian Bridges

Dorian Bridges is a genderqueer English student living near Birmingham, at the perpetual mercy of demanding fictional entities and Presley the beardy dog. He is hoping to publish his first novel in the next year, but until then, has a blog of irreverent and grisly tales at theputrescentvein.wordpress.com..

'Nathan Burgoine

'Nathan Burgoine lives in Ottawa with his husband. His first novel *Light* was a finalist for a Lambda Literary Award. 'Nathan's shorts appear in dozens of publications, including *This Is How You Die, Foolish Hearts* and *A Family By Any Other Name*. Find him online at www.nathanburgoine.com.

Nick Campbell

Nick Campbell is a writer, research student and nostalgic fool who lives in South London. His blog is situated here: leaf-pile.blogspot.co.uk

Celeste Chan

Celeste Chan is an experimental artist, writer and organizer. A Lambda, VONA, and Hedgebrook alumna, she has presented work and curated in the SF Bay Area, NYC, Seattle, Austin, Vancouver BC, Glasgow, Berlin, and beyond. Alongside KB Boyce, she co-directs Queer Rebels, a queer/trans people of color arts project.

Matt Cresswell

Matt Cresswell is the kind of person whose sixteen-year-old self read the biographies in the back of anthologies. In this singular instance, the potential for for a confusing time-travel paradox from the additional information contained in a biography is too great, so *ssh*, it must remain a secret. (Oi, nosy sixteen-year-old, a few hints: you'll publish some short stories, edit a magazine, and design books. You might one day finish a novel, but you haven't bloody well done so yet.)

G.S. Crown

G.S. Crown is a pen-name. He is a married man with children, but is also gay – something his wife and family do not know. He lives in a closet and does not tell his family or his colleagues at work what he feels; the ones who know the truth are his pen, the paper he writes on and his computer.

Justin DeFerbrache

Justin DeFerbrache studied English Literature at a small liberal arts college in Indiana. For the past three years, he has been working as a TESOL teacher in China and exploring the Asian continent one bit at a time. He writes poetry and short fiction on the side.

Hal Duncan

Hal Duncan is the award-winning author of *Vellum* and *Ink*, along with numerous short stories, poems, essays, and even musicals. Homophobic hatemail once dubbed him "THE.... Sodomite Hal Duncan!!" (sic), and you can find him onstage at spoken word performances or online at www.halduncan.com, revelling in that role.

Mark Ellis

Mark Ellis lived most of his childhood in Tennessee, but left as soon as he was old enough to study, travel, work, eventually becoming a librarian and medievalist. He writes poetry and articles on medieval literature, and information technology. He loves to read his poetry at open mic events, and has published in *RFD* and *Glitterwolf* and has a forthcoming story in *Red Truck Review*.

Sarah Fonseca

A 2012 Lambda Literary Foundation fellow in nonfiction, Sarah Fonseca's work has appeared in the digital pages of *Thought Catalog, Posture Magazine,* and *Word Riot.* She effortlessly splits her time between Brooklyn, NY and Statesboro, Georgia. Fonseca believes that the only true difference between city slickers and country bumpkins is how they define a single word: everything. For metropolitan denizens, it is a literal term; for rural folks, it's a minimalist one. Mosey on up to her on Twitter @thekudzuleague.

Kieran Forbes

An aspiring actor and graduate of the Arden School, Kieran can generally be found lurking on Manchester's Canal Street performing pop staples for drag queens, and rehearsing for a bright future on the stage.

James Gent

James Gent, 39, is a freelance writer and full-time graphic designer. Between 2012 and 2014 he was HM Revenue & Customs' LGB Network Bisexuality Representative.

David Gillespie

David R. Gillespie is an author living in Greenville, South Carolina. He is the former editor of *OIA*, an LGBT monthly newspaper in Asheville, North Carolina (no longer in print). His fiction has appeared in *ByLine, Lonzie's Fried Chicken, Open Hands*, and *Best Gay Love Stories 2006*. He is a contributor to the anthology, *OUT LOUD: The Best of Rainbow Radio* and his reviews have appeared in *Gay and Lesbian Review Worldwide, Transgender Tapestry*, and *Lambda Literary Review*. His poetry has been published in *Timelapse*. He is a former Presbyterian minister — very former.

Michael J. Hess

Michael J. Hess is a filmmaker and writer who lives in Toronto. His films have played at the NYU Director's Series, NewFest, the American Cinemateque in Los Angeles, Kansas International Film Festival and Beloit International Film Festival. His writing has appeared in *Shenandoah, The Outrider Review, AlleyCat News, Glitterwolf Magazine* and in the anthology *Creativity and Constraint* (Wising Up Press).

Michelle Lunicke

Michelle Lunicke (sometimes Ryan) is a genderqueer writer and performance artist from the Cascadian region of North America. She has lived in the U.S., Canada, and most recently Australia and New Zealand. Her plays, publishing, performance works, and blog can be found at http://michellelunicke.com

Paul Magrs

Paul Magrs was born in 1969. His first novel was *Marked for Life* in 1995. He has published fiction for adults and children in various genres. His most recent books include a memoir, *The Story of Fester Cat* (Penguin US) and a science fiction novel, *Lost on Mars* (Firefly.) He lives in Manchester in the UK. You can find him on Facebook, Twitter and his blog at lifeonmagrs.blogspot.co.uk

Jeff Mann

Jeff Mann has published three poetry chapbooks, four full-length books of poetry, two collections of personal essays, a volume of memoir and poetry, three novellas, four novels, and two collections of short fiction. He teaches creative writing at Virginia Tech in Blacksburg, Virginia.

Neil Ellis Orts

Neil Ellis Orts, a native Texan, is a writer and performer. He holds an M.A. in Interdisciplinary Arts from Columbia College Chicago. His novella, *Cary and John*, was published in the summer of 2014 and has a short story in the Lammy Award finalist anthology, *Outer Voices, Inner Lives*.

Dennis Rhodes

Dennis Rhodes recently published his third book of poetry, *The Letter I* from Chelsea Station Editions. His first book, *Spiritus Pizza and other poems* was a tribute to his two homes: New York and Provincetown.

Nicci Robinson

Nicci Robinson is an avid shutter-bug and lover of all things fast and physical. Her writing often reflects both of those passions. She writes lesbian fiction when she isn't busy being the Chief Executive of a UK charity working with victims of childhood sexual abuse.

Amy Shepherd

Amy Shepherd is an IT sys admin and writer. She lives in Seattle, Washington with her wife Laura and two cats. She loves reading and writing stories of all kinds. Visit her on the web at: http://amyshep.com.

Gabbie Slaughter

Gabbie Slaughter is a twenty-three-year-old lesbian living in Dallas. She is new to the world of writing but someday hopes to write the novel that she needed to read when she was a confused girl in Texas. This is her first published piece.

Lori Smith

Lori Smith is a bisexual feminist and blogger from London. Lori has written for *SLiNK* and *Geeked Magazines*, has spoken at a number of independent UK conferences – including *SHINE, Eroticon, Cybher* and *Wowzers Festival* – and was a finalist in the Writer category of the 2012 Erotic Awards. You can find her at rarelywearslipstick.com or on Twitter as @lipsticklori.

Victoria Villasenor

Victoria Villasenor is a full time development editor for LGBTQ publisher Bold Strokes Books in New York and also runs the social enterprise Global Words, based in Nottingham. She and her partner are often off gallivanting around Europe, when she isn't chained to her desk working. www.victoria-oldham.co.uk

Mark Ward

Mark Ward is a writer from Dublin, Ireland. His plays include *The Middle Distance, Saliva* and *Blue Boy*. His prose has been published in *Jonathan* and the *Queer in Brighton* anthology. His poetry has been featured in *Assaracus, Storm Cellar, The Good Men Project, The Wild Ones* and the anthology *Out of Sequence: The Sonnets Remixed*. He has recently completed a chapbook called *How To Live When Life Subtracts* and is busy tinkering with his first full length collection, *Circumference*, which will form the first part of his American G.I. series. http://astintinyourspotlight.wordpress.com

Ben Webb

Ben Webb is a writer and theatremaker. His trilogy of plays *The Well & Badly Loved* has been translated into Spanish and produced in Mexico, and is currently being translated into French.

Jerry L. Wheeler

Three time Lambda Literary Award finalist, Jerry L. Wheeler is editor of seven volumes of gay erotica as well as his own short story collection, *Strawberries and Other Erotic Fruits* (Lethe Press, 2012). His first novel, *The Dead Book,* is forthcoming from Lethe Press in late 2015. His letter is addressed to Irving because when he was sixteen, his sense of humor was being molded by Mel Brooks, Carl Reiner, and many other Jewish comedians. Oy.

Rhian Williams

Rhi Williams is a poet and anxious geek living in West Wales with her wife and too many animals. She writes a blog about anything and everything, writes a lot of poetry, has self-published a collection and writes bits of science fiction. Eventually she'll finish a novel.

Printed in Great Britain
by Amazon.co.uk, Ltd.,
Marston Gate.